Sheila Tyrer Hughes

THE BRIDGE MAKERS

AUSTIN MACAULEY
PUBLISHERS LTD.

A CIP catalogue record for this title is available from the British Library.

ISBN 9781785544286 (Paperback)
ISBN 9781785544293 (Hardback)
ISBN 9781785544309 (E-Book)

www.austinmacauley.com

First Published (2016)
Austin Macauley Publishers Ltd.
25 Canada Square
Canary Wharf
London
E14 5LQ

'If you would be king
First you must build a bridge.'

Chapter 1

My Name Is

Gareth's Diary

I'd love to see your face when you read this. Does it read like the words of a twelve (almost thirteen) year old? No. I'm sure you'll agree. I mean, you know what it's like when the teacher tells you to write a story. You're expected to turn on some magic switch and come up with something great. And you end up with some feeble waffle with a few similes stuck in here and there. And Miss says, 'Could do better. Try using your imagination more.'

Well, all of a sudden this imagination thing kicks in and I'm thinking strange thoughts. I don't know how or why, but something has changed lately and I keep getting these weird ideas. Mum has always encouraged me to write a diary so that I can practise my English. She didn't have a great education and wants me to make the most of mine. To be honest, I've never been that keen. Diaries are more of a girl's thing – but now, strangely, I want to write things down, keep a record – maybe just to prove to myself that these things really happened. So here goes.

My *name is* Gareth Jones. I'm nearly thirteen, not brilliant looking, but not bad either. I like painting tiny metal models and creating landscapes for them. I like to read. I like playing computer games too – but just lately I find they interfere too much, stop me thinking my own thoughts. They take control. My name is Gareth Jones. It

7

has been my name for almost thirteen years yet now when I write it down it feels wrong somehow, as if ... as if it's not really my name at all, but one I have borrowed because my own is lost to me along with everything else. What a weird thought! See what I mean? But it keeps coming to me in dreams. AND – get this! One day last week, when I put in my password for this new game I was playing it was rejected. It asked me if I had forgotten the password and actually gave me a clue T. A. L. Computers, huh! I thought.

I haven't always felt like this. I don't always feel like this now. But there are moments when something washes over me. If I believed in that sort of thing I would say it was like magic dust, a spell – or maybe a curse!

A couple of weeks ago, Grandy (that's what I call my grandfather), took me walking, a place called Crumlock Hill. A distortion of cromlech, I think. Cromlechs are megalithic tombs marked by standing stones. But you will know that, of course. It was an ancient site, a sacred site, a place where people have walked for thousands of years, where they have talked to their gods and left offerings. It was a biting cold day and we were alone on the hill. Our breath made small white clouds and our footsteps crunched on the brittle autumn grass. As we climbed the stony path that wound to the summit I touched Grandy's arm to halt him. "I can hear voices," I said. "Listen!"

Grandy nodded – and smiled in that secretive way he has. "We walk the way of badgers and foxes," he said. "Perhaps you are tuned in to them – for I am sure they listen to us as we trespass on their land. Or perhaps it is simply the wind that you hear, playing the silver birches like a lyre."

He strode on and I stood for a moment, turning my head this way and that. One voice came to me, stronger than another. Though I couldn't understand the words, there was a desperation in them that seemed to be dispersing like breath in the air around me, echoing and re-echoing before it faded and was lost.

That's really when the difference began – and the strange dreams – after that walk on Crumlock Hill with Grandy, in his long overcoat, striding out like an ancient wizard, with his carved staff in one hand and his grey beard flowing back over his shoulder.

In the last year lots of things have happened in the world. I don't mean wars and such, for as long as there are men there will be wars. There is nothing new in that. But the world is changing. The world, I think, has had enough of human beings and their terrible ways. First, a tsunami to shake us awake, then earthquakes and volcanoes erupting everywhere. The Earth is taking us by the scruff of the neck and shaking us until our teeth rattle. Perhaps, at last, we will take notice – for how can such anger be ignored?

We move house on Saturday and my stomach is churning, because something is about to begin, something to do with the dreams and the voices – and who I really am. And I'm starting a new school of course.

P.S. I will write down the dream. When you read it you will know that I am not imagining all this. But I shall keep it for later, for the right moment. Perhaps, with a little help, I will write a book.

P.P.S.

I have just read this and am shocked by what I have written – and by the (for me) brilliant English. It really is as if someone else is in my head. I'm not imagining all this! I do feel different – since that visit to Crumlock Hill – since I heard those voices – as if my skin is changing. Is this what happens when you become a teenager? If it is – no one warned me!

9

Chapter 2

Tara – The Source of the Voices

My name is Arawn Silverhand, Lord of the Tuatha, the Children of the Dawn. I am standing on the city walls of Tara, facing south, shielding my eyes against the pale sun as I scan the horizon. Is it only five seasons since Longspear passed through the gates of Tara? It seems an eternity. Never before has he failed to return at the appointed time.

"It must be worse than we feared in the World of Men."

My eyes search the plain from east to west and back again, straining to catch a movement on the straight path across the Field of Moytura, imagining a ripple in the stillness of the dark and withered corn.

"Henwas[1], your beard will turn to snow and your stout heart will break when you see how the Light fades, how the City of Tara is dying."

I feel old. A piercing wind comes from behind like an arrow from the Black Hills. It tugs spitefully at my cloak and speeds away, cutting through the dead corn like a scythe. In its wake, I hear a stone crumble, and see dust falling upon the silver tree where birds no longer sing.

---

[1] Old servant

Twelve nights ago, the city walls were besieged by the howling of Fenrir's whelps. Morgana sent them, and though we fought to drive them back to the Mist of Niflheim, I know their coming is an omen and I grow weak with fear for my people and for the Children of Men.

"It must not be! It cannot be! And yet I feel that Ragnarok, the fatal destiny, is nigh. Without the Lady Mariandor to keep it alight, the flame on Earth dwindles.

"Without her to whisper in their dreams we can no longer touch the hearts of Men."

"Courage, My Lord!" It is the gruff voice of a dwarf, Gwystil Stagshank, a faithful warrior and man-at-arms. "See how my toes curl and my beard stands on end. Something is stirring in my old blood. 'tis a sure sign that brother Longspear is not far away."

I turn to him, attempting a smile. "But I have no sight of him," I say. "There is not even a wing beat in the heavy sky."

He bows his head in sorrow and turns away, then stamps his feet impatiently, for dwarfs are not endowed with the gift of patience. "Forgive me, My King," he rebukes me, "but your hand lacks courage for want of a sword."

I am his king and yet I feel no anger at his words. Instead, I tell him, "That is the teaching of your father Ymyr, not the word of our father Nwyvre. A dwarf is never happier than when his fist is full of iron and his beard is thrust arrogantly in the face of his enemy. But the Tuatha are different. They are lovers of beauty and peace. They seek only to live in harmony with all that surrounds them. But Men close all the gateways and will not let it be so."

Gwystyl continues to shuffle and stamp. His nostrils are twitching and he is taking great noisy breaths. "Your memory is short, My Lord. Was it not Nwyvre who sent

11

Lugh Lamphada and the giant Dagda to your aid with their weapons of war? Nwyvre knows that when evil threatens, the powers of good must also take up arms and go forward into battle."

I bury my head in my hands. "You are right, my friend. It was my dearest hope that when Morgana overstretched herself we had seen the last of war, but I know in my heart that here and in the World of Men it is not so. Peace is the reward at a long journey's end, but the road seems to go on for ever. I know we must be patient, but I grow old and weary. Another doorway beckons and the grey mists cloud my thoughts, but I must confess I have thought of it, the mighty Caladbolg, sword of the first Nuada Silverhand, crafted by your father, Ymyr, before the mountains found their places. I have seen it in my dreams, the jewelled hilt held fast beneath the waves. So too, I hope, are the lance of Prince Lugh and the great cauldron of Dagda held by the Guardians, returned to them when your ancestors and mine washed the Field of Moytura with their blood."

The dwarf lifts his broad, ugly face to the wind and sniffs noisily. "There is a tingling in my bones," he says, "that tells me the Black Hills will echo again with battle cries, and that before many moons have set. The wheel of iron turns and the shades deepen." He turns to me. "Has there been no word of Mariandor, no sign of Lia Fail, the Stone of Destiny?"

I am shaking my head. "Nothing, my friend. Neither word nor whisper, and too many winters have passed for me to carry much hope in my heart. We are bound in chains to the World of Men, but without Mariandor moving among them, opening their hearts and colouring their dreams, the links between us weaken and the bridges are swept away by the Powers of the Dark. As the World of Men slips into shadow, so too do we lose sight of the sun and Morgana's evil grows apace. See, how the Mists of Niflheim creep across the land and begin to choke the life out of it. I feel

*my life is fading and there is none to replace me, to breathe
new life into Tara."*

"But My King," says my faithful servant, *"is it not
written that a boy will come, that in his hands lies the fate
of the Tuatha?"*

*"Aye, it is written. It is also written that Myrddin the
Traveller will set him on his way. But Longspear has
brought no word of them, and time grows short. It strikes
me that Myrddin chooses his own path and forgets his
ancestors. But perhaps the Dark has taken them all.
Perhaps Morgana ..."*

"No!" roars the dwarf. *"If it is written that a boy will
come then we must have faith in the word. We must lift our
heads and turn our hearts to the Light. We must not be
turned into milksops by shadows and the howling of
Fenrir's miserable hounds."*

I nod and place my hand on the dwarf's shoulder. *"The
boy must come! For it is written in blood and sealed by the
hand of our father."* I stare once more at the silent plain.
*"Make haste, Old Warrior, for without your words of hope
we are doomed. If the Light of the Tuatha is extinguished
the stars will fall and men will return to the chaos from
whence they came. If the boy, a true son of Gwydion, is not
found and set upon the path then the prophecy cannot be
fulfilled. The Earth Mother will have failed us and her
children will be lost."*

I push open the heavy oaken door. *"May Ymyr, from
whose flesh you came, grant you safe and speedy return,
Urion Longspear. And bring word of the boy. I wish it with
all of my heart."*

As I pass through the archway the great oaken door
swings shut.

On a granite crag south-east of Tara a brown, leather-
clad figure is thrusting his hazel staff into a pocket of

13

barren soil, and leaning on it, staring bleakly before him. Urion Longspear, one time warrior, now Watcher in the World of Men, is bone-weary and heartsick. The sight of Tara's ragged walls eaten into by writhing coils of mist, does nothing to raise his spirits.

"Forgive me, My King," he murmurs in the Old Tongue, his voice gruff with emotion. "My return is ill-timed and the stench of Fenrir's breath shrivels my beard. It is as I feared. Morgana gathers strength from every corner. The wild places of Earth are a wasteland. The oceans and the stones beneath them cry out in an agony of despair and weep blood for their dead."

For a moment Longspear's eyes, speedwell blue and sharp as ice, glisten wet with tears. But anger soon takes the place of sorrow. He leaps into the air three times, shaking his enormous fists. Then he tugs his staff from the ground and thrusts it wildly at the sky.

"She will not win, no matter what she summons from the Mists of Niflheim and the Fogs of the Northern Fastnesses. For I, Urion Longspear, have found the boy, the youngest son of Gwydion."

He sets off down the hillside at a wild, loping gait. As he flies over rocks and fallen branches, he is shrieking at the top of his voice, "Sucks and sogwashes to Morgana! Take heart, My King, for the wanderer returns. The Guardians are stirring and the smell of battle fever turns my blood to fire."

High overhead, unseen by the dwarf, a dark speck wheels in lazy circles before spiralling downwards. Claws scrape the granite crag as the bird flaps clumsily for a moment, watching. Then it lifts, beating southwards through the empty sky.

Gareth's Diary
(Saturday)

We have moved house. I start the new school on Monday. It feels strange. I feel strange. I keep thinking about that first entry in my diary. For now, when I think, the words that come to me are even stranger. Maybe it's normal. Maybe it is what happens when you reach thirteen. The real you begins to emerge, like a moth or a butterfly — or a daddy longlegs! Hope Grandy comes soon. I so need to talk to him.

Chapter 3

Foxhole Cottage

The Joneses' new home was a stone cottage built on a crossroads. It looked to be part of the living landscape, rooted in the earth like the rocks and the trees. Bedded in the grass verge outside the gate was a lump of stone a metre wide.

"It's like an iceberg," Gareth thought as he stepped down from the removal van. Probably a marker stone, placed there when two track-ways crossed, maybe thousands of years ago when people first passed this way in search of salt. Grandy had told him about the old roads and the people who travelled them.

He looked around him at the stone walls of the cottage, at the tall trees and the crossroads and the lane that disappeared around a bend. He had studied an Ordnance Survey map to see what kind of place this was, to look for any clues. He knew there was a mill – or the remains of one – in a valley nearby, and a hill on the other side of the river, and it struck him as strange that the new model landscape he had made out of balsa wood and polystyrene also featured a mill, a hill and a river. On the hill he had placed twelve standing stones. He was itching to explore, to search for them, but first there was work to be done.

"What do you think, then?" his dad had asked.

"It's OK."

"Is that all? Just OK?"

"No. I like it. It feels right."

His dad nodded sombrely. "Aye, well, it's not as if we had much choice in the matter. It's not far to the village," he said. "You'll soon make new friends."

"I know." Gareth's eyes narrowed, studying his father's face.

"And school's not much further."

Making friends was the last thing on Gareth's mind at the moment. There was something else far more pressing, though as yet Gareth didn't know what it was.

Gareth's Diary

I like it here. We were meant to come here, I'm certain. It feels like home and maybe that's because it's all part of a plan. But whose plan is it – and where do I fit in? Crumlock Hill is only a couple of miles away. The garden's enormous. Mum said everyone should have a garden and be able to walk right round their house. She reckons that people with gardens don't go around mugging old ladies and breaking into shops. She thinks gardens could cure half the world's problems. I thought she was talking crazy, but now, coming here, feeling as I do I know she's right. It's another connection between us and the world we live in.

Dad's just relieved that we both like it. He is so down to earth – tries to keep everything normal, ordinary. He married into the wrong family for that, I'm thinking. The move was all so quick and unexpected. I suppose it could have been a disaster. As it is, Mum can have her apple trees and grow spinach and beans forever. She might even have some hens. She's always wanted hens.

Now some more of the weird stuff.

Dad was driving home a couple of weeks ago when a strange little man, a kind of dwarf, Dad said, stepped out

17

*from the hedge and waved him down. Dad gave him a lift —
said he was a funny little bloke. He had a strange way of
talking and smelled as though he'd been digging — or
sleeping in a cave. He told Dad about the job looking after
a new Hereford herd at Millhouse Farm.*

*The house — our house — is old, built on a crossroads
from great blocks of sandstone, and the first thing I noticed
when we arrived was a boulder outside the gate. I think it's
a marker stone. I've read about them in one of Grandy's
books. If I'm right then it means the crossroads has been
here for a very long time, maybe two or three thousand
years, maybe more.*

*I can't wait to explore, but everywhere is so wet after
the downpour that Mum said I must stay in. It was just an
excuse. She doesn't usually fuss. She wanted me to sort out
my room. First thing I did was find a place for the new set
of models I bought last week. I still haven't painted the
wizard or the children, and the dwarf's trousers are all
wrong. I think he should be brown from head to toe, as if he
were a creature of the earth, like the creatures in that
computer game. The landscape is coming along well. The
bridge and the mill are looking good, really old and
crumbling. And the stone circle is short of one stone. I'm
sure there should be thirteen though I've no idea why.*

*Then there was the storm today, just after we arrived
here! One minute the sun was shining and it was a perfect
autumn day, brassy and bright. The next, it was as if
someone had hauled a dirty great tarpaulin across the sky.
And the wind was — well, alive, changing direction and
whipping around me! I know it sounds crazy but it's just
what it felt like and it gave me another queer feeling in my
stomach.*

*It was a bit like that day Grandy took me to Crumlock
Hill. The wind was full of* voices *then. I wondered after if I
had imagined them — whether they were nothing more than
the wind. But I remember the sadness in them — and*

something else, desperation – and fear. I could almost feel it on my skin.

As for the storm today; it came from nowhere. No one even saw it coming – and there was no mention of it on the weather forecast. The removal van was just leaving when the first thunder crashed. I was closing the gate. Mum and Dad had already gone inside, but when I turned the wind hit me like a battering ram. Then it stopped and swirled around me throwing leaves and twigs into my face. It was like somebody was controlling it, making it attack me. Where did that idea come from?

I put my head down and pushed through it, but just as I reached the door it slammed shut so I headed for the back of the house – and that was when I saw the bird. I like birds, but this was a big ugly thing perched in the lilac tree at the corner of the garden. As the branches bounced up and down it had to flap its wings to help it hold on. It was enormous, black, and bigger than any crow I've ever seen. It had yellow eyes and a long, ugly grey beak. I waved my arms about but it took no notice, only stared at me. So I stared back, but it made me feel a bit sick. Then a flash of lightning seemed to crack the sky open like an egg. I dropped to the ground – I don't know why – and when I looked up the bird had gone. Then the storm was gone, too, just like that – as if someone had whisked it away.

7 p.m. Same Day

My room's tidy, by my standards anyway, and I've just finished painting the wizard and the dwarf. Although he's only five centimetres high the wizard looks just like Grandy. Same long legs and that wild, scatty look.

It's my birthday next week and I shall be a teenager. I wonder if Grandy will come. I haven't seen him for ages.

WHERE DOES HE DISAPPEAR TO?

Mum has no idea. At least that's what she says. He's always done it, disappearing for weeks, ever since she was *a child. So she must know more than she lets on – as if pretending things are normal will make them so. She just says he's a bit odd. Eccentric, she calls him - missing a few marbles, can't stay in one place for long. Perhaps he has Romany blood. But it's so much more than that. I know. Sometimes, when we've been out walking in Snowdonia, just him and me, I've seen him change. He looks taller, older, and has a way of standing and looking at the mountains around him as if he is the creator who finds something wrong with what he's built. I hope he comes on my birthday. I believe he will. I want him to see the models when I've finished painting them. But I must finish the stone circle first and scratch the name on the old gateposts. 'Worlds' End', that's what I shall call it. The name's been in my head for weeks, ever since we went to Crumlock Hill.*

P.S. Dad's just been in my room. When he saw the models he picked up the dwarf and laughed. Said he looked just like the little bloke who told him about the job. Thought it was funny but it made me look, I can tell you."

Gareth put down his pen and went over to his box of modelling materials: seaweed, balsa wood, polystyrene and paints. Model-making had been his hobby for years. He rooted amongst them and pulled out a lump of tissue paper. Holding one corner he let the five tiny metallic figures, his latest acquisition, roll out on to the bed. Then he stood them up on the landscape he had made. Four of them were boys, one short and plump, two tall and thin, one medium-sized. The fifth was a girl in jeans and anorak with a long pigtail hanging down her back. They were different from anything else he had bought. The others had all been warriors and sci-fi heroes, the landscapes he'd built of another world. But he had spotted the odd collection in the window of a junk shop when he had been passing and had only paid fifty pence for them. Two days later, Grandy had sent him the wizard and the dwarf.

He looked at them curiously now. "I must paint them all," he whispered to himself, "then perhaps I will be able to name them."

Chapter 4

Kit's Place

On the other side of the crossroads, at the top of the steep lane that led down to the river and across to Rundle Hill, was Millhouse Farm, where Gwyn Jones, Gareth's dad, was going to work as herdsman. There, the Talbot family had been caught completely unawares by the sudden storm. It had even caught the doves off guard, and sent them packing back to their whitewashed house.

Reg Talbot was puzzled as he considered himself better than all the weather men put together.

Even Kit, his daughter, would brag about his talent. "My dad can smell rain in the next county," she would tell her friends. "He always knows when to cut hay and carry bales." But this storm was anything but normal. Strange forces were at work, Kit was certain. Probably something to do with the new millennium. Folks reckoned all kinds of queer things were going to happen, give or take a few years.

"I've never seen nowt like it!" Reg's words were sucked away and shredded by the whirlwind gusts as he fought to stay on his feet and clip a halter on to Kit's pony. "The sky's gone crazy, just like the rest of the world."

Kit had seen it coming only seconds before it struck. She'd been kneeling on her window seat, elbows on the sill, a pair of binoculars focused on the tiny valley below the farm. She had traced the path of the brook, under the trees, down to the ruin of the mill and scoured the hill on the other side. She had been hoping to spot one of the buzzards that nested year after year in the tall sycamores further down the secluded little valley. But each time she scanned, a movement on Rundle Hill drew her back. It was a strange, flat-topped hill rising through scattered beech trees on the other side of the Wych Brook. Each time she returned to look at it more carefully there was nothing. Cloud shadows, she thought for a moment, but there were no clouds – then, and the world she could see shone with the blue and gold of a perfect autumn day. "The stubble fields are like butter dishes with only the scrapings left; the last of the Granny Smiths hang like emeralds in the orchard, and at the end of the drive the giant horse chestnut is a fiery beacon in the sun."

"Must write all that down," Kit whispered to herself. "Miss March would be impressed."

Suddenly she shivered. The sky had darkened and there was a chill in the air. She put down the binoculars and flew downstairs. "I must feed the hens before." Before what? By the time she had reached the back door Kit knew. A grey cloud was moving like a tidal wave from the west, washing all the colour from the sky. Already the Welsh Hills had been obliterated. The cloud blotted out the sun and left in its wake a scene from an old black and white film. The ridges and furrows were turned into swelling seas and the beacon tree was being battered and doused by angry surges of wind and rain that shredded its leaves and bore them away.

Kit grabbed her anorak and fought her way across the yard. The hens had already found shelter. Even the ducks, which wallowed in the average rainstorm, were waddling like clockwork toys through the puddles, heads like arrows, aiming for the barn.

23

"I'll put Jenny in!" Reg Talbot's words were broken by the wind. "You shut the barn door!"

Kit heaved the door shut and pushed the bolt. She put up her arm and turned to head back to the house. She could feed the hens later. As she ran, the sky blew up with a terrifying flash. Kit heard Jenny scream with fear, and in that moment, frozen by the electric light, she saw the purple rooftops gleaming and the red walls awash with water that was proving too much for the old gutters and downspouts. She turned to go in but something made her look back across the yard. Perhaps, like the movements on the hill, it was just a trick of the light. But Kit could have sworn there was a tall hunched figure scurrying along the lane away from the farm. A blast of wind and rain made her close her eyes for a second and when she opened them there was nothing. She shivered and pushed open the door.

"Come on through, love," Meg Talbot called. "The kettle's on and I've just put a big log on the fire."

Kit shrugged off her anorak. "Mum, has Dad had any visitors today? Any reps or anything?"

"No, not that I know of. Why do you ask?"

"Oh, nothing. Daft question, really. They'd come in cars, wouldn't they?"

"What?"

Kit looked with horror at her slippers. She flung them off under the old dresser and padded through in her dripping socks.

Mrs Talbot shook her head when she saw them. "Get them off. There are some clean ones on the clothes maid. Wonderful day for the Joneses to be moving in, isn't it? I hope they beat the storm."

"Probably brought it with them," said Kit meaningfully.

Her mother smiled.

"Well they have got a boy, haven't they? If he's anything like those morons who are always hanging around here he'll be a right pain and nothing but trouble."

Mrs Talbot laughed as she poured tea into three large mugs. "Now then! They're not all bad."

"Really?"

"Really. You might have a pleasant surprise."

Chapter 5

The Girl with the Pigtail

On Sunday morning, Gwyn Jones pulled on his boots, ready to go to the farm.

"Why don't you come with me?" he asked Gareth. "Unless Mum needs you, of course."

Mary Jones shook her head as she unwrapped another tumbler. "The further away the better," she laughed. "I want the china for another day. Besides, there's no hurry. A frantic life's a short life. Any fly will tell you that. I'm only going to sort these few boxes today and then I'm going to take a look at the garden."

"Come on, then," said Gwyn, "get your skates on. There might be some pocket money to be earned there at weekends. Mr Talbot has no boys of his own and there's always something wants doing on a farm."

When they arrived, it seemed as if someone else had the same idea. A plump boy with spiky orange hair was wobbling across the yard pushing a barrowful of logs. Watching him, a stony expression on her face, was a girl sitting astride the gate. She was dressed in faded jeans and an old anorak with the hood up.

Gareth stared at her as she came forward to meet them.

"Hi," she said, grinning at Gareth. "I'm Kathryn Iris Talbot, Kit for short. Your name's Gareth, isn't it? Dad told me." She looked up at Gwyn. "Dad's in the kitchen, Gwyn. I'll show Gareth around if you like."

'Huh!' thought the old Gareth. 'Not if I can help it! I'm not going to be working here, not with her around.' He sent his dad a withering look that said, 'Don't leave me here with her!' She sounded so bossy and sure of herself. 'It's because she's an only child, Mum would say. Well, I'm an only child,' thought Gareth, 'and I'm not like that.' Just the opposite, in fact. Fancy calling his dad Gwyn like that! What a cheek!

But his dad seemed to think it was funny. He ignored Gareth's pleading look and winked at him. "Thank you, Miss Talbot," he said maddeningly. "I'm sure Gareth would love to see the farm. I'll see you later." And he strode away.

"Thanks a bunch," muttered Gareth, his face crimson.

Then Kit turned her head, flung back her hood and shook free a long, thick pigtail.

"Right!" said Kit, pretending she hadn't heard his mumblings. "Let's go to the barn first. I'll show you my swing." And away she walked, leaving Gareth standing in the middle of the yard. He looked around. There was no sign now of the carrot-haired boy.

"Come on!" yelled Kit, when she realised he wasn't following her.

Gareth glared back. Bossy little cat! Just like Miss Fitch at his last school. Be quiet! Do this! Don't do that! But try as he would, he couldn't ignore the pigtail. A pulse quickened inside him. He shrugged and walked slowly after her.

"Who's that boy?" he managed to ask as they stepped from the sunshine into the gloom of the barn.

He couldn't see anything at first. Specks of dust floated before him in the light that flooded through the doorway.

Behind it, sunlight scarcely penetrated the dirty, grey windows, hung with cobwebby curtains, torn and heavy with dust and hay.

"That's not a boy!" replied Kit, pulling a hideous face. "Boys are human, I think." And she grinned wickedly. "That was Barry Thomas, Baz for short. At least, that's what his mates call him. I don't call him anything. I don't talk to worms. And he's worse than a worm. Actually, I like worms. He's a snoop. Comes nosing round here, pretending to be helping Dad. Then he goes back to that Roddy Spinks and that silly Carter boy and tells them all our business. I know because I've heard them talking at school. I guess this place is different from the estate they live on. They can't seem to stay away and Dad's too soft to tell them to buzz off." She didn't even stop for a breath before she said, "Gareth's Welsh, isn't it?"

He nodded.

"It's nice," said Kit. "A strong sort of name like Geraint and Gwyn and Gwydion. Must be the first letter that does it. I wonder if girls' names are the same. Iris is such a wimpy sort of name and old-fashioned. Can you think of any girls' names? I know Glenys, Gwen, Gwyneth. I like that one. Gwyneth Talbot. Funny how most names starting with G are Welsh?"

Gareth's glare silenced her. "Do you ever stop talking?"

Kit sucked in her lips and stared at him saucer-eyed. He couldn't help but laugh.

"I talk a lot when I'm nervous," she said. "You might not believe this but I'm really very shy. It comes of being an only child."

"You're right. I don't believe you."

"It's true!" She pretended to look hurt.

"Where did you hear that name, Gwydion? It's not a common name."

"I dunno. Probably on TV – or in some book – or maybe I dreamt it. Yes, I'm sure I did. But dreams have a habit of vanishing, don't they, even if you try hard to hang on to them? Come on!"

She leapt away like a cat, jumping on to a vertical ladder that was secured to the wall, and shooting up it with the agility of a monkey.

"Hurry up!" she yelled as she disappeared through the square hole in the wooden floor above.

Before Gareth was halfway up he heard a blood-curdling scream. Kit had leapt from the wooden platform and was swinging to and fro on a thick rope fastened to a central beam in the roof. Another unladylike yell and she had dropped, landing like a cat on the heap of hay and bales below. Hmm! The girls at his last school, the ones he knew anyway, seemed to think of nothing but make-up and clothes and sleepovers. They wouldn't be seen dead in a barn, swinging on an old rope. 'She's such a show-off,' he thought - but he couldn't help smiling, couldn't help feeling glad that this crazy girl was more than likely going to be his friend.

"Your turn," she said, following him up the ladder. How could he refuse? He didn't want her calling him a worm – or a wimp. She showed him how to hook the rope and draw it back with an old shepherd's crook.

The jump was pretty good, though the rope hurt his hands. He gave it all he had, and on the first swing his feet touched the platform on the other side of the space. The landing was not so good. More like a hippopotamus than a cat. He misjudged it and hit the bales with a thud. His foot slipped down between them and he rolled over backwards. Even through the layer of loose hay he felt the shock of the stone floor.

"Goodness!" exclaimed Kit, slithering down the caught rope and landing beautifully beside him. "That must be a first. I do believe you've dented the floor. What will my dad say?"

"Very funny!" said Gareth, rubbing his back and staring very hard at his feet.

"You're not really hurt, are you?" she asked.

"'Course not! Don't be daft!" He pushed his hand through the hay until it touched the cold stone.

"Did you bang your head? Your eyes have gone all funny."

"No."

"Want another go? Practice makes perfect."

Gareth didn't answer.

"Want to see the pigs, then? Mabel's got a new litter."

Still no answer.

"You got concussion and you don't know it. What about the bantams? I've got two called Solomon and Sheba."

Gareth hadn't heard a word. He turned and stared at her. "How far is the old mill?" he asked, taking her quite by surprise.

"You mean the one at World's End?"

Gareth frowned and turned away from her, brushing the hay from his clothes. A pulse began to beat in his throat.

"It's just down the lane."

"How far?"

"Not far – five minutes' walk."

"What kind of place is it?"

"It's an old mill. You just said. Hasn't been used for over a hundred years. Falling to bits. Don't go down there much. Dad doesn't like me to."

30

Gareth thought about the models he had painted – the one that looked like him, the one that looked like a dwarf, and the girl with a pigtail down her back – and made a decision. "Can you keep a secret – a real secret, a weird secret – not the silly childish sort?"

Kit crossed her arms and said solemnly, "My brain shall turn to fish and chips if ought of this should pass my lips."

Gareth scowled at her. "It's not kids' stuff," he said, moving towards the ladder. "You've got to promise properly. You've got to swear before I tell you anything. By the way, where's that boy gone?"

"Don't worry about him. He'll be in the garden with the other worms. Actually, I think he's helping Mum pull up the runner beans. And I do swear, honestly. I'm not silly all of the time, you know."

They made a hay igloo on the floor above and sat inside it cross-legged while Gareth told Kit about Grandy and the visit to Crumlock Hill and the voices he'd heard. "You'll probably think I'm completely nuts by now," he said, "but I know we were meant to come here. And the funny little man who told Dad about the job, I know it sound insane and I'm not sure how I know but I think he's a dwarf. You see, I found these tiny models to paint – five of them. I've got lots, but these are different. I found them in a little shop down a narrow street in Chester and when I went back I couldn't find it again – the shop, I mean. One of them looks just like you and one of them looks like me. Then Grandy sent me a dwarf and a wizard. The wizard looks a lot like him. I made a landscape for them to stand in – before we ever thought of coming here – it's not to scale or anything but there's an old mill and a hill rising through trees, and there are stones on the hill, like Stonehenge only not as big. And before I came here, before I'd ever heard of it, I called it 'World's End'"

Kit listened without interrupting. She didn't fidget or laugh even once. "Five of them," she repeated. "You said five. Who are the other three?"

Gareth shrugged, trying to push away the thought of Barry Thomas and his snooping friends. "You're the only person I've met so far."

"Hmm! Rundle Hill. The place you're talking about sounds like Rundle Hill on the other side of the river from the mill. It's kind of flat but there aren't any stones. I don't go there. No one does much. Will Gresty – he's another farmer on the other side of the river – says the place is haunted, but not by an ordinary ghost, whatever that is. Dad says he's daft, been living on his own so long with only his dogs and sheep for company. But I don't know. Ages ago, Mum and I took Jess and Bill up there. We threw sticks for them, but they just whined and headed for home." She chewed on a piece of hay. "Dogs are funny like that, you know. They sense things, usually nasty, wicked things. Dad says there must have been a fort up there once, years ago. It's so flat on top. I think there must be bodies buried there, human sacrifices and things."

Gareth shook his head. "It doesn't have to be a bad place. At least, I don't think so. And I bet you the stones *are* up there."

Kit looked at him as if he were mad. "No, they're not. There's nothing up there – except rabbits and foxes and trees."

"They might not be there now, but perhaps they were there once. And so many weird things have happened lately. That storm for one thing. It came from nowhere."

Kit was staring at him and nodding. "Actually, I saw something a bit odd yesterday," she said. "It was in the storm. There was someone in the lane, tall, weird. I thought I'd imagined it, that it was a trick of the light or something

32

– you know how funny the light can be when the sky goes that queer yellow colour and the lightning flashes."

"Weird? How – weird?"

"Sort of gangly – like an enormous crow – or a scarecrow."

"See!" said Gareth excitedly. "It all fits! You're part of it too. That's why I'm here, why we're both here, and why I'm telling you all this." He stretched out his legs and leaned back. "Just then, when I landed on the hay and felt the stone floor underneath, I realised what could be happening on the hill. Perhaps the stones are beneath the surface. Perhaps they've sunk – or been buried. Perhaps they're not very big."

"You said they were."

"I know I did – but not like Stonehenge. And I know it doesn't make much sense. I mean, stone circles have been around for centuries. They don't just disappear underground – not unless someone wants them to. Perhaps they exist in another time – or another dimension, one parallel to this one."

"What?" Kit sucked on her pigtail and shivered.

"Like layers of an onion," said Gareth, remembering something Grandy had told him once. "Peel one away – and abracadabra. It was there all the time. We just couldn't see it."

"And if we can see it," said Kit, "it must be for a reason." Her voice shook with excitement. "This is crazy. You're crazy. So what do we do now?"

Gareth's frown became a smile when he heard the 'we'. "Are you sure you want to get mixed up in all this?" he said. "It is pretty mind-blowing."

"Are you kidding? It's like something in a book. Until now I never believed those adventures could ever really happen. *A dwarf, a real dwarf!*"

"OK. We look for the stones – then we wait to see what happens."

At that moment, Gwyn Jones's voice splintered the atmosphere in the igloo. "You ready, Gareth? I'm off home now."

Gareth crawled out. "Coming, Dad," he yelled, and ducked back in.

"I've got stuff to do tomorrow – I have to help Mum – but Tuesday, after school?"

"I'll meet you down the lane by the mill. Shall I bring a spade or something?"

"OK. But I'll see you at school, won't I? Are you in year eight?"

Kit nodded.

"Yeuk! School! I hadn't given it much thought," he fibbed. "What's it like?"

Kit pulled another incredibly hideous face and then grinned. "It's OK. Some of the teachers are a bit feeble but most are OK."

As he stepped off the bottom rung of the ladder, Gareth's eye caught a movement at the other end of the barn where a doorway led to the old cow byre.

"Have you got any ginger cats?" he yelled up to Kit.

"Yes, three." Kit's face appeared in the square above him. "Why?"

"I hope I've just seen one – or else that Barry person has been snooping again."

As he walked away from the barn, Gareth glanced back. Kit was standing in the doorway. She had shaken her hair loose and she reminded him of someone, someone buried deep in his memory, someone from long ago.

Gareth spent the rest of the day helping to establish some order in the house. He was just finishing his tea when the telephone rang.

"It's for you," said Mary Jones, her eyebrows raised. "You don't waste much time. Miss Kathryn Talbot, no less, and she sounds in a bit of a tizzy."

Gareth swallowed quickly and dashed into the hall.

"Hi."

"It's me," said Kit in a loud whisper. "Have you got the local news on?"

"No. I don't think we've unpacked the TV or the radio yet. Why?"

"You'll never believe this. Perhaps it's nothing. I mean nothing to do with what you've been telling me. But it does seem odd happening now. And it's only about a mile from here. It was that weird storm."

"Kit, what on earth are you talking about?"

Kit took a deep breath.

"Kit, are you still there?"

"Yes, of course I am. Only Mum was by me. Listen! There's a tree. There was a tree – and it's been struck by lightning. It was hundreds of years old, part of an old row of trees on the other side of Rundle Hill."

"So? Go on. I am listening."

"Well, when the farmer who owns the field finally got around to investigating he found this big old pot under the roots of the tree. Absolutely ancient, they reckon, and made out of bronze. It's covered with swirly patterns and stuff – and wait for it! It hasn't got legs but it's got a handle, just like a witch's-"

"Cauldron," whispered Gareth, his stomach lurching. "Where've they taken it?"

"To the museum at Chester, for now at any rate. They said some experts are coming to have a look at it. Do you think it's important? It is, isn't it?"

Silence.

"Gareth! Will you answer me?"

"Sorry. Yes, it must be important."

"Wow! Do you think so? Gareth. Gareth?"

Gareth's head began to buzz. Hot and cold waves flowed through him. The telephone felt like a lump of ice and his hand shook. "It's the cauldron of Ceridwen," he whispered. "I think she must have stolen it from the Dagda – perhaps that's why her plans were scuppered."

"What? Who? What are you talking about?"

"I don't know. I honestly don't know. A dream that's coming back to me. Things – names – just seem to come into my head from somewhere. It's really weird."

Suddenly there was a crash above his head.

"Gareth, I can't hear you!"

"Mum's here. I've got to go. I'll see you tomorrow." And he slammed down the phone.

"What on earth was that?" said Mary Jones, rushing out of the kitchen and towards the stairs.

"It's OK, Mum," said Gareth, reaching the foot of the stairs before her. "I must have piled too many things in the closet. Sounds like the LEGO box has fallen down."

Gareth's Diary

OK. So this is getting seriously crazy. Ceridwen? And the Dagda? Where did they come from? I need some answers – but I'm not really sure what the questions are. Grandy is the only person I can talk to, the only one who might have a clue about what is going on. I feel like a snake peeling off its old skin and when I look in the mirror (which is not something I do often) I swear I look different, older somehow – more handsome (hopefully). Ha, ha! It's as if the person in the mirror is more real than I am.

Chapter 6

The Book of Gwydion

Next morning a box arrived, delivered to the back doorstep before Gareth and his mum had even had breakfast. Mary was throwing out some scraps for the birds when she saw it. Gareth's name was scrawled on the top. An early birthday present? But they had only been here two days and they had not given everyone their new address yet.

Grandy. Who else could it be?

Mary Jones put the box on the table and turned quickly away, afraid to let Gareth read the anxiety in her eyes.

"It's OK." she said with her back to him. "You don't have to show me if you'd rather not. I know you and Grandy have secrets. I know he's planning something. You think I know nothing, but you're wrong. He's my father, Gareth, and sometimes I don't know who he is – but I know he is good and I have to believe that you will come to no harm – though it's difficult sometimes."

Gareth didn't know what to say. He picked up the box, his fingers tingling, itching to discover the contents.

"It'll be OK, Mum, I promise. I'm not on my own, you know. There are others."

"Others? What do you know about 'others'? No no. Don't answer that. I don't want to know. Go on. Away, and open your parcel quickly while I make breakfast. You don't want to be late for your first day at school."

Gareth found his hands were shaking as he slit open the box. Inside, all he could see was bubble wrap – layers of it. He snipped them off carefully until he reached brown tissue paper and knew that in his hands he held a book. He lifted his pillow and slid the book under it, but it was no good. He couldn't possibly wait until after school. He drew it out again, removed the tissue paper and simply stared.

Gareth's Diary

At break today Kit showed me where everything was and took me on a tour of the school. Everywhere we went we seemed to be shadowed by the same three boys, Roddy Spinks, Barry Thomas and Luke Carter. We turned a corner by the gym and Kit signalled to me to stop. There was a tall one, a medium-sized one and one I recognised – a short, plump one with spiky red hair. They ploughed into each other when we stepped out and surprised them.

"Spinks and Company," introduced Kit, wrinkling her nose and waving her arm dramatically. "What's up, boys? Want our photographs or something?"

The tall one pulled a face, while the other two just looked embarrassed, waiting for their leader to speak.

"It's a free country," he said. Very original, I thought.

"Who's your new friend?" That was Barry Thomas.

"You'll meet him in English."

They wrinkled their noses as if we were a bad smell – and turned away. All we heard were mutterings. "Looks like a swot to me."

"Don't reckon he'll be much good at football."

"Probably got a poncy name like Giles or Rupert."

"Hair like a girl's."

The Book of Gwydion

When the last bell rang, Gareth raced home. The name 'Gwydion' was running through his head. It was the name on the book. It was also a name that Kit had mentioned. Where had she seen it? Flinging his bag into a chair, he shouted 'Hello' to his mum and took the stairs two at a time. That morning, when he had removed the tissue paper he had sat staring at an ancient, leather-bound book, sensing its antiquity, curious and nervous at the same time. Then Mary had called and he had hidden it under his pillow again without even looking at the first page. Half afraid now that the book would have disappeared, he slid his hand under the pillow and sighed when his fingers touched the warm leather. He drew it out and laid it on his knees while his fingers traced the curious swirls and figures that decorated the cover. He held it to him instinctively, breathing deeply, searching for knowledge of its origins in the feel and smell of it. Then, slowly, carefully, almost afraid to expose its fragile contents, he lifted the cover.

The pages were yellowed and brittle, the ink brown and faded. Each leaf was edged with gold and in every outer corner was drawn the head of a bird or the curved horns of a ram.

On the first page was a pattern of lines with wedge-shaped characters above and below them. Gareth was dismayed. "I can't read this!" He looked up. "Grandy, I can't read this!" He ran his fingers over the strange letters, frowning, concentrating, and drawing on everything he knew – or had once known. Over them and over them he went until the fog in his mind cleared and a light shone through. "Gwydion's Dream," he whispered breathlessly. "It's written in Ogham, the language of the trees. But how do I know that? And how am I able to read it?"

The answer came from somewhere deep within. 'The knowledge is brought to you through the blood of your forefathers. Your eye throws back the light that was Taliesin's. Your mind awakens to the wisdom that was his.'

Gareth sighed and nodded. Taliesin. Of course. That was the name from his dreams. Why had he doubted, been afraid? The dreams had told him where he came from. How could he do this if he didn't have faith in those whose beckoning hands he followed? Suddenly, reading this ancient language seemed the most natural thing in the world. As he buried himself in the comforting warmth of his duvet, he felt his old life slipping away into a mist of unreality and the call that came to him then through the words of Gwydion awakened him to a greater truth, more real, more important, than anything he had ever known.

He turned over the first page and was lost in its spell.

I, Gwydion, Son of Nwyvre, Warrior-Magician, Defender of the Light and Teller of Tales, cast now this dream upon the waters of time and commend the truth of it into the hands of those who would seek and believe.

Gareth swallowed hard, remembering the dreams, the voices, the sense of everything changing inside him and around him. "I believe," he whispered. *In the beginning, when the Light was new, Nwyvre found a land that was good and pure. Long had he sought such a place, for his own world had seen the last setting of the sun.*

He set down his people to live there in harmony with the great spirit of the new world, with the creatures of earth and air. He gave them knowledge of all that surrounded them, the power of stone, the language of trees, the music of streams that is the living expression of the earth mother, and the secrets of the four winds. He called them Tuatha de Dana, the Children of the Dawn. He appointed them guardians of meadowland and mountain, river and forest,

41

and for many years they lived as one with nature and the forces of the Universe.

Then others came from distant, darker shores. First, Ymyr, father of dwarfs. His people were wild and shy and sought the secret places beneath the ground. They were cunning goldsmiths and masters of the red ores they hammered from their tunnels and caverns. In a gesture of peace, Ymyr himself crafted a magnificent sword and bestowed upon it a deep Earth-magic, that it might never be used against the Light. He made a gift of it to Nuada Silverhand, Lord of the Tuatha de Dana, and the sword was named Caladbolg, Consumer of All, and it was the First of the Four Treasures.

In the wake of the dwarfs, others followed, wave upon wave of them. They came in ships from a lesser land, armed with shields and helmets and swords. They thirsted for power and gold. They sought neither knowledge nor friendship, but lived only to conquer and subdue the land and its peoples. They scorned the Tuatha and their ways of peace. They trampled their wisdom into the dust of the battlefield.

Against their nature, but out of necessity, the children of Nwyvre became warriors, with sword and sling, bow and lance. But on all sides the earth moved further into shadow, and out of the darkness came new enemies. Against their might the Tuatha could hold out no longer. They were driven to the high, wild places of the land – but in time, these too fell into shadow and Nwyvre led them through gateways to another world, the land of Tir na nog, where the most ancient spirits slept and the Tuatha might find peace once more.

Out of the stone of the Black Mountains of Urd they built for themselves a city, a stronghold against the Dark. They named the city Tara, which, in the old tongue, means 'bracken'. For, like bracken, when shards of sunlight pierce the shield of winter, they would heave against the darkness of the earth and shine once more in the Light.

When the city was complete there arrived at the gates of Tara a warrior, Lugh Lamphada. He sought permission to enter the city but was denied. He carried with him a lance and a sling, weapons of war. But the Tuatha believed they had done with war. The World of Men had cast them out and they would not return until human hearts were open to receive them. Until that day, dreams of them must be kept alive on earth. Thus it was that Mariandor, fairest of Nwyvre's children, was destined to move between worlds, weaving threads of memory and whispering in the dreams of the Children of Men. And thus it was that Lugh Lamphada, bearing his weapons of war, was denied. But it was not in him to turn his back to Tara.

"Hold fast!" cried he that would enter when Cadw, the gatekeeper, barred his way. "If, as a warrior, I bring nothing of value to your city, then perhaps as a smith or wood-carver I may be granted entry."

When Cadw asked for proof of his words Lugh Lamphada cast over the city walls a hollow branch of the rowan wood whereon was carved in pictures the history of the Tuatha de Dana.

"How know you of this?" cried the gatekeeper, suspecting some deception. "Only Nwyvre, our father, can know so much of his children."

For answer, Lugh Lamphada smiled and cast over the wall an amulet, wrought in silver of the finest crafting. At its centre, like the eye of a living god, was set a jewel, greener than the rock-held moss, pure as dawn light on the first leaf.

At sight of it Cadw knew it to be Lia Fail, Stone of Destiny. Its origins were deep in the heart of Falias, an ancient realm wherein it was formed at the centre and beginning of all time. And the Stone possesses power over

43

Destiny for which all men strive. Long had Cadw heard its name whispered; oft had the sons of Nwyvre sought it in their dreams.

Thus it was that Lugh Lamphada crossed the threshold of Tara, bringing with him the lance, Answeror and the Stone of Destiny, gifts from Nwyvre to strengthen the hearts of his people. And it was written that the voice of the stone would cry out when a new king was chosen; that its heart, deep in the mystery of all life, would shatter if the song of the Tuatha de Dana were silenced forever.

In the wake of the warrior another arrived, a giant named Dagda. He was of the Old Race, but his sleep in the Black Mountains of Urd had been disturbed by the building of Tara. He came now, bearing his Cauldron of Plenty, offering his services to those whose labours had disturbed him.

Thus it was that Nwyvre, hearing the winds of discontent blow between worlds, sent help to his children.

Now the Treasures numbered four. And their origins were in the Four Realms: Falias in the north, Murias in the west, Gorias in the east and Finias in the south.

The Tuatha waited and listened.

Without the light and the wisdom of the Tuatha de Dana, Earth slipped further into the shadows of ignorance and greed. As Darkness ebbed and flowed, the substance at its centre thickened and grew again into the form that is Morgana, essence of Evil, possessor of a thousand faces. Pride and greed were her masters. She drew her followers from the blackest memories of Earth and sought to wipe all thoughts of the Tuatha from the minds of Men. In the destruction of hope and the shattering of dreams she grew stronger, and though Earth-born, was able to move between worlds at will. Now, she had power enough to wake the Old Ones who crawled the darkness beneath the rocks of Tir na nog.

But wind, like rain, moves freely between worlds, and on the wind a whisper was borne from Mariandor's lips, uttering Morgana's name and purpose, breathing its message through the leaves of Tir na nog.

Swollen with pride, and with none to challenge her, she of a thousand faces rose above our worlds to summon magic from forgotten places, a dark magic, asleep since the rising of the first white moon. And on the back of a roaring wind she entered Tir na nog to seek out the source of the tiny flame that flickered yet on Earth, to take possession of the Stone, Lia Fail, that she might destroy it and the hopes of those who worshipped it.

As she and the shadows of her vile swarm drew a dark line across the Field of Moytura she was met by three armies. Lugh Lamphada was their champion, leading those elves he had instructed in the art of war. On his right hand rode Nuada Silverhand with Caladbolg and another company of Elves. On his left marched the foot soldier dwarfs, led by Dalldaf Stagshank.

Though short of stature, the dwarfs have never lacked courage or strength. They have ever scorned the use of horses, and on this day faced their enemies with stout hearts and bold eyes.

On the left flank of the dwarfs came the Giant Dagda, wielding his mighty club and filling the sky with his anger. For the name of Morgana awakened old memories and opened old wounds. Morgana was outfaced. Her anger made her terrible to behold. "Spies!" she cried, casting her livid eye over those who scuttled and crawled behind her. "Who told of our coming? WHO, I ask you!"

When none replied she lifted her contorted face to the sky and snapped her fingers to summon her servant, the bird with the yellow eye.

"Go forth!" she screamed when a ragged outline appeared and darkened the sun. "Seek out whatever *grummel dared to speak my name. Tease it with a song or drag it by the ears. Only bear it to the arms of Sinadon.'*

As the armies of Tir na nog drew closer, Morgana's features sharpened into a mask of hatred, evil oozing and dripping from every pore. She stretched out her bony arms and called on all the Dark Magic of the world, all the power and energy generated by Earth's black history.

Seeing her, Nuada held up his right hand and the armies moved sideways, drawing another line across the Field of Moytura. Before them, Morgana grew in stature until her tortured shape brought night to the Plain. In that moment of darkness she swooped upon her enemies, piercing them with shards of blue ice, harder than moon rock, colder than the first light. And the shards rained down until Lugh and his warriors and the Giant Dagda were frozen into stone.

It happened in a moment.

Nuada was struck dumb. He had no idea that the Dark had grown so powerful, that Morgana could wield such strength. At last he spoke. "Release them! In the name of the Light and all that our father taught us, release them!"

Morgana laughed. "The power is not mine," she screamed. "The call must come from another." Then she took on the shape of a monstrous bird and bore away the lance, Answeror, and the Cauldron of Plenty, carried on the belt of the Giant Dagda. Lost from sight, she bore them towards Enzor, and from there she cast them from the highest cliff, with a wish that on the rocks below they would be dashed to pieces.

Too late she felt her power wane and saw the measure of her mistake. As she returned, her venomous form lacked substance. She had not paused to consider, so great was her anger. The task had proved too much, and she did not possess the Stone. With a hoarse shriek she summoned

46

Baldor of the Old Ones, whose name was nothing more than an echo haunting black and stormy nights.

"Baldor!" she cried again, and the sound of her summons met the screaming of horses and the thunder of a thousand burnished hooves as Baldor and the Savage Hunt broke like the dawn from a distant hill, flooding the horizon with a river of blood.

As they came, the curve of Baldor's horns flashed lightning through the clouds; his wild hair streaked the sky with crimson light.

"Who wakes the Savage Hunt?" he cried, his voice an echo of pounding seas and a wind that knows no peace.

"One greater by far than Baldor, he who visits battlefields only when the day is won and the mighty are slain."

"Morgana!" roared Baldor. "Your name has darkened my dreams."

"And will darken more than dreams if he does not bow to my bidding."

Baldor's eye held hers. It was in him to mock her yet something troubled him. She was of a newer magic, drawn from a different source. She had power over him he did not understand.

"Speak or I leave on the wind," he said.

"A greater purpose calls me," said Morgana. "Find for me the stone that is called Lia Fail, whose name is born with each of us."

"And if I do not?" roared Baldor to the shadow at his feet.

The shadow lifted, sliding over Baldor like a shroud. "Then you will die as humankind dies. Die and rot. It lies with the stone. You can change it not, but I, Morgana, have the power." And with a hiss, as of water on sun-baked rock, she was gone.

Baldor raised his arm and the Savage Hunt bore down on the Field of Moytura, scattering the diminished army. In his wake, and at his signal, the creatures of the Dark moved like a winter tide upon the Plain, spilling the blood of dwarf and elf, though all fought bravely. And, when the battlefield was strewn with the dead, Baldor moved on in search of Lia Fail. He found the amulet wherein the stone had been set, but of the stone itself he found no trace. To ride was all to him, and if his fate lay with the Stone, then it must be found, and not for Morgana's sake. He roared and cast about him and searched the sky for Morgana, but nought was left of her or her swarm save the choking smell of evil and the scent of death that hung like a pall over the Field of Moytura.

The Tuatha de Dana were not destroyed. Their destruction would not bring him Lia Fail. Baldor threw back his head and looked beyond the stars.

"We ride!" His voice was the winter wind.

Behind him hooves pounded air and the Savage Hunt lifted as one into the sky, a storm of horsemen, faceless, grey. They caught the wind and flew before it, leaving only fiery strands to mark their path across the sky.

When they were gone, a wounded Nuada Silverhand ordered his people to seek out a place of safety for Lugh Lamphada and his warriors. The dwarfs found such a place, a deep cavern at the edge of Moytura, beneath a mound that was named Talebolion. And there they sleep, until the day when a call from the Children of Men should reach their ears and awaken them. The Giant Dagda was of proportions so immense that to move him was an impossible task. He stands now at the edge of the Plain, awaiting the call that might waken him, that he might rise and make amends.

When the battlefield was silent, and the dead buried, Nwyvre wept for seven days, washing the blood of good and

48

evil into the soil. His grief and anger were greater than the first rains and fires from which the mountains sprang. And in his anger, though it was not in him to meddle with the will and ways of Men, he smote the land beneath him, carving his words in rock.

The loss of the stone was a terrible blow to Nuada and the Children of Tara. They knew not who had taken it. It held their dreams, their hopes, and it was gone. Its absence dragged at their spirits and clouded their thoughts until they half-believed their father, Nwyvre, had deserted them.

Crazed with wrath and anguish, fearful for Mariandor, Nuada Silverhand blamed the downfall of the Tuatha and the rise of Morgana on the metal, iron, bane of our worlds. He flung his mighty sword, Caladbolg, into the swollen river and cursed the day when dwarfs, wherever they dwelt, had become masters of the iron-craft, discoverers of the red ore of death.

And so it came about that in seven days the Four Treasures of the Tuatha de Dana were lost.

At this time, Mariandor was a wanderer in the World of Men.

She brought dreams to the sleeping children of Earth. She told stories at their hearths in exchange for bread. She touched their hearts with snatches of song, kindled their curiosity with fragments of memory and filled them with a longing for something they had never known and could not yet understand. She brought comfort to Aegir and Cernunnos and the creatures in their realms, in the seas and on land, who were beset by Evil, whose songs and voices were no longer heard.

In her wanderings she has looked into the eyes of Men and sought the good in their hearts. She taught them how to tread the old paths, to seek solace in silence and listen to the language of the trees.

Of these men Arturo was the purest in heart. Into his hands Mariandor delivered Caladbolg, for Mimir, the Wise One, had taken it from the ocean and cast it up on the shores of Gwynant when a storm gathered in the north. During his lifetime it served him well in his crusade against Evil. But when the hounds of death snapped at his heels, Myrddin, his guide and friend, cast Arturo's failing body upon the half-silent water and returned Caladbolg to the arms of Sinadon."

The book fell from Gareth's hands and he stared at the wall, numb with shock and disbelief. He had tried to be prepared for anything but now, his heart and head were pounding. He picked up the book and opened it again. The names swam before his eyes. Arturo - Arthur? Myrddin-Merlyn? And Caladbolg. The sword Excalibur? But surely they were just stories. At least, that's what most people seemed to think. Ten per cent fact, ninety per cent fiction. But the shores of Gwynant – where he had been many times with Grandy – where Grandy had often stood and stared out across the water with a solemn face – as if it held a memory – or a secret.

"If it's written in a book and called history we believe it; if it comes to us by way of song and story we doubt the truth of it and call it legend." That's what Grandy had told him once. But where does one end and the other begin? Perhaps everything we know of the past is a mixture of both.

Gareth took a deep breath and turned to the last written page.

"The years stride onward, heavy-laden. Darkness and Light live side by side in the world and in the hearts of Men. They thrust and parry, gain ground and retreat. I am burdened by the knowledge that the Earth will move into

50

deeper shadow. The Dark will rise, Morgana's power will be renewed and the Ancient Ones will be shaken from their rest.

"At such a time, when it seems that Ragnarok is nigh, when the Light of the Tuatha is all but extinguished by the darkness on Earth, and memory of them buried deeper than the roots of Yggdrasil, a boy will set out on the long, straight path. Through his veins will course the blood of Gwydion and Taliesin and of Myrddin, and Myrddin will set him on his way.

"This I tell you, is the word and design of our father, Nwyvre, written in the blood of the battlefield, cut into rock and foretold by Lugh Lamphada in his carving of the rowan-tree wood. Keep it in your hearts and doubt it not, for doubt and despair open doors to the Dark, and where there is no hope the Light cannot shine."

Beneath this last line was a row of swirling lines and careless, tangled shapes. Under them, in darker, newer ink was written.

"Many winters have passed since Mariandor crossed the threshold of Tara. The winds that blow between our worlds no longer breathe her name. The waters are silent and mountain walls have long ago lost the echo of her song. Who, now, can colour the dreams of the children. Who but Mariandor can unshackle their minds, their hearts, and guide them back along the old straight track, the pathway to the Light?

"My heart is locked in sorrow. Even for me the days grow short and the shadows lengthen. My only hope lies in the words of our father. The boy will come. For without him our peoples will be divided for ever. The children of Nwyvre will be borne away like chaff on an autumn wind *and the World of Men abandoned to the Darkness of Ignorance and Despair."*

Beyond this nothing more had been written.

Chapter 7

Worlds' End

Gareth turned over the fragile leaf and stared at the blank pages beyond, wondering what might yet be written there. As he did so his field of vision diminished until he was no longer aware of the room about him. His bed, the floor, the desk and the pale green wall beyond them had all slipped away. All he could see, as if through a microscope, were the yellowed fibres of the page as the book grew to fill the room. Suddenly, he was on his feet, standing between its pages, and as the book closed about him he was drawn into another place as a sleeper is lifted out of himself and into a dream.

He was standing by a hedge. It was a mixture of hawthorn and holly, splashed with the pink of young maple shoots. And at his feet, amid the unruly grass, spikes of cuckoo-pint fought for space among the clambering vetch.

Beyond the hedge a field, horse-shoe shaped, fell away steeply to where a house stood. It was built of pale, old brick, patterned with holes where sparrows could nest. The windows were blind and two cold chimneys pointed at the sky.

Gareth turned and followed the cobbled track down to the house. Before its hanging gate he turned ninety degrees down a muddy slope that fell gradually and rose again over a stone bridge, mossy and grizzled and rooted into the hill.

Under the bridge water drained from the hill, gathered in a choking bed of watercress and moved slowly on, where once a spate had rushed to power the mill-wheel. And where the stream from the hill joined the meandering river there stood the ruin of a water-mill, its broken wheel lodged in the shifting bank.

"Worlds' End," whispered Gareth, as if being here was the most natural thing in the world.

Within the crumbling walls of the mill, splintered beams and grinding stones were strewn about the muddy floor like the toys of a careless giant.

Gareth crossed the stone bridge and followed the riverbank to another. This one was wooden and looked as old as the first. At each end was a gate, fastened to a leaning post by a loop of heavy chain.

Across the second bridge another stream trickled down to feed the river. It had gouged a deep gully in the hillside and from its banks spindly trees leaned drunkenly, as if the ground had suddenly tilted. Violets grew in the mottled shade and larger patches of sunlight picked out the starry shapes of anemones and the spotted leaves of the early orchid.

Gareth stepped carefully between the flowers and scrambled up the side of the gully. He followed an animal track that traced the contour of the hill and was soon stepping over the line of an old sandstone wall between thorn bushes that sprouted from the heaps of fallen stone. He stopped for a moment, enjoying the scent of wild garlic and wet earth before moving on into an army of beech trees that stormed the hill, their heads in the sky and feet lost in a haze of bluebells. He was aware of their presence, their strength, all about him. In the rustle of the leaves he heard them breathe; he felt their roots stir beneath his feet. They knew he was there and welcomed him.

He clambered over fallen branches, torn by winter storms, now deep in new bracken and slippery with fungi and rotting bark. Their smell was rich and earthy in his nostrils. 'Soon,' thought Gareth, 'I shall break from the trees and see a ring of dark stones crowning the hill.'

No sooner had he thought it than the trees were behind him, pressing him forward. Up the grassy slope he ran and over the rim of the hill, striding towards its centre, searching all around. But there were no stones. In his head he thought, 'I have fallen asleep and am dreaming. If this is the landscape I have created from a dream then where are the stones?'

The hilltop was as flat as an arena, its surface broken only by thorny bushes and tangled clumps of briar and fern.

He felt disappointed, cheated somehow. He placed his feet apart and looked up at the sky. "Where are they?" he cried out loud. "They have to be here!"

Imagine!

Imagine!

He recognised his folly immediately, and that in this, his first test, he had failed. In answer to his impatient cry, darkness descended upon the hill. Angry clouds stampeded across the plains of the sky, driven by a relentless wind. The change was like the turning of the year. Gareth shivered and began to run. Across the hill he sprinted, head down, boring through the wind, crashing through the darkness. As he reached the rim, ready to leap and roll into the welcome shelter of the trees, he tripped and fell, pitching forward heavily, arms and legs flailing as brambles tore at his bare skin.

Suddenly, he was back in his room. There was something going on in the garden, a commotion, a cat yowling as if its tail was on fire. When Gareth reached the window he was in time to see the animal, hair on end, streaking across the square patch of light thrown on to the lawn. Behind it, a piece of darkness, bigger than any bird, broke from the silhouette of the apple tree and glided into the deeper shadows beyond the hedge.

He drew the curtains and looked down at the mud on his jeans and the tiny beads of blood that were drying on the back of his hand.

Gareth's Diary

Sorry diary. No time tonight. I have a story to write for Miss March. She's testing our English, checking to see if we possess any imagination at all – or if we are brain dead on account of watching too much TV and being glued to a computer. Actually, my story will be part of my diary. Strange, that she should ask us to write about a dream.

Chapter 8

Kit

At four o'clock on Tuesday Kit left Old Mill Farm. She had changed her clothes and fed the bantams in record-breaking time.

"Where are you off to in such a hurry?" Reg Talbot called as she rummaged through the tools in the barn, looking for an old spade.

"Just off to do a bit of exploring with Gareth, Dad. Won't be long."

"Down to the old mill, I'll be bound."

Kit nodded.

"Well, just be careful. That place is none too safe. Wants pulling down altogether, I reckon. Make sure you're back for tea, now."

"OK, Dad. See you."

And she was off, running down the lane, wondering if Gareth had beaten her. Carrying the spade, her eyes picking out the easiest route down the rough track, she didn't see the three bicycles dropped in the high grass behind the hedge, or the three pairs of curious, mocking eyes that watched her.

Gareth had beaten her. He had deliberately set out early, wanting to follow the map in his head. The lane and the house, the mill and the stream were just as he had seen them. He sat on the parapet of the bridge until the coldness of the stone struck through his clothes and made him shiver. He rubbed his hands together, stood up and walked through the scattered rubble towards the ruin of the mill. He put both hands on the bare brick of the sill and leaned forward to peer inside. The walls were thick, made to last. It was strange how buildings could stand for decades, centuries even, as long as they were useful and cared for. They were just like people; unloved and deserted, they lost heart and began to crumble. He wondered which beam had given way first, which stone had been the first to fall after years of wind and weather, gears grinding and wheels turning; which crumb of mortar had broken away and started the rot.

As his eyes adjusted to the gloom he saw among the debris, in the dark mud that covered the floor, the pale, squat form of a toad. Its eyes stared back at him, unblinking, two tiny pools of yellow light. Gareth didn't dislike toads, but something in the colour of its eyes made him shudder and step back. As he did so a shadow fell across the broken window frame, darkened the pale bricks for a moment and was gone. Kit, he thought, and turned. But there was no one, just a bird high in the sky. When he looked back up the lane he saw Kit, spade in hand, running jerkily down towards him.

"We'll have to hurry," she called before she reached the bridge. "Mum reckons there's another storm coming. You can tell by the funny clouds – and the birds."

Gareth didn't answer. He took the spade from her and turned, following the river bank towards the wooden bridge.

"What *about* the birds?" he asked at last as he opened the gate and waved Kit through.

"Oh you are talking then. I thought for a moment you were one of those moodies. I can't stand moodies."

58

"Sorry. I was just thinking about something."

"The rooks. Surely you know about rooks. When a storm's coming they perch lower down in the trees. There was even one in the apple tree closest to my window. At least, Mum said it was a rook. I thought it was a carrion crow. Dad said it was neither and must be a raven or something. I've never seen a raven, have you? But there are some living on the sandstone crags. And anyway, it had the weirdest yellow eyes. It gave me the creeps."

"I know," said Gareth. "I've seen it too." He was scrambling up the side of the gully now. "Did you know there were orchids growing here?" he asked her.

But flowers were the last things on Kit's mind. She was thinking of the bird, glancing behind her now, determined to keep up with Gareth as he hurried along the track, trodden nightly by badgers and foxes.

Before her, Gareth moved into the deepening shadow of the beech trees, into a net of darkness. Kit was close behind but he was hardly aware of her. He could only think of the stones now. He ran from the trees, up the grassy slope, and stood beneath the rim of the hill. He turned then and shouted her on.

Halfway through the wood, Kit had stopped and was looking back. Gareth couldn't see the frown of concentration on her face. She took a few steps forward and turned to look back again. She put her head down and scrambled after him.

"Someone's following us!" she managed to get out between gasps. "I could feel it. And every time I looked back they disappeared behind bushes and trees."

Gareth stared back down the hill. "I can't see anything now."

"Doesn't mean it isn't there, does it? I wasn't imagining things!"

"Perhaps it's the weird light," suggested Gareth. "It's hard to make anything out properly." He turned towards the rim of the hill. "Come on, I'll race you to the middle."

"There was someone," muttered Kit, following him slowly. "Boys, huh! They think all girls are idiots."

At the centre of the plateau they turned around slowly, like the hands of a clock. There were no stones to be seen, no grassy bumps, nothing to indicate that a circle had ever been built there. But Kit wasn't even looking at the ground beneath her. She was gripping Gareth's elbow and pointing. All around the hill the air was thickening, darkening, weaving itself into a muffler of grey fog.

"I've never seen it come down that quickly," whispered Kit.

Gareth shook his head slowly, unable to take his eyes away from the disappearing landscape. The fields and trees on the other side of the river were taking on the appearance of charcoal drawings. Their grey outlines were being smudged sideways by the fog, as if some giant, dirty eraser was rubbing them out. As the children watched, the world beneath Rundle Hill was swallowed completely, and the hill was an island rising from an alien grey sea.

"It is October," said Gareth at last, trying to sound light-hearted, but failing miserably, "the season of mists and all that." He looked anxiously at Kit. She was unusually quiet. "Mum's favourite poem. She's always quoting it at me, trying to educate me." Kit was still frowning. "You're not going to chicken out, are you?"

The old Kit returned rapidly. "Rubbish!" she said in disgust. "Season of mists, my big toe! You don't have to pretend for my sake, you know. And besides, there's no way I'm walking back on my own. I still don't see any stones, though."

Gareth circled the hill. He knew the exact spot where he had fallen, thought about the stone floor beneath the layer of hay in the barn. Stamped his foot. He was right. There *was* something there beneath the turf, a rise in the grass that was barely visible. He slammed the spade into it. Too hard! Too eager! A stupid thing to do! The impact jarred his wrist. He began slicing at the turf, carefully to begin with, then frantically when he heard the scrape of metal on stone. He dropped to his knees, tossed the spade aside and tore at the earth with his bare hands.

Kit wanted to help, but she was distracted. They were being watched, she was certain. She couldn't take her eyes off the trees – in case someone – or something – emerged from the shadows.

"Look!" yelled Gareth. "Kit, look!"

Kit dragged her eyes away from the trees and dropped to her knees. She stretched out her hand and brushed away the dark soil so that she too could touch the cold stone.

Gareth leapt to his feet. "I'll look for the others." He moved away from Kit, never lifting his eyes from the hill, telling himself that beyond the fog the world he knew was still there. He followed the edge of the circle and almost stumbled again. There was another mound and another, like the heave formed by a mushroom just about to break the surface. He ran around the circle, counting.

There were twelve, just as he had known there would be. He had completed the circle and was back at Kit's side. She was kneeling still, hand on the stone, eyes locked on the trees below. She beckoned him to join her, to lay his hand beside hers on the stone.

"Can you feel it?" she whispered.

Gareth nodded, unable to speak. He closed his eyes, so that his fingers would tell him more. And beneath them the hill trembled.

"Did we do it?" asked Kit. "Did we wake them?"

Gareth shook his head slowly, his eyes on the centre of the circle. "No. I don't know. Maybe. Something has – and we're a part of it." The Guardians are stirring. The wheel turns. More thoughts that came from nowhere.

Kit followed his look. As they watched, the earth heaved, bulged upwards, stretching the skin of the plateau until it burst. Beneath them the bones of the hill stirred as the splitting turf revealed a stone, grey as the fog, rounded like the dome of a giant mushroom.

Kit's fingernails dug into Gareth's arm. Neither of them could move. For a moment that seemed endless they were like the stones, rooted in the hill. Then the trembling stopped. They felt a wind in their faces, a keen, rousing wind, though they could hear no rustle of leaf or bracken, no soughing through grass or tree.

Gareth snatched his arm away suddenly and began tearing frantically at the turf around the stone. The light was fading fast, the green hill losing its colour. It seemed the fog would devour them all. But in the darkness of the stone, strange characters appeared, cut deep into the rock.

"It's some sort of writing," whispered Kit, kneeling beside him, "like hieroglyphics."

"It's Ogham," said Gareth, scraping the grains of soil from the grooves.

"Never heard of it," said Kit. "How do you …" She was going to say, "How do you know?" but thought better of it. He just knew, that was all. And besides, he wasn't even listening. He was tracing the patterns with his fingers, staring straight ahead of him, like a blind man reading Braille.

"See the lines, the way the letters are formed."

"It's getting dark," said Kit. "I've got a torch in my pocket. Do you need it?" More wasted breath.

Gareth was frowning, his thoughts lost in the words of the stone. When he did speak, his words sounded hollow as if the voice was not his own.

"Moonstone full and scarlet light,

Touch the old ways, bend the ring

And bring the keeper home."

"It's a riddle," said Kit. "What does it mean?"

Gareth traced the pattern again, to be sure. At his touch the words came alive and burned in his mind. He nodded at something made known or understood, then dragged his thoughts away. "It's raining," he said.

Drops, as big as old pennies, fell on the stone, first one drop, then a dozen, then a hundred – filling the grooves, washing the words back into the rock.

Gareth opened his mouth to speak, but before he could make a sound another came to them from the trees. Whether human or animal, they could not tell, but they recognised the sound of fear.

"We have to go!" said Gareth. "Now! Come on!"

Across the river the fog was dispersing rapidly. Any last clinging remnants were blown away by an unnatural wind that raced towards the children, gusting, tearing, spinning, lifting leaves and twigs high into the air.

They fled down the grassy slope and into the thicker darkness of the wood, legs whirring wildly, out of control. As he ran, Gareth's eyes caught a movement across the hill, beyond the thinning trees; a grey shape, vague in the poor light, scuttling through the barberry and gorse like a hunted rabbit.

But that was not all. The fog had brought something else to the hill. Gareth felt it now, moving behind them and beside them, driving them on. He glanced sideways and almost fell when he caught sight of them breaking from the deepening darkness, separating from the trees, long, thin shadows moving with the wind.

He said nothing to Kit, but kept her in front of him. When they were clear of the trees she stopped, panting, sucking in breath, hands on knees. Then she looked up and grinned at him. She was pointing in the direction of the gully where three heads were slipping out of sight. "Spinks and Co.," she got out between noisy puffs. "I might have known it. Can't keep his nose out of anything. I told you the worm was a snoop."

Now Gareth was alongside her. Barely slowing down, he grabbed her arm and yanked her forward. "Come on!" he yelled against the wind. "We can't stop yet!"

Kit stumbled forward, indignation in every step. "You idiot! It was only Roddy Spinks and his gang. Didn't you see them?"

"Yes, yes, I saw them!"

"Then why are you pulling me? I can't run any faster, and the light doesn't help." To prove her point, she misjudged the size of a grassy hump and went sprawling. Gareth dragged her to her feet.

"Come on! We must get to the bridge!"

"What is the matter with you? Didn't you hear me? It was Roddy Spinks and his little friends − and they're probably half way home by now."

Gareth yanked her forward again. "If that lot are in front of us then who's behind us?"

Kit threw a look over her shoulder, and almost fell again. What she saw − or thought she saw − made her run faster than she had ever run in her life. Against the backdrop of the wood a tall spidery shape was moving, weaving to and fro, restless, changing direction with the wind. In that moment another figure joined the first, and another. They converged and separated again, heads lifting as if they were sniffing the air. Stooping and swaying, they moved forward like beaters flushing out their quarry before the kill.

Gareth and Kit didn't look back again until they reached the bridge. Once over it, they stopped for breath and knew they were alone. THEY had stayed on the hill.

"What are they?" said Kit at last.

"Watchers, shape shifters. Who knows?" said Gareth. "They belong to her."

"Her? Who?"

"Ceridwen, Morgana. I'm not sure."

"Can they harm us, do you think?"

"I don't know that either. I don't think so. I think they're just out to scare us, stop us interfering. If they can destroy our belief in ourselves and turn us away from the Light then our greatest enemies will be ourselves."

Kit gave him a funny look. He really came out with the strangest things at times. "Oh well, if that's all …" She grinned wryly. "We can't let it happen, can we?"

"No, but it won't be easy."

"Where's the spade?"

"In the trees somewhere. I couldn't really run with it. We'll have to come back for it."

The rain had stopped and the wind did nothing more than tease the feathery strands of the willow tree. Although now it was almost dark, they left their fear behind with the shadows on the hill. Only excitement remained when they recalled the words on the stone.

"I wonder when the next full moon will be," said Kit. She searched the sky, but the moon was nowhere to be seen.

"It would make sense if it was Hallowe'en, but there's more than a week to go and it's nearly full now. What about scarlet light? Do you think it just means fire?"

Their whispering voices sounded too loud as they walked up the lane. They were aware of every footfall, every breath. It was as if time itself were trapped in the silence after the storm and they felt as if they were the last two people in the world.

Gareth left Kit at the gate to the farm. He watched until she was in the yard then he turned the corner and headed for the crossroads. As he did so he heard a low, grumbling noise in the high grass behind the hedge. He sighed. "Goodnight, Spinks. Goodnight, Baz. Goodnight, Carter."

But Roddy Spinks and his friends, frightened half out of their wits by what they had seen on the hill, were already a mile away, pedalling furiously towards the lights of the village.

Gareth's Diary

Today was so ordinary it was boring. Sorry, Mum. That word is banned in our house. I said it once and she gave me so much to do I made sure I never said it again. "No one with two hands and a brain has any right to be bored," she had told me. But it was as if someone had offered me this amazing adventure and then said, sorry, but you are just not up to it. We shall have to look for someone else. To make it worse, those three creeps kept hanging around. I reckon the word 'bored' is one of their favourite words. I guess I surprised them in the P.E. lesson. That was fun. None of them could catch me on the rugby pitch.

Seriously, though, what will Kit think of me if nothing does come of all this? She'll think I'm a real loser.

Chapter 9

The Story Boy

"OK, who's first?"

Miss March, Gareth's form tutor and English teacher looked around the class. She had said that hearing their stories was a good way of getting to know them. She'd shown them some paintings by Klee and Dali and played some music that made them think of forests, alien planets, waterfalls and armies marching – to name but a few.

Roddy Spinks had sniggered at the idea of dreams – and grinned at his two mates, Barry Thomas and Luke Carter. Miss March had sighed, anticipating the silly essays they would write. The girls would try harder, especially Kit. She knew she shouldn't have favourites but Kit was different from the other girls with their frivolous love of clothes and sleepovers and such. She didn't possess a computer like most of the others. She loved books and had the most wonderful imagination. She was pleased and not a bit surprised that Kit seemed already to have made friends with Gareth, the new boy. There was something about him. He looked like a loner, and that had bothered her, but in four days she had noticed a difference in him. It was something she couldn't put a finger on. He had the most incredible blue eyes – and such a smile – when you were lucky enough to catch it. The girls would love him; she hoped the boys wouldn't give him a hard time.

"No volunteers, then?"

Most of the boys shrank visibly, eyes downcast. Some of the girls, though keen, were reluctant to put up their hands. They knew they'd be mocked for being 'prima donnas' or 'teacher's pets'.

Reluctant to single Kit out again, she was curious about Gareth and took a chance.

"What about you, Gareth?"

Gareth stood up and looked around him, at the sea of faces turned his way. He heard the sigh of relief that went up. Then he walked to the front of the class and, when everyone was quiet, began to read.

"I am sitting beside a fire in a clearing in the forest. There is a dwelling nearby. It is made of wood and mud and the roof is covered with sods of earth. There are tall red flowers growing from the roof and vines curl and climb around its walls with here and there a glowing white flower, bright as a lantern. There is a doorway but no door, only something hanging, thick and dark, to keep out the cold. It is not my home. I am given food and drink, mostly hard oat bread and a pale mead that tastes of the bitterness of nettles. I am grateful for it. Times are hard and the work is easy. I only have to stir the broth in the cauldron that hangs over the fire. Nothing more. Only that. And carefully, that not a drop may be spilt.

"There is an old man with me. He never sits properly on a log, as I do, but squats on his haunches, his hands constantly moving before him, measuring the heat from the fire. It is his job to keep the flames alive, though he is blind and searches for the firewood on hands and knees, using his long fingers like rakes as he forages beneath the trees.

"I know that I have been sitting here for a year. I began when the forest itself was aflame in colours of yellow and red and now the trees are on fire again and the days

grow short. *Every morning a woman comes out of the house and goes deep into the forest. When she returns, she drops flower petals and herbs into the pot.*

"'Stir, boy,' she commands, never calling me by name. And though I ask her what it is I am stirring, she says nothing more, only silences me with a glare as cold and empty as a winter sky.

"Sometimes I see a girl standing at the edge of the clearing. She is more beautiful than anything I have ever seen. She has auburn hair that hangs to her waist and although her gown is grey and simple, nothing she might wear could make her more enchanting. And sometimes I see a boy in the doorway of the house. His back is bent and his face seems aged and wizened, dark and knotted like the bark of an old apple tree. The two are such opposites, not like a brother and sister at all – though their mother is the woman who lives in the house.

"Today, something is different. The boy is being brought to the fire. The woman is telling him to wait by the cauldron. She is touching his head, patting him as you would a dog, muttering strange words. The girl is apart from them, still as a rock, her face pale, unmoving.

"'Once more,' the woman says to me, 'then I am done with you.' She opens her fist and drops something into the cauldron. It bubbles, and before I can stir, three drops of the mixture have flown from the pot to my hand and my scalded fingers leap to my mouth for comfort. In that moment I see three images flash before me - of a world in chaos, a world empty of life, and a world crawling with people and machines.

"The woman leaps towards me, bowling over her crippled son, screaming oaths and howling as the cauldron cracks and the broth hisses in the fire. I am running for my life now, making for the darkness of the forest, wishing I was a hare. Suddenly, I am leaping over fallen trees,

tunnelling through bushes, and I hear the baying of a hound behind me, almost snapping at my heels. I reach the bank of a river and as I dive into the swiftly flowing water my soft fur changes into silver scales. An otter slides in after me so I shake my muscular tail and propel myself into the air. Scales become feathers and as I curve and swoop over a corn field a hawk soars in the sky above, watching. I dive into a pile of wheat, becoming a single golden grain, and a black hen seeks me out and devours me."

Gareth stopped and lifted his eyes to the window. He had the curious sensation that he was flying somewhere above them all, looking down from a great height.

The room was silent. The girls were open-mouthed, staring at Gareth with a new kind of awe. The boys were embarrassed and resorted to glancing sideways at each other and grimacing.

"Is that it?" asked Miss March, softly. "Is that where your dream ends?"

Gareth shook his head. *"I wake up,"* he said, *"and when I go back to sleep I am floating on the sea. I can see myself from above as if I am in two places at once."* He looked away from them all, and stared again at the window. *"I am a baby now, tied up in a leather bag. I can see the woman's face, still hard and cold, still hating me for stealing what had been intended for her son. For I had reasoned while locked inside her body, that the mixture would give power and knowledge to her ugly son. And as she pushes me into the ebbing waves I see a flicker of love and sadness light up the shadows of her face. I sleep, and when I awake different eyes are looking into mine, bold, blue eyes in a face framed with golden hair and beard. I want to tell him who I am. My name is Gwion. I come from the Vale of Sinadon. I am bewitched. But I cannot speak*

70

and the man smiles down at me and says, 'Never have I seen such a beautiful child. The gods must have sent you and protected you. I shall call you Taliesin and you shall live in the court and bring honour to my house.'

"And so," continued Gareth, without looking at his book now, *"Gwion becomes Taliesin. Taliesin, who knows the name of every star and the birth day of every moon – who was present at the launching of the Ark and the birth of Arthur. Taliesin, who was carried nine months in the womb of Ceridwen, the witch – who can live in every shape, who knows all that was and is and will be. Taliesin, Radiant-Browed and Silver-Tongued, whose words and memories were destined to weave themselves into the fabric of the world and the soul of every man."*

The silence seemed to be made of glass. No one moved or spoke for fear of shattering it. Even Roddy was gawping, speechless for once.

Gareth walked back to his seat and slowly, without a sound, the rest of the class closed their books. He hoped they couldn't see him shaking.

"That was astonishing," said the teacher. "Do you always have such colourful dreams?"

Gareth smiled. "I know what it feels like to fly," he said.

Then the bell went and the class was dismissed.

"Did you really dream all that?" The whispered question came from Kit, trailing him as they walked home from school.

Gareth turned and frowned at her. "I didn't make it up."

"Roddy says you've probably read it somewhere. He says he's going to look it up on the Internet."

Gareth shrugged. He didn't particularly care what Roddy Spinks thought. "Ceridwen had five fingers on her

71

left hand and a wart underneath her thumbnail. The Internet won't tell him that."

He walked away quickly and Kit, refusing to take the hint, ran after him

"I like writing stories too."

"It wasn't just a story."

"I know, it was a dream – but you must have added bits, made it more exciting. That's what people do."

"Do you think I was just showing off?"

"No, but it was – well."

"Weird?" Gareth looked up at the sky and all around him before his gaze settled back on Kit. "Life *is* weird. Every time I have that dream I bring something back with me – a feather, a leaf, a thread of cloth. Sometimes my clothes smell of the fire – and sometimes my fingers sting where they were scalded."

Kit stared at him, tugging at her pigtail. This Gareth was somehow different from yesterday. She didn't know how to respond, what she was meant to say. Instead, she changed the subject. "I heard you were good at rugby. All the boys are talking about how fast you can run."

Gareth shrugged.

"Roddy won't like it. He's already the star of the under fourteen team." She looked behind. "Uh-oh! Talk of the devil."

Roddy and his two mates were quickly catching up with them. The three boys were wielding their bags like weapons and there was something primitive about the way their shoulders were hunched, their legs bowed. Then Roddy yelled, "OK. Now! Let's see how fast story boy can run!"

They threw their bags over a hedge and ran towards Gareth and Kit as if planning to launch into a rugby tackle. Kit leapt aside and Gareth turned. He left his bag with Kit and sped away from them with long, light strides. It seemed to Kit that his feet barely touched the pavement. He turned down Willows Lane, and the distance between him and his pursuers increased. Then a tractor came, a beast of a thing, taking up the full width of the lane. Gareth slowed, scrambled up the bank to let it pass, saw the others gaining on him and pushed through the hedge.

Roddy was in front. He saw Gareth disappear from the bank and clambered over a gate into the field before the tractor reached him. He ran down the hedge line, yelling to the others to stay in the lane and watch for him there. There was only the hedge and the field. Nothing else. Nowhere to hide. But the field was empty.

Roddy ran up and down. "Where'd he go? Did you see him?"

The other two lifted their hands in the air and shrugged.

"He must've jumped on the back of the tractor."

They looked back down the lane, but the tractor had turned off and was out of sight.

"Ah well," said Roddy, "there's always tomorrow."

Hands in pockets, they headed back to the village.

The hare lifted its ears and listened. A robin sang in the hawthorn above him. It was safe to move. He lifted on his haunches, sniffed the air and set off in a steady lope across the field.

Gareth's Diary

Thursday

Sorry, diary. Maybe later. I don't know which is shaking more – my hand or my stomach. And I simply don't know what to write. It's all too crazy.

73

Chapter 10

Stirrings

"You'll need your waterproof on today,' said Mary Jones as Gareth finished his breakfast on Friday morning. "Sounds like we're in for some rum weather. They've had it up north and in Europe. It's all those contraptions up in space, your grandma used to say, and I wouldn't wonder. We were lucky on Tuesday by the sound of it. The storm must have circled around and missed us."

"It didn't miss me," said Gareth.

"I'm surprised you didn't see it coming. You must've caught the tail end of it."

"Some tail," muttered Gareth.

She passed him his lunch box. "It's lucky Kathryn didn't get a chill."

"Don't worry. She'd soon scare it away. Where did you hear about the weather?"

Mary Jones nodded towards the windowsill. The radio had been found.

"Has the paper come yet?"

She shrugged.

"I'll go and check."

The newspaper was inside a piece of drainpipe stuck in the hedge by the gate. Gareth unrolled it and stared.

'FREAK WEATHER HITS EUROPE,' was the main headline, with a picture of cars half-buried in snow. The other headings were smaller but mainly concerned with the weather. 'WINTER COMES EARLY TO SKI SLOPES,' 'FLOODS IN ITALY,' 'ICY WINDS IN THE SOUTH OF FRANCE,' and 'METEOROLOGISTS BAFFLED BY FREAK WEATHER PATTERN.'

In Scotland hailstones as big as golf balls had smashed windows and dented car roofs. In North Wales trees had been uprooted by gale force winds. It wasn't at all what the weathermen had predicted for October.

Gareth opened the paper, scanning each page, until he spotted a tiny headline in the bottom corner of one. 'MUSEUM THEFT'

The cauldron had been stolen from Chester Museum. Police were mystified. Nothing else had been taken or tampered with. There were no obvious signs of a break in, no fingerprints, and the thief or thieves had disappeared without trace.

"Have you seen the paper?" Gareth asked Kit when Mrs Talbot had dropped them both off at school.

"No, but I heard the radio. You mean about the weird weather everywhere?"

"Yes, but there was something else, too. The cauldron's gone, stolen by an invisible thief, someone who gets in through locked doors and leaves no fingerprints."

They stared at each other. Kit shivered, imagining those tall, gaunt figures stalking the city streets as people slept.

"Do you think it was them?" she asked.

Gareth shrugged. "Maybe. Or maybe she came herself."

"The witch in your dream, Ceridwen."

"She has other names."

"It's like a jigsaw puzzle," said Kit. "Each piece is enormous, but none of them fit together."

"They will," said Gareth. "Have you thought about the rhyme?"

"Yes, but." Kit stopped speaking and spun around. "Want something? A photograph, maybe? Or a kick in the butt?"

Baz had appeared from somewhere and was walking quietly behind them. He pulled a face at Kit. "What are you pair up to then?"

"Nothing that's any of your business."

"We saw you the other night, Spinksy and me. And we heard you – playing at witches or something daft. They burn witches, didn't you know that, Talbot?"

Gareth and Kit looked at each other and back at Baz in disgust.

"Get back to your cow-pat, Wally. That's where worms belong," said Kit.

"Tell me what you were up to then, because me and Spinksy saw something really weird, and we might just tell on you if you're doing that black magic stuff."

"No chance!" yelled Kit. "And anyway, you're too thick to understand. You haven't got the imagination of a wood louse." She lifted her school bag and swung it around her head. "Tell who you like, creep. No one would believe you anyway."

Barry Thomas fled, knowing full well that Kit wouldn't think twice about clobbering him.

Gareth frowned. When Baz was well out of sight he said, "I think the scarlet light is probably just fire."

Kit nodded. "Moonlight, firelight and the ring of stones. We must be there when the moon is full."

"Monday night," said Gareth.

"I'm glad it's not actually Hallowe'en. That would have been really creepy," said Kit – and she shivered.

"You OK?"

"Uh-huh. I'll see you at break." They walked together in silence towards the main door.

At the corner of the first building, Roddy Spinks, Barry Thomas and Luke Carter were huddled together like conspirators. Gareth's stomach lurched when he saw them.

"Kit, who do you think the other three are going to be?"

Kit looked hard at the threesome and laughed out loud. "Not those prats anyway."

"Who, then? Who could they possibly be?"

Kit frowned and turned her back on them. "It's like a snowball, isn't it," she whispered, "rolling downhill and getting bigger all the time."

"We couldn't stop it even if we wanted to," said Gareth. "No."

"Would you stop it if you could?"

Kit shook her head. "It has to happen," she said. "We can't go on like this, can we, always spoiling things. There has to be a turning point. Someone has to make a stand."

Her words surprised Gareth, reassured him too. He felt sure he could count on Kit, that she understood the nature of the task ahead.

"Hallowe'en," he said. "The night when witches fly."

"I thought it was just an excuse for dressing up and telling ghost stories."

They were in the cloakroom now. "It's more than that," said Gareth. "It's the evening before the feast of Samain, when two worlds come together and creatures from the Otherworld walk in ours."

Kit leaned closer to him and whispered. "Perhaps they're doing that already."

After morning break, Miss March involved the class in a discussion about the strange weather. They were full of wonderful ideas about the causes.

"A magnetic meteorite," said Tim Sharpe, "passing too close to the Earth."

"Satellites," said Carter, "interfering with the atmosphere."

"Alignment of planets," said Sophie Parton, whose mother wrote 'Starguide' for the local paper. "My mum says that weird things are happening in the sky, things that have never happened before."

"Like what, Sophie?" asked Miss March.

"Like stars fading." She blushed crimson when her words were met with rude sniggers. "I know it sounds stupid, but that's what she said."

Gareth came back from Rundle Hill and stared at her.

"Your mother's not a scientist," said Barry Thomas. "She doesn't know anything about the stars. She makes it all up."

"Astrology is an ancient science," said Miss March, "but even today, with all their marvellous telescopes, do people really know much more about what goes on out there? It's all so vast."

"The seas are rising on the shores and there is a restlessness in the skies," whispered Gareth, unaware of his audience. "The stars will be beyond his reach."

"What did you say, Gareth?"

"Pardon? Oh, nothing, sorry. A poem … I was just thinking out loud."

Behind him, Baz and Carter giggled, pulling faces and pointing at their heads.

"What about you, Roddy?" asked Miss March. "Do you have an opinion?"

"Yes, Miss." (To nudges between Baz and Carter) "I think the weather's lousy. Roll on summer, that's what I say."

"Is that all?"

Roddy stared at the table in front of him. "I dunno. Maybe the earth's had enough. Maybe it's fighting back like when the Titanic went down."

"Huh?"

He'd completely lost Baz and Carter. "What you on about, Spinksy?"

Kit looked startled. Roddy Spinks had actually said something intelligent, something that showed he could actually think. She couldn't let it pass. "What have you had for breakfast, then?"

He glared at her.

"Go on then," said Baz. "What's the Titanic got to do with it?"

Roddy shut his mouth like a clam and stared out of the window.

"Shall I tell them?" asked Kit, more than happy to be the centre of attention.

Roddy shrugged.

"Well," she said. "When they built the Titanic they thought they were really clever. They said she was unsinkable. They reckoned she could take whatever Nature and the elements threw at her. But they were wrong. They were too big for their boots and Nature taught them a lesson. We are all a part of Nature. We can't ever be bigger or better than it. While they were building a ship, she was building an iceberg. It was a lesson in humility, but we don't learn, we don't ever learn. We think we're so clever, but look at us, we're ruining everything. Nature won't stand for it any more. She wants to put things right, to restore the balance, because without balance none of us can survive."

"Wow! That's an interesting point of view, Kathryn. Is that what you meant, Roddy?"

"I s'pose so."

Beside him, Baz and Carter looked at each other and screwed up their noses.

"Thank you, everyone," said Miss March. "Now, pass these around, please."

She gave out a pile of newspapers and asked them to read some of the articles before deciding on a topic for their own writing – a newspaper report, an interview or a story. There was an undisguised groan from one corner of the room, but Miss March simply raised her eyebrows and the groaners put their heads down and picked up their pens.

Gareth's fingers were tingling. He couldn't wait to begin. He didn't need to read the newspapers. He picked up his pen, then saw Kit frantically trying to attract his attention. She was pointing at the paper in front of her and putting four fingers in the air. When it was clear he understood she passed the paper along to him. Gareth turned to page four and read; 'LAKE DISTURBANCE: A student, walking near the shore of Llyn Llydaw in Snowdonia, was puzzled by what he described as 'severe turbulence' in the middle of the lake. It lasted, he said, for several minutes before subsiding, and he half expected to witness the appearance of a Nessie look-alike. Scientists, already investigating monster reports in another Welsh lake, feared the report was a hoax until the pilot of a light aircraft seen in the area was located. He bore out the walker's story and added that the surface of the lake had been choppy for several days, even when the weather had been relatively calm. No similar reports have ever been recorded. Local legend claims that King Arthur died near here, and that his crown or something equally valuable, lies at the bottom of the lake. A team, led by Doctor Janus Winstanley, is planning to investigate the phenomenon, but at this point he declined to comment on the possible cause of it.'

Further down the page, Gareth saw, 'EARTH TREMOR IN SCOTLAND' but he was too impatient to read any more. His fingers were itching to begin. "Earth, air, fire and water," he murmured to himself. "The Guardians are stirring, just like the stones on Rundle Hill."

He gripped his pen and released the words that, like the pictures in his dream, were exploding in his mind.

Chapter 11

Mariandor's Song

When the Children of Men are ready, Mariandor will return. When their thoughts flow together and they yearn for that which has gone, the joy of nature that is not born of metal or machine, then she will enter their world to touch their dreams and show them the path to the Light.

In a secret corner of the Earth, at the gateway to Tir na nog, the whisper was born. From the mouth of the great North Wind it leapt into the sky.

At the top of their frozen world the snow bears heard it. Thalar, their king, left his palace of ice and climbed the highest glacier, lifting his great white head to listen.

"The elves are coming.

The elves are coming."

The whisper flew on the icy wind and drew frosty patterns in the air all around him. The snow king roared to the world beneath his feet. Then he slipped into the Arctic waters, carrying the whisper on his back.

In a blue valley beneath the sea the whales and dolphins heard it. They swam to the surface and Balee, their king, heaved his great, glistening body into the air and crashed back into the waves.

The whisper swirled through the sandy ocean floor and was cast up on the rocky shores.

"The elves are coming.

The elves are coming."

Balee drew wide circles in the blue waters and called to his brothers.

In the last peaceful jungle of the world a small herd of grey giants stood quietly and listened. They looked up as the whisper burst apart and words, like petals, showered down upon them. A warm breeze gathered them together and carried the whisper from tree to tree.

Bosca, the great grey king, swung his trunk from side to side. Then he lifted it high in the air and bellowed.

The creatures of the jungle heard it and stopped to listen as the whisper vibrated in the sir around them.

On a mountaintop, high above a green valley, a lonely eagle heard it. Aquila, queen of birds, caught the wind as it raced past her rocky shelf. With the whisper on her wings she swooped down the valley to the forest below. As she flew, she passed on the word to her sisters.

In the treetops the whisper grew into a song and lifted into the air on a thousand voices. High on the back of a cloud it floated down the valley towards the town.

Above the town the song went on.

No one heard it.

The people were too busy.

Their machines were too noisy.

The song grew weary.

Only the whisper remained.

SOON, thought Mariandor, from whose lips the whisper had been born – soon, the people will be still and their machines will be quiet. Then they will listen and be glad.

But even when they were still, the people clung to the ground like ants. Not once did they look up or open their hearts to listen.

And their machines roared on into the night.

At dawn, rain fell upon the grey town.

The whisper tapped softly on rooftops and windows.

But still no one heard.

In a field at the edge of town was a boy. He was searching for mushrooms as he did every day, and he was humming softly to himself.

Suddenly, his tune became a song as words fell upon his clothes with the gently falling rain.

"The elves are coming.

The elves are coming."

The song filled his head and trembled in the air all around him. He began to dance the steps to an ancient dance, a dance he had never been taught.

He stopped and looked at the grey, smoky town, spreading like a stain, swallowing fields and trees. The sadness inside him was like a stone. He pictured the people scurrying about like ants through tunnels, heads down, always on the move. Machines woke them, fed them, and transported them. Machines were their servants and their masters. They grew more like them every day.

They had forgotten the old stories, the old ways of magic and miracles. They had shut them out with their walls of concrete and steel.

The boy knew what he must do.

He ran back to the town. Surely, the people would be glad when he told them the news. For the Elves had disappeared long ago. They had taken with them all the wisdom and knowledge that was earth's gift to Man.

"Listen!" he called to the people as he passed. "The Elves are coming! The Elves are coming!"

But the people only looked at their watches and hurried by. They thought he was mad, singing in the streets, smiling at everyone.

"Go home, boy!" they said. "Find something useful to do."

And on they rushed to their shops and factories.

The boy walked sadly to the edge of the town and climbed Witch-Wither Hill. He didn't hear the footsteps that followed him. For the children of the town had woken from one dream and had felt something good in the air. They had listened and heard the whisper.

Now the song was beneath his feet, trembling through his toes, rippling over him like warm, and summer waves. Louder and louder it grew until the music drummed all around him like a marching song.

"The Elves are coming!

The Elves are coming."

Beneath his feet the heart of Witch-Wither Hill began to beat – as up, up they came – in their thousands.

From the roots of trees.

From rabbit warrens and mole-hills.

From fox earths and badger setts.

And out of the air.

Their long, pale faces shone like stars; their limbs were shafts of light.

The boy sprawled like a cat on the hill, afraid to breathe lest they disappear. And still they came, carrying books and brooms, spades and hoes, saplings and seeds.

They turned north and south and west. Not one of them went east, towards the town.

"The Elves are coming.

The Elves are coming."

Now, the air was alive with music. Thousands of slender feet tapped out the rhythm, their reed-thin voices singing, humming and whistling as they went.

With each step they stooped gracefully, planting a columbine here, a cowslip there, sprinkling seeds where a hedgerow had once been.

Their sigh was like a lonely wind when they saw the stump of a felled oak tree. By its side they planted an acorn.

Where they had walked, flowers sprang and shone like stars, and the acorn sent up a pale shoot.

Now, Witch-Wither Hill was covered with children. They joined hands in a circle, crowning the hill, laughing and dancing and singing.

"The Elves are here.

The Elves are here."

In the town the machines roared louder than ever. But the voices of the children lifted into the air and hammered on the walls of concrete and steel.

At last, the people stopped to listen.

They pushed buttons, turned handles, pulled levers, and every machine in the town shuddered, hissed and ground to a halt.

Clocks stopped ticking, motor cars were still, radios were silent.

When all was quiet the people straightened their backs and lifted their heads to the sky.

Above the grey rooftops and chimneys a rainbow hung, and the blue sky was full of birds – finches and orioles, lapwings and doves.

The people rubbed their eyes and smiled to see them. They had forgotten how beautiful they were. They heard children laughing and singing. They walked to the edge of the town and saw forgotten flowers blooming on Witch-Wither Hill. And when they saw the Elves a seed of joy burst inside them like the memory of a wonderful dream.

Now the children were leaving the hill. They turned north and south and west, their feet treading in the footsteps of the Elves. And the people followed, laughing, singing, lifting their faces to the sun.

The whisper returned to the mouth of the Great North Wind.

But the song of Mariandor lived on in the hearts of the people and the light returned to our world.

***

Gareth had noticed neither the bell ringing nor the children leaving the classroom, and Miss March hadn't the heart to disturb his concentration. She sat quietly and waited at her desk. At last, Gareth put down his pen and stood up. He held his book on the palms of his hands, like an offering, and walked slowly towards her. Miss March blinked. Had she been dozing for a moment? Was that music playing softly somewhere – surely not! For a moment she had thought she could she hear children's voices chanting, singing? At lunchtime? She shook her head briskly.

When she looked up at the boy standing with his arms outstretched it seemed to her that his face shone like the stars and his limbs were shafts of light.

When he had gone and the door was closed, Miss March sat down on Gareth's chair and opened his book. She scarcely heard the bell ring and was suddenly aware of bustle and noise outside the door. "Let them wait a moment," she thought, as she finished the story for the second time.

Outside, the day was darkening. An autumn mist had all but smudged out the Welsh hills, and the poplars at the perimeter of the school field were restless, shaking down the last of their leaves as purple clouds rolled across the sky.

"So, how'd the first week go, then?" Gwyn Jones asked his son later.

"Fine," said Gareth. "You'd think they'd never seen a Welshman before, though. One of them calls me Taffy Two."

His father laughed. "Nothing changes then. Always one idiot in the bunch. You can't be the only Welsh kid at the school, surely. We're only just over the border."

Gareth shrugged. "I think Taffy One is a teacher called Emrys Williams. He teaches geography."

His father laughed again. "We had an Emrys when I was at school. Taught P.E. We used to call him Emrys the Boot, he had such a kick on him. Threatened us with it sometimes."

Now it was Gareth's turn to chuckle.

"You can laugh. Terrified, we were. Seriously, though, you gonna be all right here?"

"'Course I am. Why shouldn't I be?"

"Don't be daft, man. You know what I'm talking about. You're different from them."

"Don't worry, Dad. I can handle it, though I must admit I do feel kind of strange sometimes, like I'm two people. Tomorrow, perhaps I'll know more – when Grandy comes."

"Sure, I know, if he comes, but I just wish …"

"I know. So do I sometimes, but we can't change things, can we? We are who we are."

"We *had* to come here, didn't we? It's part of your *destiny*, as Grandy says. What's it all about, this destiny he talks about? He's not just talking about being an engineer or a doctor, is he? Have you any idea at all what he's on about?"

"Not yet, though I'm getting a few clues. But I'll be thirteen tomorrow and I've a feeling my birthday present will be something unexpected."

Gwyn held out his hands. "All of this was unexpected – to me anyway. That odd little bloke with a beard thumbing a lift and telling me about this job at the farm, just a week after being made redundant. It was uncanny. *He* was uncanny, smelt like, I dunno, a cave or something. Must have been wearing some weird new aftershave. Can't see it taking off somehow."

"Don't be daft, Dad."

"Sorry. All this stuff makes me uncomfortable. Your mam doesn't say much."

"I know. I'll deal with it. Me and Grandy. We'll sort it, you'll see. You don't have to worry. Mum understands, I think, more than she says."

"Ay, I reckon it's in the blood, this weirdness, something you've inherited. Makes me feel on the outside, like. You know what I mean."

"Sorry, Dad. But you have to be there – just so's we have something to hold on to." Gareth looked at his feet, embarrassed, glad when Mary called them for tea. Gwyn grinned and cuffed him on the shoulder. It was the nearest they got to hugs.

Half an hour later, Kit phoned. "I've got an idea. Let's go to Chester tomorrow. We can visit the museum – see where the cauldron was stolen from."

"Can't, sorry. Might be going out. Anyway, we're not detectives. We don't need to be. We know who stole the cauldron. At least, I think we do."

At that moment, Farmer Will Gresty was out checking his sheep, less than a mile away as the crow flies from Foxhole Cottage where Gareth was now making himself a cheese sandwich. Every evening for thirty years Farmer Gresty had performed the same ritual. "It settles me somehow," he said when asked, "knowing they're safe and content." He enjoyed the walk down the rutted lane; he liked the feel of the lichen-encrusted gate under his hands and the green and earthy smell of the air at the end of the day. Beyond the field was the Brook, and in a loop of it was Rundle Hill, circled with beech trees and with gorse bushes and hawthorns that were scattered about its slopes like the pieces of a broken coronet. His mother had had strange ideas about the hill. "It has moods," she used to say, "like it's haunted or something. There are times when I don't want to go near it – and there are times when I want to spread myself upon it under the sun and simply melt into the earth."

Will had laughed. His mother had been full of funny ideas, but he had to admit that the changing light does have a habit of playing tricks on your eyes and making a fool out of you. Familiar landscapes can soon appear alien and hostile when a wind rises and the skies darken. A wind was rising now. He could hear it coming from the west, playing in the willows and alders by the brook. He could smell a change in the air and thought of the plate of liver and onions waiting in the Aga. He turned away from the gate and headed back up the lane.

Behind him, darkness settled in deepening layers upon the hill and somewhere, lost in its own past, a dog lifted its head and howled at the rising moon.

Chapter 12

Grandy

Gareth's Diary
Saturday 8a.m.

Today is my birthday. I woke suddenly, before it was light. There was movement in the room, cold air punching my face like a playful wind. I reached behind me for the pull cord and saw the light fitting swinging in the middle of the ceiling. On the floor, by the desk, sheets of paper were flapping like dying fish. I threw back the bedclothes and crawled across the bed to the window. I pulled back the curtain, but the window was closed tight. The draught of air wasn't coming from there. Where, then? I looked back into the room, but the light was still now and the papers neatly stacked. It must have been the leftovers of another dream. I was about to drop the curtain when a movement caught my eye. The moon was almost full and riding high, filling the garden with moon-shadows. There was no wind, yet, beyond the hedge, and half the height of the apple tree, a single thin shadow moved – and this time, I felt certain, I was not dreaming.

Trembling, but unable to take my eyes away, I saw a second tall thin shadow on the other side of the crossroads, moving with long, spidery strides down the lane. I searched again for the first shadow, but lost it in the ragged darkness of the hedges and trees. I drew back from the window, turned to look again and there it was, only now it was standing in the middle of the garden, and, though I couldn't see its face, I knew it was watching me back. I lunged at the curtains, drawing them together until every inch of window was hidden. Slowly, silently, afraid to breathe, I put my feet to the floor and stood up, facing the window. For ages it seemed I stood, unable to take my eyes away from the square of grey light. Then I moved my frozen feet forward until I could just reach the curtain. I uncovered an inch of window and peeped through. Nothing! I let out a great breath of relief. The garden was empty. So was the lane. There was no movement anywhere and the trees looked like cardboard cut-outs silhouetted against a silver-grey sky.

I dropped the curtain and turned to look for the light switch. My hands were shaking and I suddenly realised how cold I was. I knocked the switch down and saw the light in the middle of the ceiling swinging gently to and fro. As I watched, it slowed down and was still. The curtains rippled once, and on the floor by the desk sheets of paper flapped like dying fish.

I gripped the door handle, thinking of Mum and Dad, warm in their bed. My hand fell. It was years since I'd gone crying to them in a thunderstorm and we'd hidden together, giggling, under the duvet. I couldn't do it now, could I? I wasn't a baby any more.

I frowned, deep in thought, then unhooked my dressing-gown from behind the door and pulled on my slippers. There was no point in going back to bed. Sleep was out of the question.

I picked up the sheets of paper and sat down at the desk, struggling to remember the dreams, to piece together the shards before they crumbled and were lost. They were different from the other dreams. In those I was one of the players, every thought and emotion playing over me – but these were like pictures from a film I was watching, fragments of a story that had yet to be told.

I picked up a pencil and began to sketch. I was astonished by the way the soft graphite skimmed over the page, bringing these new dreams to life. When, at last, I put down the pencil, daylight was flooding into the room and I could hear Mum bustling about in the kitchen.

"I wish Grandy would come," I said out loud as I stared at the two sketches. They were good, better than anything I had ever drawn, just as sometimes the words I speak and write were the words of another part of me, a part I am struggling to remember. The first was the outline of a city carved from stone. Though the stone was dark it gave out light as if veins of quartz or threads of silver were reflecting the sun. Before the city was a wide plain and beyond it, brooding darkly, a high ridge of naked, black rock.

The second picture was of a now familiar hill rising through a circle of trees and crowned with a ring of stones. When I looked at the model I had made out of wood and polystyrene and imagination – at the ring of tiny standing stones – my heart began to race. I looked back at the picture. In the centre of the ring was a fire. Its flames lit up six, pale, blurred faces. I knew that one of them was mine, one of them was Kit's – and another, the bearded old face of a dwarf. Who were the other three? The question made my stomach churn – because suddenly I knew.

I pushed back my chair and stared, aware of the blood pumping hotly through my veins, my heart thudding against my ribs like a caged rabbit. I turned the sheets of paper this way and that, looking at them from every angle. Then I took them to the window. The drawings were like the words that had come to me lately - not entirely my own. They couldn't be. I'm just not that good at drawing either. I wouldn't show them to Mum. I wouldn't say anything. She'd say I'd been dreaming – about everything, the curtains, shadows, *wind. 'Too much imagination, that's your trouble.' I'd heard it before, many times. Grandy usually got the blame for 'Filling his head with poppycock and nonsense.' Poor Grandy! Poor Mum! But she isn't like most grownups who can't see beyond the ends of their noses. She knows that things are different for us but still she tries desperately to pretend that our lives are normal. And I don't want to give her any more cause for concern.*

But Grandy will know. Grandy will explain. I wish he would come.

Gareth looked down the lane in the direction of the village, willing him to appear, desperate to see his wild, white hair, to hear his voice and be comforted by his presence.

He lifted the pictures to the light, frowning. On each drawing a grey patch had appeared, like a water-mark or shadow. It was so faint you had to blink and look again to be sure. On one it was as shapeless as an ink blot, spreading up the hill, engulfing the trees. On the other it lay upon the walls of the city like a long, clawed hand. Like some kind of warning!

When Mary Jones came in with a glass of orange juice she was surprised to see him already dressed.

"My, you're up bright and early," she said. "Too excited to stay in bed, I suppose."

Gareth grinned, glancing at his desk where a sketchpad hid the two pictures. If only she knew.

Mary Jones sighed. "You used to wait for the postman and catch the cards as they dropped through."

"I haven't done that for years," said Gareth indignantly.

"I know. I know. Happy birthday, love. Mushrooms on toast for breakfast."

"Thanks, Mum." He breathed in the garlicky mushroom smell as he ran downstairs. "Do you think Grandy will come today?"

"Your guess is as good as mine, but he hasn't missed a birthday yet, has he?"

Gareth smiled and shook his head. "I wonder what time he'll be here."

"Who knows? Clocks don't exist in your Grandy's world. He only stops by if the wind's in the right direction. Then all he does is talk a lot of twaddle, stare at a cobweb for half an hour, eat everything he can lay his hands on and drift away on the next breeze. I know he's my own flesh and blood but I do wonder about his sanity sometimes. Beats me how he knows where we are. He's not answered his phone."

Gareth lifted the last, delicious mouthful and sighed. "He knows. Grandy always knows. Why do you pretend he's just daft? You know he isn't."

At that moment the postman arrived. In spite of himself, Gareth dashed to the door. Of course there wasn't much. There hadn't been time to give everyone their new address. His cards would be late – if they came at all. But there was one, written in a familiar, untidy scrawl. Gareth tore it open and read. Then he looked at the clock.

"He'll be here any time. He's taking me out. It's OK isn't it? You don't mind, do you? I guess you could use my help here. There's a lot to do." He crossed his fingers as he said it.

Mary Jones laughed. "Maybe. But the last thing I want is a helper with a face as long as Friday. Don't worry. What I don't get done today I shall do tomorrow. It is your birthday, and you must spend it the way you choose. One day, birthdays won't be so important. I suppose you'll be needing a picnic."

"Yes, please. You know Grandy. And don't forget the banana cake." He dashed to the door, flew upstairs and flung his cagoule and wellies out on to the landing. "I wonder where we're going," he yelled, hardly able to contain his excitement.

"Somewhere weird and wonderful, I'm sure," Mary Jones called back dryly. "You haven't opened your presents yet." She sighed. "Never mind. You can do it this evening. We'll be a bit straighter by then. I'll make a nice tea."

Gareth went back into his room and slid out the pictures. He traced the outline of the hill with his finger and then he looked again at Grandy's card. It was a picture of a bird of prey perched on a rock and carried nothing as ordinary as a birthday message. Instead, it said, 'Make ready. Courage in one hand, Wellington boots in the other. Tell your mother we'll need a picnic and don't forget the banana cake. The skies are restless. Ergyriad calls. We must journey to meet him. Until nine o'clock – or thereabouts. Yours in haste, M. PS Happy birthday, Gareth S.o.G.'

It was cryptic to say the least. Who was Ergyriad? And what on earth did S.o.G. mean? "It's beginning," whispered Gareth. "It's really beginning – and I've been expecting it."

The idea hit him in the stomach like a football. He looked at the landscape he had built, at the tiny figures standing by the old mill and sat down at his desk, deep in thought.

Grandy's drum-roll on the half-open door startled him out of his daydream. He looked over his shoulder and grinned. Grandy was wearing a bright blue sweater covered with yellow moons and stars. Around his neck hung a long, striped scarf. His eyes were a deeper blue than Gareth's. Sometimes they were flecked with pinpoints of light and darted about like fish. At other times they were bottomless pools, glowering from beneath a tangle of eyebrows at things that weren't there, secrets that no one could share. Today, they were a mixture of both. When he entered the room Grandy's face was awash with wrinkling smiles. But in a moment Gareth was aware of the darkness lurking beneath.

"Happy birthday, lad," he said. "Did you get my present?"

Gareth nodded.

Then the old man's eyes alighted on the drawings and the disguise slipped. "Tara," he whispered hoarsely, as though he spoke of a long-lost love. "You have seen it then?"

Gareth nodded. "Only in a dream. I drew it because it was so real – and sad, as if something terrible had happened there."

Grandy lifted the picture.

"What does it mean, Grandy? Where is Tara?"

But Grandy didn't answer. "And the shadows?" he said. "Did you see those in your dream?"

"No. They just appeared. I thought I'd imagined them like the shadows in the garden. But I know now that I didn't."

"The garden? Here? What did you see in the garden?"

"People, figures, shapes – I don't know what they were. Tall, thin, black. Human, but not human. I couldn't see their faces."

Grandy looked hard at him, his eyes as sharp as steel, his face full of words that Gareth could not read. "They know you are here," he said quietly.

"Then they should have sent me a birthday card," said Gareth.

Grandy looked right through him.

"Who?" said Gareth. "Who knows I'm here? What are you talking about, Grandy? I know weird things are starting to happen but I don't know what they are."

Grandy walked to the window and looked out. "My daughter will enjoy this house," he said.

"There was a wind in the night," said Gareth. "Things blowing about in my room. It woke me up, but I hadn't left the window open."

The old man turned and nodded. "It begins," he said. "I had hoped it would not be so soon, that you would be a little older, better prepared. But you have grown so quickly and the choice isn't mine to make. I feared as much when I heard Ergyriad calling." He paused and looked hard at Gareth before continuing. "There is an alignment, a coming together of powers and circumstances that no man can halt. It is written and it will come to pass. There is no changing that."

Gareth made to speak, but Grandy lifted a long finger and carried on. "The dreams are more than dreams. They come to you from a past you have forgotten, a fount of knowledge that rises to the call it hears and bursts into your mind. But the shadows and the creatures you saw, they are a different matter altogether. They are her creatures. She holds them in her hand, for without her they are even less than shadows."

"Morgana!" Gareth's lips shaped the word and the sound of it made him shudder.

Grandy nodded. "Morgana, Ceridwen, call her what you will. She has had many lives. The Ancient One, the Shapeshifter who sucks her poisons from the darkest corners of the Earth, who feeds on evil and multiplies it, who gathers strength in the midst of darkness and despair. She has a bone to pick with you."

"The cauldron?"

Grandy's eyes grew black and dense as woodland pools, his mind dwelling for a moment on some deep and distant memory, while Gareth was bursting with questions, biting his lip, swallowing his words, trying to be patient.

"And Tara?" Grandy's voice softened and the blue light returned to his eye. "Tara is the last stronghold of the Children of the Dawn, the Tuatha de Dana." He looked directly into Gareth's eyes, searching for his thoughts. "The Elven Folk." He nodded, seeing no flicker of amusement or disbelief in Gareth's face. "In our hearth stories through the centuries we have called them elves, and in giving them faces and wings and pointy ears we have mocked and diminished them. We have lost sight of them, but they were – are – a people of great stature, the embodiment of grace and wisdom, in tune with all that is natural, all living things and the elements and forces that govern our universe. Yet they have courage too, and fight with stout hearts when Evil threatens. It was a dark day when they were driven to the Otherworld by Man's arrogance and ignorance. Their going left a void that Mankind felt but could not name, a divide between Man and Nature that widens with every passing year.

"Sadly for the Tuatha they share our blood, the source of our being, and are inextricably linked to our world. But if Morgana succeeds in spreading Evil and despair, in severing the links between Man and the spirit of the world, then the light of the Tuatha will be extinguished forever and Man will have lost a part of himself that can never be replaced. The stars will be beyond his reach. He will be like the mole, blinkered and blind to the wonders that lie beyond the exit of his long, dark tunnel."

Gareth scraped a thumbnail with his teeth. He was struck dumb by the knowledge; his mind was bursting with a jumble of words and emotions. It was as if Grandy was turning the first page of a story he had known all his life.

But where did it leave him? What was his part in all this? Grandy touched his shoulder.

"You and I, Gareth, are of the line of Gwydion, a warrior-magician and poet held in great esteem and friendship by the Tuatha."

"S.o.G," murmured Gareth.

Grandy nodded. "Son of Gwydion. And you too have had many lives. Once, you were a poet, the greatest Wales has known. Hence the words that find their way to you now."

Gareth gaped. "Taliesin! But what do I –?"

Grandy wagged his finger. "Let patience be your master. I have said enough – for now. The doing must begin. You have come of age, Taliesin."

Gareth held his head in his hands. "Is that my real name?"

Grandy smiled. "Maybe. It is one of them."

"I feel as though ..."

"You feel as though a door was slowly opening?"

Gareth nodded.

"And so it is, and there are many doorways. But for you this particular door has never truly been closed. Do you remember Crumlock Hill? I was testing you then."

"Yes, I think about it every day."

I saw the light in your eyes when we walked there. I saw your hand tremble as it moved over the rock. And when the wind spoke through leaf and grass you bowed your head to listen. You heard the voice of the Tuatha, though you knew it not. You trod in their footsteps on the Ancient Path. Their memory is held fast in rock and tree, and there are those who have seen images of them printed upon the air." He threw back his head and took a deep breath. "I know you are only a boy, but your mind is

100

unclouded; the doors in it are still open to realms of possibility that logic and reason shut out. You are every child who dreams, every child who has imagination, every child who strives to find the world that once was ours. You are the hope of the Tuatha, the hope of children everywhere."

No sooner had the words been spoken than a breath of cool sweet air touched Gareth's fingers and moved on, lifting the corners of the papers on his desk, ruffling the bright peacock feathers that stood above them on a shelf.

Grandy sprang to his feet and touched the old book that lay on Gareth's desk. "Have you read it?"

Gareth nodded.

"Guard it well. There are no cheap copies, no paperback editions. It will answer many of your questions. And now, Caer Cadarn. We shall see what Ergyriad can bring us from the skies. Are you ready, Gareth, Son of Gwydion?"

Gareth took a deep breath and nodded and felt his teeth chattering. "I think so. Ready as I'll ever be."

In a single motion, Grandy turned and was leaping down the stairs, scarf in one hand and banister in the other.

Gareth looked quickly round his room, trying to quieten the butterflies waking in his stomach. He hid the book under his mattress, covered his pictures, grabbed cagoule and boots and flew after him.

Chapter 13

Ergyriad (the Striker)

They were already getting into the car when Mary Jones came dashing down the path clutching a rucksack.

"For goodness' sake, Dad! You don't get any better with age. It's like having two children, it really is. Are you sure you've got a licence for that old heap?"

Grandy chuckled. "Throw it in the back, woman!" he yelled. "We've got more important business to worry about."

He turned the key savagely and Mary jumped back as the old Morris 1000 spluttered into life.

"Have a good time," she called lamely. "I don't suppose you'll tell me where you're going."

Grandy cupped his ear and shook his head. "Back in time for tea," he shouted. "Hope you've remembered the banana cake." Head and shoulders bent over the wheel, he eased his foot from the clutch and they crawled up the lane towards the village and the main road.

Gareth looked sheepishly back at his mum and waved. He thought she looked lonely standing there, knowing nothing, but fearing everything. He felt guilty going off and leaving her when they had just moved in. But Dad would be back from the farm soon. She'd be OK. He turned to look at Grandy. The old man's head was like a rocky headland sculpted by sea and wind, his craggy brow tufted with spiky grass - or else it was the figurehead of an old ship with chiselled nose and chin thrust forward, sailing into battle.

"What are you thinking about?" said Grandy.

"Ships," said Gareth, and turned away.

They left the sprawling village behind and turned onto the main road.

"Who's Ergyriad?"

"A friend."

"Where will we find him?"

"Didn't I say?"

"Caer Cadarn. But where's that?"

Grandy didn't answer. He could be infuriating at times. Instead, he murmured something soothingly to the car and threw his scarf back over his shoulder. Then: "When I was a boy," he began, "a long, long time ago ..."

Gareth smiled, wriggled down in his seat and closed his eyes. It was the best thing to do when Grandy told one of his stories. Poppycock, Mum called them. Stuffing the boy's head with nonsense. Poor Mum! It was wishful thinking on her part. She knew they were anything but nonsense.

"... I lived in a stone cottage on the side of a mountain. It was a rare and beautiful place to be in the summer. To walk between earth and sky with only ravens and sheep and peregrines for company, and the sharp edge of the wind biting at your bare legs.

"Winters were something else, long and dark and wild. Storms blowing up suddenly, coming from nowhere and everywhere. No warning except a silence in the sky and sheep huddling against the slabs. Then the old house would tremble, its corner-stones move like the roots of old teeth."

103

Grandy pushed himself back and tried to stretch his legs. "It was as if the mountain wasn't ready to be still, as if it was remembering its youth of fire and brimstone, darkness and upheaval. As we listened to the wind tearing at the twisted trees I could feel the mountain shuddering, ridding itself of the rubble and debris that clung to its shoulders and clogged its throat."

Behind his closed eyes Gareth could see it. "I am still a force to be reckoned with. You cannot own me. That's what the mountain was saying."

"Perhaps," said Grandy.

"That's where we're going, isn't it?"

But Grandy's thoughts were buried deep in his story.

"One night there was a storm so terrible it must have been born in the deepest, darkest lairs of space. It was the winter of '43. Your great-grandmother spent the night under the table wrapped in an old eiderdown. I didn't understand her fear. She should have known that no harm would come to us. In the morning, it seemed as though half the mountain had rained down around us. One slate had blown from the roof, but otherwise the house was undamaged."

"The mountain took care of you," said Gareth. He opened his eyes for a moment, puzzled by his own thought. "But that's crazy! Rocks can't have —"

"Feelings? Is that what you were going to say? I'm sure the world and his wife would agree. Rocks can't have thoughts, memories. Are we so clever? Do we know so much about the universe that we can be sure? Think, my boy! Were they not there at the beginning of all things and all time? Did they not shape themselves out of darkness and move forward into the light? Did they not cradle the first living thing, echo the first heartbeat, the first cry? Pah!" He snorted. "Man gives them names, tries to conquer them, make them bow to his will. What does he know of their true nature? What does he understand of the earth and the trees and the power of good and evil that makes all things breathe, gives everything purpose? The little he knew he has cast away, trampled into the dust. Believe me."

As Grandy spoke, Gareth saw in his mind's eye a tall figure in light, flowing robes. He was standing on a hilltop, a long staff in each hand. Beyond him, on another hill, a beacon burned.

"Believe me. Nothing can be lost forever, neither sound nor echo, thought nor memory, spirit nor essence – when there is a rock to hold it fast."

Gareth blinked and shook himself properly awake. The robed figure was gone. Now, it was Grandy's voice he could hear.

"Ah, yes. Now, where was I? The storm – yes, the storm. All that day I was busy clearing stones from around the house and out of the stream where we took our water. That's when I found it – or it found me, whichever you like."

"Found what, Grandy?"

There were traffic lights ahead.

"Betws or Bala?" said Grandy. "Betws, I think." He turned and winked. And when the lights changed they carried straight on.

"The stone," he replied.

"But there were lots of stones."

Grandy turned for a moment; his blue-green eyes drilled into Gareth's. "I know," he growled, "but not like this one. Oh, yes, there was granite, glinting like ice in the sun. There was mica, feldspar, quartz. Their names are enough. All magnificent. But nothing like this. It was golden, pale as the morning sun and round as the autumn moon."

"Like topaz?" said Gareth, proud that he knew the name.

"Like nothing you or I have ever seen."

"It must have been valuable, then." But valuable was not the right word, not what he meant at all.

"Beyond any price a mortal could pay," whispered Grandy. "To hold it was enough. The finest birthday present a boy could have."

"Your thirteenth birthday."

Grandy nodded. "I knew I couldn't keep it; the time was not right, but I didn't want to give it up. Looking into it was like looking through a star, glimpsing a world beyond it, a world full of light and hope – a new beginning. When I took my eyes away they ached with the beauty of it. I closed my fingers around it and felt the power trapped inside like –"

"A fly in amber?"

"Yes." Grandy smiled. "Something like that."

"But where had it come from?"

"From the mountain, cast up by Mimir, the Wise One, Guardian of spring and lake and pool, Watcher in the subterranean caverns, that echo now with only the memory of dwarfs."

"You *sent* me a dwarf. I've just painted him. I meant to show you."

"I saw him," said Grandy. "His clothes are his own but he needs a little more silver in his beard and a brighter blue in his eye. Then, you'll have him, Old Brownskin himself in the flesh – or Urion Longspear, if you want to honour him with his proper title." He glanced sideways and smiled to see Gareth's head nodding. "Talking to myself, am I?"

Gareth tried to rouse himself.

106

"I know. Dreams trespass on sleep. You look shattered. Forty winks you may have and no more."

When Gareth awoke he was alone in the car, parked on the gravelly edge of a narrow road. On both sides of the road, rivers of scree hung like widows' weeds about the dark, rocky slopes. Above him their summits were wound about with wisps of cloud that curled and clung like remnants of hair.

He looked around for Grandy and saw him beckoning from the hillside. He was standing in a green rectangle, marked by a low wall of grey stones and littered with shards of slate. Gareth left the car and ran to join him.

"This is where I used to sleep," said Grandy, flinging out his arm to encompass one corner of all that was left of the cottage. The ruin looked ancient, nothing now but a windbreak for sheep if the droppings were anything to go by.

"And there's the stream."

They followed the stream with their eyes, tracing it to its source above the clouds, behind the high, sheer face of the mountain. Grandy turned, nodded, but no smile passed between them, only a look of deep understanding between equals. Gareth felt a tremor run through him. There was no going back now. He was beginning to find out who Grandy really was. They moved together, picking their way back through strewn rocks and stunted tufts of fern and heather.

They drove on, and in a short time the road rounded on a lake of reflected blue and gold. Above the water, from a shoulder of rock, rose the ruin of a castle. A single tower and some tumbled stones were all that remained.

Grandy parked the car and they took their picnic with them up the hill. Beneath their feet, the worn path was slippery with rotting leaves. Gareth stood for a moment, looking up at the tower. "Caer Cadarn," he whispered, "Castle of Might." But he spoke only to the wind, for

Grandy, nimble as any thirteen-year-old, was already halfway up the hill and would reach the tower first. Behind him, Gareth turned to follow the path of the foundations, to establish the plan of halls and chambers once contained within the high stone walls. The walls themselves were long gone, their stones plundered. Only a few grassy mounds showed that they had ever been there at all.

He climbed the tower, amazed at the view, gulping the sharp air as he moved through it. From the top he saw a panorama of rock and sky, earth and water that bore not a single trace of humanity. "It probably hasn't changed in a thousand years, in ten thousand years." The thought made him shrink so that he felt less than a seed on the wind. He turned to go down, fingering the cold stone as so many before him had done, letting his feet slip into the hollows of the worn steps. Once down, he circled the tower three times, running his hands along the chiselled stones, thinking about Grandy's words, wishing the stones could speak.

"I like this place," he called, holding his hand flat on a band of cool, smooth slate. A mixture of granite blocks and slabs of slate, the tower looked strong enough to outlive time itself. It was a pity the rest had been destroyed and plundered.

On the grass, where the north-pointing corner stone disappeared into the earth, lay a scattering of small bones. Some were bleached and dry, some half-buried; others were still darkened with blood. Gareth looked up the sheer face of the wall, to the highest part of the tower. "Is that where he lives, Grandy?" He knew by now that Ergyriad would be no ordinary friend, just as he knew that Grandy was no ordinary grandfather. From the moment they had set out it seemed that new thoughts, new names and ideas were slipping in and out of Gareth's mind. It was as if he were shedding something, like a snake – only it wasn't skin he

was shaking off but his old self. This was a different road —
and he was becoming a different person.

Grandy nodded in answer to his question. He had
settled on a stone and was sitting, elbows on knees, stuffing
tobacco into a long, thin pipe as he stared at the distant,
purple peaks and the haze of sky beyond. Gareth sat beside
him, silently for a moment, afraid to step from Grandy's
shadow, from the comforting warmth and smell of him.
Around them, the world too was silent, waiting.

"Grandy, I need to know so much."

"I know," he said softly. "But the words and the time
are not mine to choose. Have patience, and remember this —
that the memory of Nature herself can be recalled with the
right symbol, the right key. Nothing done can be undone;
nothing said can be unsaid. Everything is remembered and
can be recalled. And of all the symbols, natural and crafted,
stone is the greatest."

"Is that why we're here — to find the golden stone — to
find out what it is we have to do?"

"We?" Grandy shook his head sadly. "The stone is in
good hands. Caer Cadarn and Ergyriad have kept it
between them. And if I could I would travel with you to
restore it to its rightful place and free the power within.
Alas! I cannot choose. It is a journey for the young. When
book and stone are in your hands, Gareth, Son of Gwydion,
my part is played out, my guardianship over." He turned
away and sighed. "I step sideways along a different road."

At first, Gareth was horrified. Journey? What journey?
And without Grandy! But, he should have known Grandy
wouldn't always be there, that he would have to stand on
his own and Grandy would move on to another time,
another place. "I don't know what I'm supposed to do," he
said, "and I'm not sure I want to do it on my own."

Grandy stiffened. He was staring out across the lake.
His eyes lifted, narrowed as they scanned the shadowed

face of the mountain beyond. "See, here he comes, Lord of the Skies."

Against the dark rock, Gareth saw a darker, winged shape moving towards them. Grandy leapt to his feet and dragged Gareth up with him. "Courage, my boy," he shouted. "You will not be alone."

"But Grandy, what do I have to do? That's what I need to know."

The old man turned, his eyes like crystals, full of the sky. "Why, didn't I tell you that much at least? Go to Tara and take back the Light to the Silver City. Show them that all is not lost and there are those who still believe."

"Grandy, look! There's another bird. What's it doing?"

"The Scald-Crow!" Grandy spat out the words. Don't worry. Ergyriad is more than a match for her. He has been outwitting her for centuries. Unfortunately, like her mistress and all Evil energy, she can be subdued, but not destroyed."

Gareth watched, fascinated, as the two birds came together in the sky. Talons clawed and tore, beaks jabbed and pulled, wings jerked and flapped desperately. Together they fell, amidst a cloud of bloodied feathers. They broke apart, grasping the air, heaving against it, fighting to regain height. Ergyriad, the striker, lifted and circled the tower, gathering strength. Three times around and he rose again, higher and higher.

The other bird landed heavily in a tree that leaned out over the lake. For a moment she seemed to be looking at them. Then she rose, her wings as heavy as metal, and flapped away across the water. By the time she saw him, or sensed his purpose, it was too late. She swerved in flight but Ergyriad had the advantage and was on her in a moment, like a boulder falling from the sky. And back he came, the peregrine victor, to drop a tangle of black feathers at Gareth's feet.

For a moment, Gareth stared at the smashed beak and dull, amber eye, at the dark blood that crept like shadow over the stone. Then he shielded his eyes and searched the sky for the peregrine. Above the lake, Ergyriad was gliding in lazy circles. When Grandy raised his arm the bird coiled slowly down and alighted on top of the tower.

Grandy motioned Gareth away from the ragged shape and spreading ooze at his feet. They looked up to where the peregrine was preening his ruffled feathers. Grandy placed a hand on Gareth's shoulder; the other he lifted in salute. The peregrine stopped its grooming and watched them.

"You have brought a Son of Gwydion?"

Gareth heard the words in his head, while Grandy nodded, keeping his eyes on the bird.

"The time has come, old friend. The stone must begin its journey."

No sound waves moved through the air yet Grandy and the peregrine were communicating and Gareth understood every word. Ergyriad stretched his wings and shook his head.

"So be it, Myrddin, Son of Nwyvre. I have known the day was near. There is a restlessness in the skies; the waters are troubled and rise upon the shores, and beneath the mountains, rock moves against rock."

"Earth, air, fire and water," said Grandy, "Guardians of the four ancient symbols until such time as they are needed to drive back the Dark."

"Such time is now," spoke Ergyriad. "The Guardians grow impatient. I have seen shadows moving over the land, searching. They have darkened the skies and fouled the seas with their evil. They spread and grow and call on the Ancient Ones. When the symbols are released, be sure that Morgana will not be far away. In her hands they are no more than the earth from which they came. But it is written that when four and one are united by the hand of humankind before the gates of Tara, then birds will sing once more in the silver tree and the corn will grow tall and strong."

Grandy nodded slowly. "And if the symbols fall into the wrong hands Morgana will take them to the four corners of the earth and cast them into the deepest darkest pits where they might be lost forever."

Silence. The thought hung heavily between them.

Suddenly, like a painting come to life, the peregrine lifted its wings and swooped down from the wall. Gareth ducked and stumbled forward as beating wings brushed his face. When he looked up it was to see a ragged, black shape moving away from the rock and out over the lake. Where the Scald-Crow had lain, broken, there was only a dark stain on the granite slab that faded even as he watched. Across the blue lake Ergyriad pursued her, only returning when he had driven her beyond the mountain. He flew once more to the top of the tower and perched, frozen like a gargoyle, his eye fixed on Gareth.

"Climb," said the voice in Gareth's head. "To be worthy of the task you must first find the stone."

Gareth glanced at Grandy. Grandy raised his bushy eyebrows and nodded. Then he picked up the rucksack and sat down.

Gareth walked slowly towards the tower and began to climb for the second time. He climbed and climbed. Surely there hadn't been so many steps the first time. Up and up, each step requiring more effort than the one before until at last he could see the sky above him. He looked all around, touching the cold stone that seemed to be covered by a skimming of ice. His fingers stung as they dislodged cushions of emerald green moss and tiny plumes of pale fern. He searched every nook and cranny. Nothing! He stopped and tried to focus his mind on everything he knew, which at this stage seemed to be alarmingly little. What had Grandy said? 'Earth, air, fire and water.'

And something else! 'Let us see what Ergyriad can bring us from the skies.' Of course! The stone wasn't in the tower. It was too simple. He positioned himself in the centre of the tower and looked up. Then he stepped forward and leaned out through the crenulated parapet. He could see nothing of the ground beneath. Grandy, the lake, even the mountains beyond the lake, had disappeared. There was only a vast, shimmering whiteness as if the tower had been cast adrift in an ocean of cloud.

He looked up again. High above him the whiteness was swirling and shifting. Its motion made Gareth's head spin. His legs were not his own; his feet seemed lost on another plane as he swayed with the rolling and heaving of the tower. He flung out his arm, certain that he was falling – and out of the empty air a cool hand reached out, grasped his own, steadied the reeling body and was gone, sliding from his fingers like silk. Around him the silence was as deep as the White Sea. He could hear no other sound but his own painful breathing.

Still, the clouds swirled and spun and wound themselves about the air until it seemed to Gareth that he was looking through the wrong end of an immense telescope. At the other end was a tiny circle of sky and a dark speck wheeling.

"Ergyriad," whispered Gareth, "I am ready." He lifted his hands, stretching upwards, summoning every ounce of strength until his body was rigid, intent as an arrow, resolute as the rock on which he stood.

"Do you believe, Gareth, Son of Gwydion?" The voice came to him from the clouds and the stones and the air about him.

He smiled, closed his eyes for a moment and knew beyond doubt or question. "Oh yes, yes," he proclaimed, though words were not needed. "I believe in Tara and the Children of the Dawn. I am of the blood of Taliesin and of Gwydion and I know what I must do."

Down through the white tunnel came a ray of light, fine as a silver thread. Every nerve and sinew in Gareth's body tightened. He squeezed his eyes shut until they hurt; he put his wrists together and opened his hands. When the cold light touched them, his fingers closed around something smooth and hard, something that sent needles of ice and fire through his veins. He clutched it to him and shrank away from the light, moving through darkness until he sank to his knees on the bare rock and felt an Arctic wind on his face.

Slowly, one hand following the wall, the other clasping the stone to his chest, Gareth unwound himself from the tower. He stood for a moment, staring at Grandy who was taking great bites out of a sandwich and washing them down with mouthfuls of coffee. Gareth frowned and shook his head at the strangeness of it. Egg sandwiches – and a tower that lifted you into the sky!

Suddenly aware of him, Grandy looked up and smiled. "Hungry?"

But Gareth couldn't speak. He walked over to Grandy and sat down, his knuckles white with gripping, his hands and face frozen. Grandy poured another mug of coffee and passed it to him.

"The Scald-Crow has not returned," he said. "She's none too bright and probably thinks that we're here for one of the Four."

"She's wrong," said Gareth, wondering how he knew. "This is not one of the Four."

Grandy watched him thoughtfully and nodded his head slowly as Gareth painfully opened his clenched hand. The moment he did so a light rose from the pale golden stone and wrapped itself about him. It washed over him and through him, warming his cold hands and feet, pouring

114

strength into his aching muscles. In that moment he glimpsed, as Grandy had all those years ago, another world beyond the stone, a world of peace and harmony, enlightenment and understanding, where the Earth's past is woven into the present and Man and Nature are reunited. Gareth looked up. "There is a chasm," he said, "a deep divide – between Man as he is and Man as he was destined to be – and we are the bridge-makers."

As the words formed, Gareth became aware of the enormity of the task ahead. It was not just a game he had conjured out of his imagination, with his model landscapes and characters. It wasn't a childish make-believe to be shared with Grandy. Strange things had been happening all around the world for months now. Volcanoes, extinct for thousands of years, had erupted without warning; there'd been earthquakes and tremors, even in Britain. Violent storms, hailstones as big as golf balls in the South of France, seas rising, tides higher than ever before, flooding holiday resorts, and seasons jarred out of rhythm.

Now he understood. It was the indomitable spirit of the Earth fighting back against the forces of evil, forces that had been unleashed by Man – and aided by Morgana.

"You are right, Son of Gwydion."

Suddenly, Gareth was aware of the peregrine, perched once more on the tower, watching him, listening to his thoughts.

"Already, you are proving yourself worthy of the task, growing into your new skin. Your mind is open to the thoughts that enter it through your ancient blood. What you hold is not one of the Four. It is the Light with which you must journey. I dare not breathe its name nor hint at the essence of its being, lest knowledge of it be carried by the wind who knows no master to the ears of those who would destroy it. Question not the nature of it. Doubt not the extent of its wisdom and power. Give it no names. Only believe in it and know in your heart that it is good and will protect you and give you warning of Evil."

Ergyriad bobbed his dark head and stretched out his wings. "My work here is finished for the present. I fly to the Northern Reaches to join my sister Aquila in her search for the Four. Guard your treasure well, Old One, and may the power of the Light fly with you."

Gareth lifted his hand in salute and spoke silently. "Go in safety, Lord of the Skies, and have no fear. The stone gives me strength and courage to face our enemies. Perhaps our paths will cross again in another place or another time."

"And if they do not," spoke Ergyriad, "then be sure, Son of Gwydion, that we shall meet at our last journey's end and our thoughts will flow together in the River of Time." Gareth's eye was locked in the golden light of the peregrine's stare. Its beam forged a bond of friendship and understanding deeper and stronger than anything he had ever known. Now he was ready.

"You were right, Grandy," he said. "I won't be alone. I won't ever be alone." He looked up and raised his hand. At the signal, Ergyriad lifted his wings and fell upon the wind. He swept in an arc across the lake, lifted, circled once in farewell and was gone, flying into a wind that came from the sea and the greater mountains beyond.

Gareth picked up the rucksack. Inside was an old tea towel that Mum had wrapped around the flask. It was unworthy, but it was all he had. He folded it carefully around the stone and put it in the front pocket of the rucksack. Then he turned to look at Grandy. He was eating banana cake! How could he even think of doing anything as normal as eating banana cake? Grandy smiled and offered him some. "Battles are not won on empty stomachs," he said, "and we daren't take anything home. You know what your mum's like."

Gareth dropped his shoulders and laughed. "Myrddin. Son of Nwyvre, Traveller and Finder of the Stone – afraid of my mum? You must be joking!" He reached for a sandwich and took a bite, surprised at how good it tasted and how hungry he really was. "But we should be doing something," he got out between munches, "making plans, not just sitting here eating a picnic as if nothing was happening, as if it were just an ordinary day."

"But it is just an ordinary day for most people." Grandy drew his pipe from his pocket and tapped the ash out on a stone. As they watched, the wind took away every visible speck. Grandy touched the stone. "Vanished without trace," he said, rubbing his fingers together. "Does that mean it no longer exists?"

"Of course not," said Gareth. "It's in the air, blowing around us."

"Easy to say that when you have just seen it," said Grandy. "But to believe in something – or someone, you have never seen – now that is a gift indeed."

"Like Tara?" said Gareth. "Like the people who once lived on Crumlock Hill – and the power of the Light?"

Grandy smiled, but said nothing. He stuffed the lunch box and flask into the rucksack and leapt to his feet. "The wheels turn," he said. "The thread unravels in its own time. Tug too hard and you will become enmeshed, caught in a web of confusion. That is not the way. You must learn to move with the rhythms that Nature has devised. She knows what she is about. Ask any bird or butterfly. Now, I'll race you to the bottom of the hill. Last one to the car's a nincompoop."

Chapter 14

The Rowan Wood

The journey home began in silence. Gareth was bursting with questions he was afraid to ask, piecing together the events of the last twenty-four hours, wondering what would happen next. "One step at a time," he murmured.

"It's the only way," said Grandy, "or else you get kippers and custard on the same plate and nothing tastes right."

He indicated, and without slowing, turned sharply left down a narrow lane between high banks and crumbling stone walls. Three more bends and they were in a sombre grey village, like something from a Bavarian folk tale. Two rows of cottages seemed to lean into the street. Gareth saw a post-office and a dreary little shop that boasted 'Antiques' and 'Welsh Pottery'. Nothing stirred. The village seemed deserted, left over from a different age, but further down the street an old bicycle was propped against the wall, and as far as Gareth could see, grey net curtains hung inside the dusty windows.

Grandy pulled up outside the shop. The bulging window was in shadow and no lights were on, but Gareth could just make out the shapes of a coal-scuttle and a log-box, both tarnished, neglected. There was a heap of old flat-irons, a black kettle and an iron saucepan full of wooden spoons with ornate handles – and butter pats.

"I don't see much pottery," said Gareth, eyeing an assortment of ugly brown mugs.

"We're not here for the pottery," said Grandy as he untangled himself from the seat belt and flung open the door. "Where better to lose an antique? No! Don't get out! There's no time!" He stood for a moment on the pavement, looking up at the rugged backdrop of mountains. "I'll only be a minute."

Gareth frowned. "What do you mean?"

Grandy's words sent a tiny ripple down his spine.

But Grandy was already striding through the shop doorway, making the bell jangle furiously. Inside, Gareth could just make out a pale face hovering in the half-light. It was no higher than Grandy's elbow. Male or female, Gareth couldn't tell as a large, thick-fingered hand reached into the iron saucepan. When it emerged, it was gripping a brown, tube-shaped object.

Seconds later, Grandy was folding himself back into his car seat, thrusting the strange object at Gareth.

"What is it?" asked Gareth, instinctively lifting the tube to his eye.

"The rowan wood," said Grandy, "carved by one with the Old Magic in his fingertips, though it is well known that the rowan wood has magic enough of its own. It carries secrets well. Now, put it safely away. You will find a good use for it later." He turned the key viciously. "Hold on to your back teeth. We may be in for a rough ride."

He turned the car sharply around, bumping over the narrow pavement and racing through the gears. Gareth knew not to speak. He was aware of a change – in the air and in Grandy. He glanced around. Behind them the village had already disappeared, the autumn sun had been smothered by sullen, churning clouds and the pale, golden sunlight replaced by a smoky, yellow glow.

"Looks like we're in for more than a dumbowdash," said Gareth, using one of Grandy's expressions. "I can't believe it. Half an hour ago there wasn't a cloud in the sky."

"This is no ordinary storm," said Grandy, hunching himself over the wheel and urging the old car to go faster. "Come on, old girl. We can beat her."

As they turned on to the main road, rain swept over them in a wave, hammering the windows, rendering the wipers useless. Not even three o'clock, but the storm brought with it a ferocious darkness that closed in upon them, squeezing them along the hazy beam of light that moved weakly before them.

"I can't see a thing," said Gareth, rubbing the windscreen. "Don't you think we ought to stop until it passes?"

But Grandy was beyond hearing. His knuckles gleamed white on the steering wheel; the contours of his face were etched in stone as he directed every ounce of his energy and will against the storm. His crown of white hair, always wild, stood out from his head as if charged with electricity. In fact, it suddenly seemed to Gareth that the air inside the car was pulsing with vibrant energy – as if someone had flicked on a switch. And the source of it was there, inside the rucksack on his lap.

He gritted his teeth and braced himself as Grandy flattened his foot on the accelerator. Wrapping his long arms about the wheel, he clung to the road like an insect, anticipating every corner and flying around it recklessly into whatever lay beyond.

Gareth's eyes were glued to the windscreen. All he could see was the rain, battering across them in solid grey sheets, and the hostile shapes of the trees that bowed and twisted grotesquely, clawing at the roof of the car as Grandy willed it forward into the light.

Gareth clung to the rucksack with one hand, the door with the other. "I had a nightmare like this once," he yelled, knowing that Grandy wouldn't hear. "Someone was chasing me down a long dark tunnel. I could see the light at the end but I couldn't reach it. So I stopped and turned around."

This was just like the dream. On and on they went, pushing through the darkness as though it were something thick and tangible, like treacle – getting nowhere.

"Grandy!" screamed Gareth. "We can't outrun it!"

It was difficult to turn around and look behind, but when he did, he was aware of movement, sensed rather than seen, something that sent a trickle of ice down his back - a shadow, darker than the clouds, thicker than the grey blanket of rain, a shadow that writhed and twisted and wound the storm about them.

"It's moving with us!" he yelled, into Grandy's ear this time. "We have to stop and face it, don't you see!"

Grandy's shoulders sagged, his grip relaxed on the wheel. When he turned to look at Gareth, the chiselled lines in his face had softened into a grin. "Sorry, old chap. Hold on to your socks!"

Gareth slid down in his seat and jammed his feet into the foot well as Grandy braked, rapidly changed down and flung the car around. As they skidded to a halt the lights failed, the engine died and they were in complete darkness. Instinctively, Gareth leaned closer to Grandy, his left hand gripping the rucksack until his knuckles hurt. As they watched, two pools of red light grew out of the darkness and swam towards them. For a moment they hovered, turning the rain to blood, flooding the car with their sickening glow. Then they lifted, merging and growing into a gaping red hole that began to swirl and spin. Faster and faster it turned, throwing out tongues of fire that coiled about the darkness, sucking it, howling, into the vortex.

When the last wisp of darkness had been swallowed, the red light paled, turning in on itself, narrowing and darkening into a spiral of black smoke that threshed and flicked like a serpent's tail, breaking at last into the ragged shapes of thirteen screaming birds that beat noisily against the air and pulled heavily away from the sun.

Gareth's rigid body sagged and he let out a great lungful of air. "That was Morgana, wasn't it? You knew we couldn't outrun her," he panted at last.

Grandy shrugged. "It was only a game," he said, "for the present. I know her of old. She is testing the waters, taking stock of her opponent, trying to discover what kind of power you possess. Evil, you see, brings no satisfaction unless there is someone to contest it, or someone to observe."

"But I haven't got any power! I don't know any magic."

As soon as he said it, Gareth knew it was no longer true.

Grandy smiled. "You have more power than you know, like an ant in a hurricane. You have simply forgotten how to use it, as all Men have. Fear not. When the time is right, your seventh sense will return. Only have faith. Be who you are. You have already learnt so much."

He started the car and made a tight, three-point turn. The road was quite dry, the air motionless. At the roadside, oak and beech looked familiar and friendly. Their coppery leaves caught the last of the afternoon sun as the mountains in the west rose up to meet it.

"It's another world," said Gareth, "and we are stepping between the two."

Grandy nodded. "Other worlds are wrapped around our own like the skins of an onion. Sometimes the skin wrinkles and there is a shift in time and place."

Gareth couldn't help grinning. That's what he had told Kit.

"Like now?"

"Like now." He paused. "But even without the shift, which no mortal can control, there is a way that Man can enter the Otherworld if he has courage and strength enough to confront his own shadow there. All that is needed is knowledge of the gateways. That knowledge has been lost to all but a few. You, Gareth, are one of the chosen ones."

Gareth nodded slowly, considering the power of the dark, aware that what he had just seen was only a glimpse of its terrible strength. He drove the thought away and forced himself to think of Tara. As he concentrated his thoughts a picture grew in his mind. He saw shining walls, dulled by the shadows that moved over them. He saw a gateway through which a lady walked. She was tall, beautiful, with clusters of tiny pearls in her red-gold hair. Around her pale neck hung a torque of gold, inlaid with green stones. Mariandor. He turned to Grandy. "Tell me about the lady who stands before the gates of Tara?"

"Mariandor."

"I know her name. I think I've always known it, deep inside. But who *is* she?"

"Mariandor. The word itself is a whisper, a prayer. Listen carefully and you can hear it where cool mountain streams trickle and burble over mossy stones in quiet vales. It's there, in the water, the rocks, in the trees and the wind. Mariandor, the silver wheel that turns forever, unrelenting, touching our dreams, lifting our hearts. When you feel that unexpected surge of hope, surprising gleam of optimism, that is Mariandor. For when a star danced, beneath it was she born. Sometimes, you will glimpse her in the turn of a stranger's head, in a smile that takes you to another place. Sometimes, you will hear her voice in a phrase of music, the song of a bird, the rustle of leaves, the dancing of shadows on a sunlit path. When you do, then rejoice and embrace her. For memory of her is fading and, beyond childhood, few can see her clearly. Yet, in quiet moments, she can be with you. Hold out your hand and open the chambers of your heart and you will see her. She stands at a gateway that is higher than mortal man, its oak wood carved with the heads of eagle and dove, lion and stag. Her auburn hair is laced with tiny pearls, her gown and eyes are green, her face unclouded. Her spirit moves between worlds, keeping dreams alive in the hearts of our children. For she is the keeper of the Light, star-born, daughter of the dawn. She is hope and the builder of bridges. She paves the road to eternity. Grandy smiled and continued. "She is the essence of all our dreams. She is sunshine and birdsong and morning rain. She is the spirit of Goodness and Light. She is the torch that leads Men forward out of Darkness."

"Have you ever seen her?"

"Aye, once, long, long ago on the shores of Gwynant."

"And where is she now, Grandy?"

Grandy shook his head sadly. "None but Nwyvre knows."

"And the Golden Stone? If it is not one of the Four then what is it and why is it so important?" Gareth turned away, stared through the window at the darkening landscape, his thoughts a jumble. He closed his eyes and before him another face emerged. It was the grey face of a warrior, locked in stone. His right hand was empty and lay open on his lap; his left gripped the arm of his throne-like seat as if he would rise. Gareth opened his eyes suddenly, breathing deeply, and relaxed his grip on the rucksack. "When I close my eyes I can see her for a moment before she fades and is gone. In her place I see a warrior locked in stone, a warrior asleep on his horse, his sword hand empty. What terrible thing happened in the world to bring all this about? Though I see Mariandor, I know she is no longer there, for Tara is in mourning and their king is near death. And the army of Prince Lugh is helpless."

Grandy sighed. Such a sigh that the sound of it sent a shiver of fear through Gareth. Sometimes, saying nothing, Grandy could say so much.

"Men," he said, bitterly. "Men with their cleverness and their greed and their pride. Men are what happened."

"But what?"

"No more questions. See how much of your inner self has been revealed to you already. Answers where until a few days ago there had been no questions. Read the Book again and the thread will slowly unwind. As it does, you will be drawn beyond your earthbound self into the silver mist that lies between Dark and Light, the twilit zone where all the greatest battles are fought."

Grandy stayed for tea, devouring chicken legs and chocolate cake as if he didn't expect to eat again for a week.

"Did you have a good day?" Mary Jones asked out of habit, knowing they wouldn't share much of it with her.

Gareth nodded, staring at the salad on his plate, attempting to cut the thick stalky bit from his tomato. He was afraid to look at her, afraid that everything he knew would be written on his face. If their eyes had met he might have been surprised to see the knowing light that shone there for a moment.

"We picnicked by a ruined castle," he mumbled through a mouthful of crusty bread. "It was great. There was a lake and some birds."

Mary Jones nodded and smiled wistfully. "It sounds lovely. What was it called?"

"The Castle of Might," he said. "At least, that's what it means in English."

She smiled. "What a wonderful name. Like something out of a fairy story." She picked up the teapot. "Now then, Dad, another cup of tea?"

Grandy held out his cup. "Have you settled in then?" he asked. "Is the air vibrating kindly around you?"

Mary Jones frowned. "We've only been here a short time, but in a strange sort of way it feels as if we've been here for years, as if it was meant to be, like coming home. Sounds silly, but there you are. Did Gareth tell you how Gwyn heard about the job, how he bumped into that funny old man?"

Grandy nodded, though Gareth hadn't mentioned it. "Someone must have sent him," he said, "just when you needed him most. There is a plan, you see, a great cosmic jigsaw puzzle, and somehow, somewhere, we all fit into it." He pushed back his chair as if suddenly thinking of a reason why he shouldn't be there at all, and leapt to his feet. "Now, I must be away." He grabbed a sausage roll. "There's no peace from the wicked."

Gareth glanced at him sharply, his sensitivity heightened by what he knew. Gareth saw the hint of a frown on his mum's face but all she said was, "You haven't drunk your tea."

Grandy reached for the cup and gulped down the hot liquid. He threw his scarf over his shoulder and turned to go. "I shall see you when I see you. Thank you, my dear, for a splendid meal."

He kissed the top of her head absent-mindedly and strode towards the door. Gareth jumped to his feet and followed him to the kitchen. Grandy was about to lift the latch when Gareth touched his elbow. The old man turned and stared above Gareth's head as if his thoughts were on another plane.

"Grandy, you can't just go and leave me. What do I do next? Do I just wait until something happens?"

126

Grandy shook his head and blinked. He threw back his shoulders and seemed to grow a foot taller, his wild hair almost brushing the low ceiling. "Read the Book again," he said in a gruff whisper that expanded to fill the room. "Samain draws near. Keep your wits about you and be ready. The earth will open and dark spirits stalk the land. You will hear echoes of the chaos from which Men came and to which he must never return. It is the twilight time between the dark and light seasons when the fertility of the earth must be restored and the future of its peoples guaranteed."

He put a firm hand on Gareth's shoulder. "You must seek out your companions for indeed they have already been chosen. With them you will not be alone. The spirits of Gwydion and Taliesin will strengthen you, the voice of Ergyriad will guide you, and the thoughts that are your own will give you power over Evil."

Grandy offered his hand and Gareth held it tightly. Already, today, he had seen another side of Grandy, the side that was Myrddin the Traveller, not his own Grandy, who stood before him.

"Who are you?" he whispered. "Sometimes, most of the time, you are my grandfather. Then you become Myrddin and I see you in my head standing on a hilltop holding two long sticks and pointing the way for others to follow. Which one is the real you?"

"Why, both, of course. Take the friend from the brother and you have half the man. We are different things to different people. Husband, brother, father, friend and son are all in one man. To most people Merfyn Llwyd Thomas is just a scatty old man."

Gareth grinned. "They wear blinkers," he said, and Grandy nodded.

"I suppose I know what you mean," Gareth added, "but it's not quite the same, is it?"

Grandy shook his head. "Not quite. But it's close enough for now, and you will come to understand in time. You see, each of us has his own space to fill. We must stretch and grow in all directions, pushing our imagination and understanding to the limits in order to fill that space. And when we fill it, it grows bigger — so we must stretch some more. Do you grasp what I mean? Your mind is a fertile garden. Neglect it and the choking weeds take over; nurture it and the world — nay, the universe and all its secrets — can be yours. Sadly, the world we have created is choked with weeds."

Gareth nodded slowly, trying to take it all in. "When will I see you again?"

"Who knows?" said Grandy. "Perhaps when you least expect it, though in spirit I shall never be far away." He squeezed Gareth's hand firmly, pulled open the door and was gone, striding away from the house without a backward glance.

Gareth waited until the little car had disappeared around the corner, feeling suddenly lost. He took a deep breath of the cool evening air and went back into the dining room.

"Your tea must be cold," said Mary Jones. "Shall I make a fresh pot?"

"No, thanks, not for me anyway," said Gareth. "Can I take a piece of cake up to my room, please? I've got something to do."

His mum smiled and sighed at the same time. "Yes, of course you can. It hasn't been much of a birthday, has it? I mean, with the house in such a muddle and your dad busy at the farm."

"Don't worry, Mum. The tea was great, and Grandy and I had a good time. I wouldn't have wanted to do anything else, honestly. Anyway, I'm too old for jelly and stuff and kids' games."

"I know that. They never were your cup of tea. You're a strange boy, Gareth Jones. But you're not too old for presents. Here, take them up with you. They're not very exciting – just a couple of sweaters and a new bag for school."

"Thanks, Mum." He slung the rucksack over his shoulder, picked up the parcels and went upstairs. He hadn't really wanted another piece of cake.

Once in his room he opened the rucksack and took out the strange, wooden tube. It seemed so very old, hard as stone, toughened by time. He examined it closely with eyes and fingertips. Made from the rowan wood, Grandy had said. Power over Evil. *Protection for the stone*? He turned it over and over, frowning at the intricate markings finely scored in the wood. At each end was a narrow band of yellow horn – or bone. These, too, were patterned with delicate, swirling lines and tiny, wedge-shaped characters. He held it to him, warmed by the feel and the smell of it. It was good to see old things, to handle them and breathe in the musty essence of age, as if, in doing so, you might learn something, absorb into your own being a knowledge of the craftsman and the age in which he worked. The object itself was a traveller in time, a thread drawing past and present together, linking the hand that now held with the hand that once made.

But how could it protect the treasure he now possessed? Gareth opened the rucksack pocket and took out the golden stone. It was roughly the same diameter as the rowan tube, but there was no way it would go inside, unless – Gareth stared at the wood, at the smooth bands of horn or bone. He put down the stone. It looked and felt quite ordinary now. He gripped the tube with both hands. He was right – at one end the band could be moved. He turned it through a hundred and eighty degrees and it was free. He felt inside. There was a ridge all the way round. He picked up the stone, a pulse throbbing in his temple as he held his breath and slotted it gently but firmly into the rowan wood. With the band replaced, the stone was secure.

Without thinking, Gareth lifted the tube to his eye and turned to look at the peacock feather. Nothing was clear. He couldn't even make out its shape in the pale disc of light. Slowly, his back to the window, he moved the tube across the room. His eye was level with the mirror on the chest of drawers when he stopped. In the smoky light there was a movement, a tiny flicker of red like the smouldering edge of paper in the dark ash of a dying fire. He dropped his hand and looked at the mirror. There was only the reflection of the familiar things in his room. But deeper in the glass was the window, and beyond that, the growing darkness outside.

Gareth moved to the window and closed the curtains sharply without looking outside. If there was something – or someone – out there watching, he wasn't ready to face it yet. He didn't know enough to be able to deal with it. "Read the book again," Grandy had said. But first, he needed a little time to unscramble everything in his head. He hid the rowan tube in the closet and sat down at his desk.

He took out his paints and worked for an hour on the dwarf and the five tiny figures, using a needle-fine brush to bring them to life. He finished by adding a pin-prick of speedwell blue to the eyes of the dwarf and a few hair-streaks of silver to his beard. "And now I have him," he mimicked, "Old Brownskin himself."

He set the children down on the hill at the centre of the stone circle. As he placed the dwarf beside them his hand was trembling. His throat was dry. Something inside him was sending ripples of excitement to his toes and fingertips. It was as if, in playing what he had thought was just a game, he was adding another piece to the puzzle, operating a trigger that would set something far more real in motion.

He stared at the scene for a moment, mesmerised by it, remembering his dream and the faces by the fire.

Chapter 15

Old Brownskin

It rained all of Sunday, washing the fields and blotting out completely the slate-grey ridge of the Welsh hills. There was no way that Kit would be allowed out. At three o'clock she telephoned Gareth.

"I don't think it's ever going to stop."

"Don't worry. I can't go out either."

"What about the stones? Don't we need to check if they're all there? There isn't much time left."

"We'll go tomorrow," said Gareth.

"And what if it's still raining?"

"I've thought about that. Ask your mum if I can camp in your garden tomorrow night – or in the barn."

"She'll think it's a bit odd. I mean, we've only just made friends."

"I know. Tell her we're working on a project together. It won't exactly be a lie, will it? Tell her it's about Hallowe'en. That'll be even nearer the truth."

Kit giggled nervously. "I've got a tent. I could camp, too. Then it'll be easy to sneak off when the time comes."

"Perfect! That's it then. We'll get everything ready tomorrow. Better go to bed early."

"I suppose so, but I'm sure I won't sleep much. We have no idea what will happen tomorrow. Are you scared?"

"No," said Gareth, "just excited."

"Are you sure?"

"Well, maybe just a little."

"Me too. I've got this weird buzzing in my stomach. Do you think we ought to tell someone what's happening? A grown-up. I mean. Two kids like us meddling in something like this."

"It's not meddling," said Gareth. "We've been chosen to do it. Something weird is happening, with or without us. We can't just turn our backs on it and hope it'll go away. We have to do our bit, you know, play our part. We might only be kids, but Grandy says we have a kind of power, and if we don't use it now when it's most needed we'll regret it for the rest of our lives. You're not having second thoughts are you? You haven't told someone already?"

"Of course I haven't! I'm not stupid!"

"They wouldn't believe us anyway. They'd only laugh and tell us what wonderful imaginations we have."

"What if they saw the stones?"

"Good point. However, I don't believe they CAN see them. They weren't there last week. How can they possibly be there now?"

"But we've seen them!"

"Of course we have. But that's only because someone, somewhere, wants us to. It's like you said. There are two worlds – skins, Grandy calls them, one on top of the other. On certain days, or when special things happen you can see right through one into the other. You can even step from one to the other if you know where the gateways are. Don't you see?"

"I suppose so," said Kit slowly.

"You're not backing out, then?"

"Idiot! Wasn't I in your dream?"

"Yes, but you weren't the only one. Look, I have to go. Mum wants to use the phone. See you tomorrow."

"Yeah. Bye."

That night, sleep took Gareth immediately and carried him into another dream. He was alone in the empty house at Worlds' End, locked in the eye of a storm while all around the valley clouds churned, winds lashed and the world shook.

He was standing at an upstairs window, unable to move, unable to do anything other than look at the unkempt garden below. Nothing was stirring. Beyond the garden he could hear the wind howling, trees screaming. He could sense chaos all about him, but here, house and garden were as still as a painting, until, in a moment, the artist grew careless and ink, blacker than the night sky, spilled across the scene. As he watched, tentacles of darkness slid silently over the grass. They crept into corners, slithered over walls and coiled around trees, until the whole canvas was steeped in shadow. Only then did Gareth see two pools of dull red light moving back and forth through the darkness, searching. They stopped at the foot of the biggest, oldest apple tree. The black tentacles were drawn in and wound themselves about this tree until the trunk was a pillar of darkness.

When every branch had been engulfed the window flew open with a crash and the apple tree burst apart, showering the ground with black, rotten fruit. Out of the heart of the tree a ball of green light rose like the last flash of a dying firework. The shadows screamed, reached for it, clawed the empty air and fell back, beaten.

Gareth looked to the sky but the green light was gone, and all he could hear was the wind shaking the last leaves in the empty garden.

Morning came quietly, jewel-bright and clear. Everything seemed so normal, so ordinary, that Gareth wondered for a moment if anything strange had really happened at all. A single glance at the closet door was enough to remind and reassure him. He could feel the energy contained within it and sensed the urgency of its need to be free.

After breakfast, Gareth got down the attic ladder. Mary needed some help putting boxes up and as it was raining, she felt she was not keeping him from anything more important.

"It's OK then – if I camp out at the farm tonight?"

Mary frowned. "What if it's still raining?"

"We can go into the barn."

"I hope Mrs Talbot doesn't mind."

"But you spoke to her. You know what she said."

"What about the jobs your dad wants you to help with? Why can't you do this at the weekend?"

"Mum! You know there are things I just have to do!"

She sighed. "OK. Well, just be careful, then. You're not as grown up as you think you are."

Gareth crossed his fingers and swallowed hard. "Mum, we're only camping in the garden, not on top of Ben Nevis. Stop worrying."

She shrugged. "Sorry! I guess it comes with the territory, seeing dangers where there aren't any but I've got this funny, restless feeling."

Gareth couldn't look at her.

"It's probably the weather and the full moon and moving house." She turned to look out through the window. "I wonder where Grandy is. I do worry about him you know. He's not quite your average old man, is he?"

Gareth smiled. He touched his mother's arm. "He'll be OK. So will I. I promise."

She gave him a quick hug. "Love is proved in the letting go."

"Huh?"

"Something I read somewhere."

"Can I go and get my stuff ready now?"

She nodded. "I'll make you some lunch first. What about this evening's meal?"

"Kit's sorting it."

"It was three-thirty when he arrived at Mill House Farm. Kit was waiting on tenterhooks. "Where on earth have you been? I thought you were coming ages ago."

"Couldn't find the tent – and then Mum kept finding me things to do, as if she didn't really want me to go out."

"Mums, Huh!"

She hauled Gareth inside and dumped his rucksack and bags beneath the coat hooks. "We won't be long, Mum," she yelled through a doorway. "Back in time for tea."

It was turning into a perfect autumn evening, crisp and bright, with splashes of scarlet and gold lighting the fading hedgerows and a vague promise of mist haunting the marshy iris beds along the river bank.

They moved in silence, their thoughts too deep and too many to share, both afraid to voice their fears. Once their feet had struck the cobbled track it was as if they already walked in another place, in another time.

They crossed the bridge, its weathered boards groaning in the high water. They scrambled out of the gully and followed the path to the wood, both now thinking of the creatures that stalked there. They sought a sky-lit way through the trees, aware of the fading light and the tricks it could play, glancing neither left nor right until the wood was behind them and they were safely through it.

Halfway up the grassy slope they caught their first glimpses of the stones, ages old, upright and still and silver-grey with lichen, a ring of ancient sentries guarding the secrets of the hill.

Gareth whistled as they came upon the flat arena, for the stones were at least eight feet tall.

Kit gaped in astonishment. She had tried to imagine the circle, but the sheer size of the stones and the weight of their presence was a shock. She reached out to touch the nearest one, needing to know that, against all reason, it was real. The contact sent a shiver through her. It was ice-cold, damp, and as solid as the hill on which it stood. She glanced back to the darkening forest and the tangled shadows where anything could hide. She felt instinctively that the circle was safe. She stepped forward.

"No!" Gareth yelled at her. "Don't step inside the circle. Not yet! It's complete, that's all that matters. Now we must wait for the right moment."

"Wise words indeed," said a voice. "There is yet hope for humans. And this one, if I am not mistaken, carries in his veins the blood of Gwydion."

The children spun around.

Behind them, moving up the hill from the trees was a short, stout figure. He was broad-shouldered, short-limbed and carried a long staff. He thrust himself towards them with bold, determined strides.

"If you had looked up," he said, "you might have seen me. But it is as clear as the rainbow to me that you have looked down so long your necks won't straighten."

"It's him!" whispered Gareth. "I have never seen him and yet I would know him anywhere. Old Brownskin – or Urion Longspear, to give him his proper title."

137

Longspear bowed low. "At your service," he said.

The voice was deep – gruff, but not unfriendly.

Gareth held out his hand, as if meeting a dwarf was the most natural thing in the world.

Kit could only stare. She closed her eyes, looked again – and put her hand over her mouth to hide a giggle. "Are you real?" she said.

The dwarf glowered at her from beneath hairy clumps of eyebrows. "As real as the Coelfain[2] Circle," he muttered, lifting his stick and pointing at the stones, then dropping it and poking Kit sharply in the ribs. "What about you?"

Now it was Gareth's turn to giggle. "We came to check," he said, ignoring Kit's indignant glare, "to make sure the stones were here. We'll come back when the moon rises."

"Are there not more of you?" said the dwarf. "I was thinking you might be leading a small army. The task is over much for two young humans with little magic and no knowledge of the Dark."

Gareth sighed. "There should be others but I don't really know who. We just moved here."

"Don't I already know that," said the dwarf. "Wasn't it Master Brownskin who pointed the way – who found you on Cromlech Hill? Pah! Rabbits indeed!"

Gareth grinned. So that was it – or part of it.

"There are others who show interest," said the dwarf. "Didn't I see them riding those two-wheeled contraptions up the lane?"

"Don't worry about them," said Gareth. "They haven't a clue about what is really going on. They're just mucking about. It gives them something to do."

---

[2] reward

138

Longspear shuffled his feet and looked uneasy. "Until moonrise then," he said.

"We thought it would be on Hallowe'en, but that's not until next Monday."

The dwarf chuckled. "A trick," he said. "The months were shifted long ago so that the true All Hallows Eve would pass unnoticed and the spirits that inhabit the earth and air could go about their business without the curious eyes of humans upon them. Hallowe'en, as you name it, is this very night." He glanced about him with an odd, jerking movement, sniffing the air and frowning. He drew nearer to them, and with him came the smell of damp earth and dark places beneath the hills. "It is written," he said, "that a boy will come, that he will restore the Light and forge anew the link between the Tuatha and humankind. But, as the tallow flickers on earth and the shadows deepen there are those whose faith in the Word is crumbling. Time grows short."

He bowed low once more and stepped back from them. "Keep your wits about you. The Shapeless One has eyes beneath every stone, and though she cannot destroy you she can fill your mind with darkness so that of your own free will, you abandon the Light and tread the twisting path that leads into shadow. Her creatures are already in your world, for the treasures are here. She possesses one of the Four, and the burden of that lies with me, though even a dwarf cannot have his feet in two places at once. She plays games. It is the way of evil ones. Be wary of games, for the playing of them oft leads to deeper, darker things."

And with that he was gone, leaping away down the hill, one more shadow in the deepening gloom.

"Did they find you?" Mrs Talbot asked as they kicked off their boots in the porch.

"Did who find us?" yelled back Kit.

"Barry Thomas and his friends. I saw them in the lane so I sent them after you."

"Mum!" Kit pulled a face at Gareth. "No, they didn't find us, thank goodness. Come on, Gareth. I'm starving."

Even as they spoke, Roddy Spinks, Barry Thomas and Luke Carter were climbing over a fence into the lane below the farm.

"You two can please yourselves," Roddy was saying, "but I'm definitely coming down here tonight to see what's going on. 'Course, if you're too chicken ..."

"Come off it, Spinksy! Who're you calling chicken?" said Carter. "I'm coming, for one, just to see what those two are up to. A couple of loonies, if you ask me."

"Well?" Roddy looked at Baz.

"It's all very well making plans now," said Baz, "but things look different after dark. I bet you won't be so brave then. That place is dead spooky."

"What a wimp! You're dropping out of the gang, then? Just when things are about to get interesting, tough old Barry Thomas can be depended on – to disappear down the nearest hole."

"I didn't say I wasn't coming, did I? But there's no batteries in me torch."

"Won't need 'em," said Roddy, kicking at a piece of fallen branch. "There'll be a full moon."

"Great," said Barry, without enthusiasm. "Anything for a laugh."

"Right!" said Roddy, slapping him hard on the back. "What else is there to do in this boring dump?"

"Hey, Spinksy, who do you think they were talking to?"

"I dunno," said Roddy. "Wasn't very big, but I couldn't see that well. Must've been another kid from school. Beats me what they're doing on that old hill. Nothing up there but rabbits and thistles."

"What about the other night?"

"What about it?" said Roddy sharply. He refused to believe in ghosts and other such nonsense.

"They weren't rabbits, were they?" said Baz, watching Roddy's immobile face.

"Let's go! None of us has any lights."

They picked up their bicycles and began wheeling them up the lane.

"It's awful quiet," said Baz.

"So what? It's that time of day, isn't it?" said Roddy. "Sort of half way between light and dark. It's always quiet then, kind of muffled. Haven't you noticed?"

Baz focused on the wheel of his bike, holding tightly on to the handlebars as it bumped up and down in the ruts of the lane. "Well, I think it's weird."

"You think pasta's weird."

But Roddy said nothing. He was agreeing with Baz. It was as if they were moving in a bubble, isolated by the eerie light, cut off from the real world. He gave himself a mental shake and was just preparing to mount his bike when there was a yell from behind.

"Did you see that, Spinksy? What the heck was it? It nearly took my ear off."

Roddy looked at the dark shape moving against the sky. "It was just a bird, you pea-brain. You know, those things with feathers and wings. Must've been an owl."

They mounted their bicycles then and pedalled hard up the lane.

"Where'd it come from?" yelled Carter, in front now. "I never saw it coming. Why did it attack me? Owls don't do that. Our Tom told me about this film years ago where birds attack people and peck out their eyes."

"Don't be daft. Must've thought you were a mouse."

Suddenly, before them they saw a bird-shape. Its ragged wings brushed the lower branches of the trees as it swept towards them. They saw outstretched claws and yellow eyes and an ugly, gaping beak.

"Watch out!" yelled Roddy. He ducked and swerved just in time. Baz had dived into the grass at the side of the lane. But the bird found a target. Its coarse wing-feathers raked Carter's face. He screamed, wobbled, hit a big stone and crashed into the ditch, arms flailing, still trying to beat off the vanished attacker.

"Where'd it go? Where'd it go?" he squealed as the other two dragged him to his feet.

"Who cares?" said Roddy, in a voice unlike his own. "C'mon, let's get out of here. This place is beginning to give me the creeps."

"What about tonight?" Baz shouted across to him as they cycled three abreast now. "You still coming?"

"Stupid question!" yelled Roddy, head down and pedalling like crazy. "'Course I'm still coming. It'll take more than a stupid bird to stop me."

What else could he say? He was their leader. They looked up to him. It was a good job they couldn't see the blood on his lip or the white of his knuckles on the handlebars.

Chapter 16

Moonstone Full

After a hearty warming meal of homemade burgers and jacket potatoes followed by nutty apple crumble and custard, Gareth and Kit put up their tents on the lawn at the edge of the orchard. There was no sign of a moon yet, but the night was crisp and clear. That done, they returned to the house and spread their books over the kitchen table. Without speaking, Gareth took out his drawings to show Kit. Instinctively, she covered them and moved to the window to drop the blind.

They sat close together, lost in the pictures and 'The Book of Gwydion', fitting together all they knew and felt. Gareth started to say something but Kit stopped him. She was staring at his drawing of Tara and frowning. "Wait a minute! I've seen this before. I'm sure I have." She jumped up and dashed from the kitchen.

When she returned, she was carrying an old notebook with a stained and faded brown cover. She closed the door and leaned against it for a moment.

"What's up?"

"It's my great-grandfather's diary. It's kept on the bookshelf in the spare bedroom with a lot of other old stuff." She held it out to Gareth. "See. I'm right, aren't I? It is the same."

Gareth looked at the faded sketch, drawn with a purplish pencil. He shrugged. "It does look a bit like it. But it could just be a coincidence."

"Rubbish!" Kit glared at him. "Look at the gate and the arch in the wall. It is the same. You know it is." She turned over the page, glanced down it and gripped Gareth's arm. "Listen to this!"

"They live beyond the Hill,
Beyond the ocean and the sky,
Yet, still they are with me
Still their faces shine.
I walked on the Hill
And felt their sweet breath
On my face.
Their pale hands touched mine,
And together we trod the same path.
If only the key were mine,
That I might speak with them as before,
Walk with them under the moon and stars,
Breathe the same air,
The same light."

"Is there any more?"

Kit shook her head. "I don't think so. Not like this. Isn't that odd? The rest is just a diary, stuff about the war mostly."

"He knew about them," said Gareth. "I wonder how."

"Look at the date," said Kit. "Nineteen-sixteen. He was injured in the Battle of the Somme and spent months in hospital. Perhaps, in the middle of all that horror he had a

144

dream or something, just like you did. Perhaps lots of people did. Perhaps they still do. Perhaps Mariandor's voice found a way.'

Gareth nodded slowly. "Then maybe she wasn't imprisoned by the Dark after all. Maybe Morgana didn't find her. Maybe she grew weak and lost her earthly form, trying to keep the Light alive when it seemed that the world had gone mad. She is a spirit of Nature. Perhaps Nature took care of her. Snatched her from the jaws of Evil and is keeping her safe until the time is right."

"Then how do we find her?"

They didn't hear Mrs Talbot come in. As soon as he was aware of her, Gareth moved his arm to cover the ancient book. She walked to the table and stared at the diary, but the faraway look on her face told them she didn't really see it.

"It's part of our project," said Kit quickly.

"What? Oh, yes, it's very good," said Mrs Talbot absentmindedly. She was frowning, not looking at them. She moved to the window, lifted the blind and peered out for a moment. "How very odd," she said at last. "I had completely forgotten about the apples."

"What apples, Mum? What are you talking about?"

"Your picture made me think of them. And that's odd, too. How could a picture of a castle remind me of apples?"

With that, she left the kitchen. In a moment, she was back, carrying a bowl full of apples which she dumped heavily in front of them. "Would you like one? I picked these straight away – after she'd gone."

"Why not?" said Kit, more puzzled by the minute. "After who'd gone?"

"You too, Gareth."

Gareth took one and bit into it with a loud crunch.

Mrs Talbot picked up an apple herself and stared at it. "I can't see any worm-holes in them, can you? Put a couple in your bag for tomorrow."

"Mum, what's all this about apples? You are behaving rather strangely."

Mrs Talbot put the apple down. "It's all rather odd. This afternoon a woman came to the door wanting to buy apples. She was a bit eccentric looking, to say the least, and Jasper wouldn't come near her, just skulked in the kitchen the whole time she was here. I decided she was one of these New-Age travellers or something. Talk about mutton dressed as lamb. She was wearing an awful fur coat and black stilettos. Anyway, I gave her a couple of pounds. I told her I didn't want any money for them, but it didn't please her in the least. She said she wanted all of them, every last one. I said they weren't for sale, that I used all the apples myself. I told her I made chutneys and pies, and we only had one really good tree. She wasn't a bit interested. In fact, she was quite rude and said the apples were probably rotten anyway. Then she turned around and stamped out of the yard in a right paddy. What a madam! I was so taken aback I stood and watched her going up the drive."

"Oh," said Kit. "Is that it?"

Mrs Talbot shook her head. "No, not by half. The strangest bit is still to come. When she was half way up the drive she stopped. I couldn't see her properly, but I could see the apples as they flew over the hedge. Such lovely big apples. I'd chosen some of the best. When she was quite out of sight, I went to the field." Mrs Talbot shuddered. "I couldn't believe what I saw. They weren't the same apples. They couldn't have been. They were black, rotten, and full of disgusting worms. I don't understand it." She picked up another apple from the bowl and examined it. "Look, not a single worm-hole."

146

Kit could think of nothing to say.

Gareth was remembering his dream about an apple tree. The hair on the back of his neck stood on end, and an icy shiver ran down his spine. "Are there any apples left in the orchard?" he asked.

"Only a few," replied Mrs Talbot. "They're on the highest branches. I think I'll get the apple-tree ladder and pick them right now just in case that dreadful woman comes back. I wouldn't put it past her. She was like Cruella de Vil."

"But, Mum, it's dark."

"I'll switch the big light on." And she left the kitchen, quite determined that that *woman* would scarcely find a single apple if she came back.

"Creepy!" said Kit when they were alone again. "Are you thinking what I'm thinking?"

Gareth nodded. Morgana! They both knew it, though neither would speak her terrible name. She had been here, *here* to the house.

"She must be watching our every move," said Kit, "But why did she want apples?"

"Maybe just an excuse," Gareth said lamely, "to come sticking her nose in."

"Can she harm us, really harm us?"

Gareth shrugged. "I don't know. I have this feeling we've got something she can't break into, a kind of power she is incapable of understanding. I don't think she can hurt us as long as we stand firm and believe in what we're doing – as long as we have-"

"Would you credit it?" Mrs Talbot flew into the kitchen, a half-eaten apple in her hand.

"What's up, now?" asked Kit, impatient at being interrupted again.

"She's been back! That dreadful woman's been back and this is all that's left, this and half a dozen windfalls. Some guard dog we've got. He never even growled. I think I'll phone Constable Evans and warn him that there are some unsavoury characters about. Who on earth can she be?"

"I reckon she's a witch," said Kit, unable to resist. "You know how witches have a thing about apples – and it is almost Hallowe'en."

"As long as we have what?" said Kit as they piled everything into the tents.

"Huh?" Gareth was still thinking about the apples.

"You said she can't really hurt us as long as we have what? You didn't finish. And I *do* think I ought to know – *if* I'm coming along." She knew that would get his attention.

Gareth glanced sharply at her. "You wouldn't back out now, would you?"

Kit grinned wickedly. "I don't quite believe what's happening, but until this week, the most exciting moment in my life was when Mr Riley's ram chased me across a field."

"I'd like to have seen that."

She thumped him, then turned to look at the sky. "There are no clouds," she said, serious again. "Now, answer the question."

"It'll probably sound stupid."

"Not the right word," said Kit. "Strange, maybe, but not stupid. Tell me anyway."

"Faith," said Gareth, watching the moon climb higher in the starlit sky. 'It's our secret weapon, something SHE knows nothing about. We must keep to the straight path in our minds, I mean. We must never stop believing in Tara.

The future of the world depends on people believing in the right things, keeping faith with the spirit of the Earth and the forces that govern all life the magic that is life itself."

Kit nodded slowly, staring at him. "Yes, I know. I think I have always known, just like Grandfather Joseph did. Perhaps Mariandor's dream has survived. Perhaps her words are locked away inside us waiting to be set free again, at the right time."

Gareth nodded and smiled. It was a wonderful, warming thought.

"It's not going to be easy," said Kit.

Gareth shrugged. "No one said it would be. But nothing worth having is free. Come on, let's pack the rucksack. It's already half-full of apples. Have you got the torch?"

Gareth strapped the rucksack on his back, straightened his shoulders and took a deep breath. Kit was zipping up her anorak, staring back at the house. Above them, a perfect silver moon had sailed up from the horizon and hung like a lantern in the sky. It washed the fields in shimmering blue light and drew inky shadows from the trees and hedgerows. It seemed the world was shifting, changing. The moon was beckoning.

"Time to go," whispered Gareth. "The moon is moving towards the hill."

Kit grabbed his arm and pointed back at the house. "No going back now, even if we wanted to."

The house was being wrapped in the arms of a swirling grey mist, just like the one they'd seen from the hill. As they watched, the dark, straight edges became blurred, then the doors, roofs and chimneys disappeared. Last to vanish was the pale square of light that was the kitchen window, the comforting golden glow that meant home and safety and the world they knew.

"This is it!" said Gareth. His left hand felt for the rowan wood in his pocket; his right gripped Kit's arm. "To Tara, then."

"Yes," whispered Kit, fists clenched tightly in her pockets. "To Tara."

Chapter 17
Scarlet Light

They closed the gate to the orchard and didn't look back. They drove the fog from their minds and locked away the picture of the farm as it would be on their return. They moved through a numbing silence, as if the lane was a tunnel, its entrance and exit in separate worlds. The only sounds they could hear were their own heartbeats and the squelch and suck of their boots in the mud, though their footfalls seemed far away, like echoes bouncing off a distant hill.

As they followed the river bank, the moon was before them, riding in a halo of silver light, its reflection trapped, quivering, in the dark waters of the stream.

Gareth lifted the latch on the gate slowly, carefully, afraid of rousing anyone, anything. But nothing stirred, neither bird nor beast. Only the old timbers of the bridge complained at being disturbed. Even the waters were silent, muffled by the weight of the night. Not yet nine o'clock, but it felt like midnight, that between-time when good folk close their doors and draw their curtains against the night and the creatures who call it their own.

Once over the stream they concentrated on the path ahead – and the wood, dark as a wound in the hill. But, try as she would to look only in front, Kit found herself turning to glance back. The second time, she shivered. "Gareth!"

she hissed through clenched teeth, "There's someone following us again."

"I know! Just keep going. Don't look back!"

Their voices sounded brittle: their words crackled and froze in the moon-shadowed night. They moved faster now, intent only upon reaching the safety of the circle.

Even in the wood they had no need of the torch. Moonlight dripped through the ragged canopy and mingled with the shadows, illuminating their path. And still there was no sound save the pad and rustle of their own footsteps and the hollow rasping of their short, sharp breaths.

Urion Longspear was standing out of the shadows, at the foot of the grassy slope. He was stamping his feet and thumping his stick on the ground, looking grumpy and impatient. "Bezountee!" he exclaimed when he saw them. "So you have brought yourselves at last. And not before time, either." He looked up. "She'll not ride much higher, and once she slips we're lost." He scowled at them. "You are not an army to scare old Mouldywarp out of his hole. But, if be so you are the son of Gwydion, you will have to do."

They climbed over the rim of the hill, Gareth clutching a box of matches in his pocket. His hand was shaking. "The sticks!" he whispered to Kit. "We've come without the sticks. What are we going to burn?"

Longspear gave them a half-smile and raised his tufted brows. "You will have no need of sticks," he said. "The fire is enough. Now, into the circle with you, and move swiftly. There are vermin rising among the trees. My fingers itch to be feeling their scrimpy necks."

Without further ado, he leapt away over tussock and bramble until he disappeared into the maze of shifting shadows beneath the trees.

Gareth and Kit stepped into the circle and remained close together, looking back the way they had come. As they stood, a cold wind came from nowhere, slapping their faces and tearing at their clothes. Beneath them, the wood lay huddled and thick with darkness, as though a different night had overtaken it. Above their heads, silhouetted against the shining disc of the moon, a pair of ragged wings beat silently across the sky.

"Where on earth has he gone?" said Gareth, hugging himself to keep warm.

"Oh, please hurry!" whispered Kit, lifting her eyes to look at the moon. For in the wake of the bird, a duster of cloud was being blown from the horizon, wiping out the stars as it came.

A shriek rose from the wood – then another. Animal sounds, panic-stricken, terrified. Then a yell – and another scream.

The dwarf appeared first, breaking from the darkness of the trees. He was followed by three, all-too-familiar figures, leaping through the grass like hares. As they scrambled over the rim of the hill it seemed the tree shadows followed them. Black shapes flowed over the ground, growing, changing, lifting into the air, fingering their clothes and lapping at their feet as they ran. Wailing and yelling, swiping the air with their arms, they made for the centre of the circle where Gareth and Kit were already kneeling by the stone.

Kit was too wound up to say anything. She just stared at the three despised faces of Spinksy, Baz and Carter, whiter than white, eyes like dinner plates.

"I knew it!" murmured Gareth, resigned. "I do believe I knew it all along."

Roddy Spinks found his tongue. "Now you've done it, Talbot! What the bleeding heck was that lot in the trees?"

"Shut up!" hissed Kit, furiously. "Just shut up!"

Gareth looked at the dwarf. Longspear nodded. Gareth struck a match. His hands shook and the wind took the flame. He lit another, leaning towards Kit.

"What's he doing, Spinksy?" Baz's voice was scarcely heard above the wind.

Roddy didn't answer. He couldn't.

Carter drew closer to him, peering with half-closed eyes in the direction of the trees.

"I'm off home," snivelled Baz. "You coming, Spinksy? I'm not stopping here with these nutters."

Roddy looked at the dwarf. Then he glanced behind him and shook his head. "Belt up, Baz. There's no way I'm going back through that lot."

Kit was looking anxiously at the sky. At any moment now, she thought, clouds will darken the moon. She unzipped her anorak and held it around the match.

Gareth struck again and this time the flame held. He looked at the dwarf. "What now, when there's nothing to burn?"

A gust of wind answered him. It threw the flame back over his fingers, biting them like ice. He cried out and the fire fell to the stone.

The wind rose higher now, raking the hill and screaming through the sky. All around them, beyond the rim of the hill, shadows reared and writhed and slunk back into the shadows of the trees as scarlet arrows of flame leapt into the air like dragons' tongues. When moonlight and firelight met, ribbons of silver light radiated from the stone, cutting through the circle like the spokes of a giant wheel. Then the wheel began to turn, and in the firelight Gareth saw the five faces of his dream.

Chapter 18

Through the Gateway

Gareth was sucked into a whirlpool of darkness and for a moment, was the baby growing in Ceridwen's womb. I am a grain of sand, he thought, and will spin in this black hole for ever. Then the darkness thinned to a soft, grey light, like the coming of a misty dawn. The whirling slowed, wound away from him, and he was left behind to land gently on solid ground.

He was standing alone before a dark, sheer face of rock. Set in the rock was an iron gate. At the side of the gate hung a disc of burnished metal, ringed with bands of coloured stones – the shield of Lugh Lamphada, though Gareth didn't know it yet.

Gareth lifted his hand, and barely had his fingers touched the shield when the gate swung open and he passed through into a cavern so immense that walls and roof were only sensed, not seen. The cavern was lit by a pale, cold light that emanated from the air all round him.

With every step, the feeling that he was not alone grew stronger. He stared all around, his eyes straining to see through the light that hung about him like a curtain of blue gauze. Suddenly, out of the haze, a figure loomed. Gareth side-stepped – and saw others. He moved towards them, among them, and saw that they were lifeless. Nothing but cold, grey statues, standing and leaning, row upon row of them, like stones in a mason's yard. They carried swords and bows and quivers of arrows. Some lay on the floor, arms outstretched as if to stave off something. Others were bowed in their saddles, on horses whose eyes stared blankly as Gareth stepped between them.

In the midst of the strange army, mounted on the biggest horse, was a man different from the rest, taller, broader of shoulder. He held his right arm aloft, grasping a fistful of air; the other lay empty at his side. His mouth was open and his eyes issued a challenge. He looked as though any minute he would rise in the stirrups and dismount. Instinctively, Gareth dropped to his knees, bowed his head and touched the long, widespread fingers of the soldier's left hand. Expecting ice-cold stone, he recoiled in horror when his own fingers felt the warmth of human flesh. Beneath his anorak, tucked safely into the inside pocket, the golden stone was pulsating like a second heart. He looked around him at the inert bodies, the frozen faces, and in that moment it seemed their eyes were not quite so dead. He reached out to them, but the whirlpool snatched him again and when he looked back the cavern and its silent occupants were disappearing like the light of a lamp in a vast, deep ocean.

He hurtled away from them towards another pinpoint of brightness. It grew rapidly, flowing about him until he could feel the light washing over him, lapping at his feet.

When he opened his eyes he was lying on wet sand at the edge of a sea or a vast lake. He remembered the sleepers in the cave, awaiting the call that would awaken them. Then he wiped the sand from his face and felt for the reassuring bulk in his pocket. Something troubled him, niggled at his mind, something he felt he should know and understand by now. Something about the golden stone.

He looked around for the others and sighed with relief. Kit was sitting on a rock, emptying sand from her boots, while Urion Longspear squatted in a hummock of spiky grass, staring at the horizon. Not far away, three figures untangled themselves, muttering and mumbling as they shook the sand from their clothes.

"Where the heck are we now, Spinksy?"

"Me mum will be that mad."

Gareth sighed again, but not with relief. Whatever he and Kit were destined to do, Roddy Spinks and his mates were not going to make it any easier. And yet, he had to admit, it seemed that they too had a part to play in all this, unlikely as it seemed. He puzzled over it as he walked towards Kit and the dwarf.

"Where are we?" Kit was asking.

"Beyond the hill," said Urion, shaking his head violently. "I travel to and fro regularly, but not once have I ended up with sand in my beard. 'tis a bad omen."

"Beyond the hill?"

"A pebble-skim from where you were before – and a world away. 'Tis the image of your own world, the land called Tir na nog."

"It's beautiful," whispered Kit.

"As is your world," added the dwarf.

"I can hear music," said Kit.

"Your world is full of that too."

Gareth stood beside Kit. "It's coming from the sea," he said, as if it was the most natural thing on the world.

"I've never heard anything like it," said Kit. "It makes me think of -"

"Whales," said Gareth. "Whales and dolphins and seaweed and coral reefs and everything that lives in the sea."

Kit nodded and closed her eyes. "It's as if every movement of every tail and fin and tentacle was a part of the music, all moving to the same gentle rhythm."

Urion Longspear grunted his approval. "Aye, 'tis something that the song of the sea can still reach your ears. I'm certain I am that you've not heard the same in your own world."

Behind them, Roddy Spinks was scowling. "What are you on about, Talbot? You must've banged your head. I can't hear any stupid music. What about you, Baz?"

Baz and Carter shook their heads, both of them looking thoroughly miserable.

The dwarf stamped his feet and looked at them sadly. "Your part in this is a mystery beyond fathoming," he said. "For, if your ears are deaf to the music, then your hearts are in chains." He shrugged. "But I am only a dwarf, and what do dwarfs know of the workings of Skuld?[3] You are here. Perhaps, in time, we shall be seeing if your worthless presence has a purpose."

Roddy was seething, but he was out of his depth. The stupid runt had insulted him in front of his friends, and they were expecting him to respond.

"It's not our fault," he said in his defence. "We didn't plan this. We didn't ask to come here, wherever it is."

"You stuck your noses in," said Kit. "We certainly didn't want you to come. This isn't a job for divvies with no brains and the imagination of a turnip."

"Huh! Listen to it!" said Baz.

"Miss Know-it-all!" added Carter.

"Shut up, all of you!" yelled Gareth. "We're here, and that's it, like it or not. We've just got to get on with it, not squabble like babies."

"Get on with what?" said Roddy. "Don't tell me you know what's going on, Mr Clever Clogs."

---

[3] fate

Gareth sat down and opened his rucksack. "There's no time to tell you everything," he said. "Not now, at any rate. But take a look at these. You may not have planned it, and we certainly didn't invite you, but you were always meant to come."

He took out the pictures he had drawn. "See? The five of us and Mr Longspear. And this – this is Tara."

Roddy stared, feeling uncomfortable. It was all a bit beyond him, and yet something like a tiny bubble of excitement began to swell inside him. "Where d'you get them?"

"I saw them in a dream, and I drew them."

Carter sniggered. "You're a good one for dreams, Taffy."

"Shut it, Carter! This Tara place, is that where we're heading?"

Gareth nodded.

"What for?"

Gareth hesitated, glancing at the dwarf for guidance. But Longspear was still watching the horizon.

"We have to return something," he said. "Something the people of Tara lost a long time ago."

"Something valuable?"

"Beyond any price a mortal can pay," said Gareth.

"Treasure?" said Baz, his eyes sparkling for the first time since they had arrived.

"Was it stolen?" asked Baz.

"Not exactly."

"Spinksy's got something he stole, haven't you Spinksy?" giggled Carter. "Can't call that treasure, though, can you?"

Roddy shot him a look of pure poison. Carter squirmed and looked away.

159

"Is it treasure?" asked Roddy.

Gareth shook his head. "Not the kind of treasure you mean," he said. "But it's more than that. We have to believe in Tara. We have to forge new links between our worlds. We have to take back the Light."

Roddy stared at his feet. "I haven't a clue what you're talking about."

"We have to save the Tuatha de Dana, the Children of the Dawn," said Kit.

"The what?"

"The ..." (She was about to say elves, but knew what reaction that would bring) "... people of Tara."

"I think we'd rather go home, if you don't mind," said Roddy.

"Impossible," said Gareth.

Roddy looked at Kit and Urion Longspear. The dwarf shrugged massively; Kit shook her head.

"Save them from what?" said Roddy in a noticeably smaller voice.

"Evil," said Kit.

"Overflowing from our world," added Gareth.

Carter swallowed hard. "Those things in the wood," he said.

Gareth nodded. "They're just a part of it. There is someone far worse, someone whose very name will empty the forest of birds."

"And what are we supposed to do?"

They hadn't noticed the dwarf twisting his beard and stamping his feet. "Enough!" he yelled at last, leaping into the air and shaking his great fists. "The path lies before you. The task awaits. If you have wit and strength enough to keep the light of Tara burning in your hearts there is hope for us all – but standing here, filling the air with

160

words! Pah! Save your breath – for it will be needed sooner than y'know."

Baz and Carter gaped. Roddy lifted his shoulders and closed his mouth tightly.

What could he say?

"Sounds crazy to me," grumbled Baz.

"Still can't hear any music," muttered Carter.

"I'd like to hear a motor-boat," said Baz. "That's what I'd like to hear. Then we could get away from this place."

The three boys wandered away to the edge of the sea and watched the waves lapping the shore.

Gareth glared at their backs, but Urion Longspear shrugged. "The fault is not theirs," he said. "Like so many of your kind their hearts and minds are in chains. They are slaves to everything their brains have built. They cannot see the depth of the lake beyond their own reflections – and the cause of it lies deeper than the roots of Yggdrasil."

"Then why are they here? It doesn't make any sense."

"Who can say? The answer does not lie between the ears of a dwarf. Yet, consider. Three unbelievers, blind and deaf to the call of Tara. Open their eyes and mayhap you can open the eyes of all who cannot or will not see."

"And until then," said Gareth, "without faith to give them strength, they will be dogged by the Dark, easy prey for Morgana."

The dwarf was silent.

"Time to go," said Gareth, beckoning the other boys. "Will you show us the way, Mr Longspear?"

"I will not," said the dwarf. "I have guided you to the shores of Tara. You, Gareth, are the chosen one. My job is to follow and obey. I am merely your servant." Then he looked pointedly in the direction he believed they had to go.

Gareth turned to the others. Kit grinned reassuringly; the other three scowled and looked down at their feet.

"Are we ready, then?"

No reply, only a nod from Kit.

"Haven't you lot ever wanted a real adventure?" she asked.

Baz and Carter shrugged. Roddy almost smiled. "Like the Famous Five, you mean? They never did anything like this."

"OK, let's get moving. We need to get higher so that we can see the land better and choose our path."

"You gonna let him tell us what to do, Spinksy?" moaned Carter.

"Stop whinging, Carter! We haven't got much choice now, have we? Unless, of course, you can show us the way or get us out of here. Come on, move your idle bones."

A path climbed steeply from the shore, winding around grassy hummocks, threading its way through strewn rocks and boulders. Gareth and Kit kept out in front while the dwarf hung back and fell into step with Roddy.

"Hm!" snorted Longspear. "I can see that curiosity is running a three-legged race with imagination."

"Huh?"

"One has a weak leg; the other is too lazy to drag him along. They will never finish the race. They will never go anywhere at all. But, mayhap, it is nought to do with wammocky legs. Maybe it is that they are cowards, the pair of them."

Roddy turned to look at the dwarf. He saw the deep lines scored into the brown face. He saw a pair of startling blue eyes searching his own. He saw a wild, grey beard threaded with strands of silver – and he thought, *this can't be happening. Any minute now Mum will yell at me to get up.*

162

"We just followed the other two," he said, lamely, "for a laugh, a bit of fun."

"Well, you're here now," said the dwarf, "for all the good it will do. So, I'm thinking, you might as well know who it is that needs your help so badly." He took a deep breath and began. "They came from the stars, as everything did," and by the time they had reached the end of the path, high above the sea, Roddy Spinks, who had rarely read a proper story in his life, knew something of the history of the elves.

When the others caught up with them, Gareth and Kit were shielding their eyes against the sky, taking in the view before them. As far as they could see there were gently rolling hills, wide plains, forests and streams. But there were no walls or hedges, no buildings or pylons, no sign of human habitation – and no sounds.

"It's like a painting," said Kit, "and it's waiting for us to step into it and bring it back to life."

"It looks like the Lake District to me," said Baz.

"I know what's happened," said Carter. "We've been transported like in the Scouts, and we've got to find our way back."

Kit almost felt sorry for him.

"I say we go this way," said Roddy, pointing west.

"Why?"

"Why not? What difference does it make? We haven't a clue where we are – unless you've got a map, of course."

Gareth ignored him. He was looking north. The furthest point they could see was a range of low hills, purple and black in the distance. At their foot something faintly silver shimmered like a mirage, caught the sky like a sliver of water. Gareth pointed. "There it is!" he said excitedly. "We don't need a map. There are the black hills, and before them stands Tara, just as it was in my dream."

"It looks an awful long way," said Kit, struggling to focus on the far horizon and the glimmer of light beneath it. "The Silver City," she whispered. "It's there, it's really there."

"Were you ever doubting it?" asked Longspear.

Kit shook her head. "Never. I don't know how or why, but it's as if I've always known – like when you visit somewhere as a tiny child, then forget all about it. One day, you go back there and all your memories come flooding back."

"Aye," said Longspear, thoughtfully, "you speak with wisdom and truth. The memory of Tara is born with you – and when the door opens..." he frowned, looking at Baz and Carter, "but some doors are held with a thousand bolts. 'Twill be a fine day when *they* burst apart."

Kit smiled at him – and then at Gareth. "North it is then," she said.

And the three set off.

Behind them, Roddy, Baz and Carter were squinting and staring at the horizon.

"What's he on about, now?" grumbled Baz. "I can't see any city."

"You always were as blind as a bat," said Carter.

"Can you see it, Spinksy?"

Roddy shook his head.

"They must think we're stupid," said Baz.

"Yeah," said Roddy. "Has it ever occurred to you that maybe they're right?"

"What?"

"Spinksy! You going soft in the head or something?"

Chapter 19

Scathack

"I wish we could hear seagulls," said Kit. "I wish we could hear birds at all. It would make the place seem more normal, friendly like."

Before them lay a wide grassy plain, flat and treeless. Beyond it was the black smear of a forest that stretched east and west as far as they could see. Even at a distance it seemed a dark and forbidding place.

"There are bound to be birds in the forest, don't you think?" said Kit hopefully. She looked up at the sky. It was a vast, lonely place without the movement of wings or the sound of birdsong. How she missed the birds. Yet, at home, she took them completely for granted. What she would give now to see a fat pigeon land at her feet as they sometimes did in the farmyard when grain had been spilt. She stopped for a moment, drawn to look at the sky above the sea. Nothing stirred, not even a wisp of cloud. Wait a minute! She shielded her eyes and pointed to where a tiny, dark speck had appeared low on the horizon. Longspear turned, saw it too, and waved his stick in the air.

"Gareth, look!" yelled Kit. "It's my fault. I'm sure it is. I wished for birds. I was longing to see birds, but I've got a horrible feeling that's not a pigeon or a seagull."

"The Scald-Crow!" said Gareth with certainty, though none of them could see the bird clearly yet.

"Never heard of it," said Carter, squinting at the sky.

"Weird name for a bird if you ask me," said Baz.

"We didn't," said Kit.

"Wait a minute!" Roddy was staring hard at the growing speck. "You might not have heard of it, Carter, but I've got a feeling you've seen it before. I think we all have."

Carter gaped as realisation dawned. "You said it was an owl. Called me a pea-brain. I knew it wasn't an ordinary bird. I'm not stupid. It's a pterodactyl, isn't it — or something like that."

Roddy looked at Gareth. "In the lane by the farm," he said. "I think it was trying to scare us off, or something. I hate to admit it, but maybe you were right, after all. We were meant to come, though I haven't a clue why. And it had feathers, Carter, so it couldn't be a pterodactyl now, could it?"

"'Tis the Scald-Crow, Morgana's eyes. And when she finds us you may be sure Morgana will follow with all the crawling, squirming, mealy-mouthed creatures she can summon. And then the fun will be starting. Her fun, I am meaning, not yours," said the dwarf.

"Then what are we standing here for?" said Roddy, setting off at a trot.

"Aye," said the dwarf, "'tis time for striking dust from the path and sparks from the stone."

And they all ran, down the long, gentle slope towards a wide plain and the unwelcoming darkness of the forest. When the ground levelled again they stopped. For a moment the Scald-Crow was lost from sight. Then she appeared, much nearer now, a ragged silhouette like a tear in the sky, labouring steadily towards them. Only now, she wasn't alone. Twelve others followed her, weaving through the air like a serpent's tail. Baz and Carter glanced

166

desperately towards the forest. It seemed a terrible, long way off.

"C'mon, you idiots!" yelled Carter, memories of the bird still painfully fresh in his mind. He began to run.

In a flash, without stopping to reason why, Gareth grabbed Longspear's staff and thrust it out in front of Carter, who collided with it and almost did a complete somersault before sprawling on the grass. He hugged his leg and yelled angrily at Gareth. "You crazy or something? What did you do that for?" He looked to Spinksy for support.

"I don't know," said Gareth, unwilling to tell them about the stone pulsing in his pocket. "But there's danger in the forest and on the plain. I have a feeling."

"Well, we can't stop here," said Roddy. "What exactly are those birds? They're enormous!"

"Shapeshifters," said the dwarf. "Remember the crawling darkness and the herring-bone wastrels who move about the hill?"

Baz and Carter moved closer together. How could they forget?

Gareth glanced at the sky and the circling birds, wishing it was Ergyriad's noble shape he could see. "Help me." He spoke the words in his mind. "How can I make them believe and give them power over evil?" He turned to the others. "Listen!" he said. "I showed you the pictures because you have to believe in Tara. You have to understand about the Light. I know it's not easy, but you have to try. Believing in Tara and the people who live there will give us power over Evil. It's the best magic we possess."

No one spoke.

Baz shuffled his feet and stared blankly at the ground. Believe in elves? Him? It was impossible.

Carter was still smarting, still seething with indignation. He was unable to take in anything. "Well," he said, "I've got a penknife and I'm off."

Longspear reclaimed his staff and rammed it into the ground where it vibrated violently, humming like a tuning-fork. "Then tread with butterfly feet," he warned, "and heed the words of your leader. Make room in your thoughts for the Tuatha and the Light will grow and give you power over Evil."

Carter stared for a moment, his resolve snagged on some fragment of memory that would not quite come into focus. Then, "Cobblers!" he yelled as he ran. "You're all nuts, completely off your trolleys, and any minute now I'm going to wake up. I had a dream like this once before."

"Bezountee!" yelled Longspear. "If his brain isn't as full of dust as the Morgana's own snuff-box. Away, and let's be following him."

"And on to Tara," said Gareth, "whatever lies between."

"To Tara," said Kit.

"To Tara," whispered Roddy, so that no one could hear.

Baz nodded and ran, trying desperately to imagine this Light they talked of, these strange people who supposedly lived in the Silver City.

Before them, the plain was green and gleaming in the pale sunlight. It was like a well-kept football pitch, inviting them to play, tempting them to run across it and feel the wind in their faces.

Across it they ran, and the wind changed. It separated them, pulling them further and further apart so that each ran on into his own nightmare.

At first there was only a feeling of isolation, a few ragged wisps of mist that fingered the empty air before them. Then a cold wind wrapped itself about their feet and the ground softened beneath them as though they trod at the edge of a swamp. Their limbs grew heavy, every step more difficult than the one before. They wanted to cry out, but every sound was sucked away by the wind – and the mist was thicker now, turning into a sea of yellow fog that heaved and swirled, wrapping them in its cold arms.

Kit's mouth opened wide in a scream of terror as pale, icy tendrils coiled about her ankles and flicked away.

Gareth didn't hear her, though he sensed her fear. "Hold on, Kit!" he called, his words moving through the air like a long, slow echo. "Think of Tara. Think of Mariandor. Think of the Light."

"How much further? I can't run any more!"

But Gareth couldn't answer. The fog burnt his lungs and stung his eyes as he strained to see the forest ahead. Then the voices came, thousands of whispering voices keening like a lost wind through winter reeds. Gareth felt their despair drawing everything from him – strength, will-power, resolve. He fought to keep the picture of Tara in his head. To remember the face of Mariandor and the eyes of the waiting warriors. But Tara was a ruin, crumbling into the plain, Mariandor had the cruel face of a hag and the Hand of Prince Lugh was cold.

Gareth was losing his mind to the voices. They were so unutterably sad, so entirely without hope. He couldn't go on without trying to help them. His steps slowed. He stretched out his arms, opened his hands, offering them comfort, consolation, friendship. The moment he did so, an icy tendril coiled about his wrist and the wailing changed to mocking laughter as the mist tightened about him and tried to drag him down.

Gareth tore his hand free and instinctively thought about the rowan wood and the golden stone in his pocket. As he did so, something sparked life in his mind, growing and flaring and lifting his thoughts, until the darkness had gone and Tara was whole again. He pushed forward, thrusting his way through the suffocating wall of fog.

As he dragged his mind away from them, the voices muttered and gabbled angrily and the fog divided, shaping itself into tortured figures that drifted and distorted in the air about him. Above each one moved a face, twisted and shapeless, with empty gashes where eyes and mouths should be. Gareth closed his eyes against them. Then he lashed out at them and cried, "You have no power over me, for I believe in Tara and the power of the Light."

Silently, for there was no breath left in his lungs, he willed the others on, his legs feeling lighter with every step. The gabbling softened to a wailing and the wailing died to the whining of a gnat. Then the fog was behind him and he was treading on firm ground again.

One by one, the others caught up with him and sank to the ground in the lee of the forest, too exhausted to speak.

Kit's face was white and strained; Roddy's eyes were wild, his lips grey and set.

Baz turned away from them and was sick. Then he lifted his head and looked around. "Where's Carter? He was in front. He should be here."

The others shook themselves and looked around and back across the benign sea of grass. There was no sign of Carter.

It was Gareth's turn to feel sick. "He wouldn't listen, would he? He thought I was nuts, just talking nonsense."

Kit plucked at the grass, staring at him. "It's not a game, is it? We knew that from the start."

"But *they* didn't," said Gareth. "*They* didn't understand. They were just mucking about. Why did they have to come? We should have stopped them."

"It's not our fault," said Kit. "And anyway, I don't think we could have stopped them. They had to come, just as you and I did."

As they spoke, a shadow moved across them. The Scald-Crow was circling above them, watching. Seeing her, Urion Longspear leapt to his feet.

Baz jumped up, too, and turned on the dwarf angrily. "What's happened to Carter? Where is he?"

Longspear shook his head slowly. "Morgana has roused the Old Ones from their sleep. We have just been allowed the pleasure of meeting Scathack and her phantoms, witches and swamp-dwellers of the Old World. Evil without cause. And if she has stirred you can be sure there are others. Your world has something to answer for, indeed, if Morgana has such power. Scathack has not risen from the dungow-dash in a thousand winters."

"But what about Carter?" sobbed Baz. "We can't just go and leave him."

Longspear shrugged. "They have him," he said simply. "Soon he will be clay in Morgana's hands, and for the present there is nothing we can do." He laid a strong hand on Baz's shoulder. "You have it in your power to help him with courage and faith as your weapons." He clenched his fist. "Hold them fast and we shall find him in good buckle before this day is out. Now, on yer leathers, or none of us will see the moon rise."

Gareth was already on his feet and heading for the forest. The others followed, heads bowed, each thinking his own thoughts. With Carter gone, the adventure took on a different, more sinister shape. Gareth realised with a shock that he'd never seriously believed they would be in danger. Now, it seemed, the danger they faced was real and terrifying. He was a fool not to have known. Longspear had said she couldn't harm them; she could only break down their will and turn them against themselves. Wasn't that the worst kind of danger? Perhaps his own will could fight against Morgana. But not Carter's. Not Baz's. Everything was happening so fast. They hadn't had time to convince them, to show them the truth about the elves and Tara. It wasn't fair.

Gareth looked back at Roddy and Baz, remembering the dwarf's words. Maybe Roddy Spinks and his pals were typical of thousands of others who believed in nothing, whose imaginations had been dulled by televisions and computers to the point of almost non-existence. Perhaps if Roddy and his pals could be convinced, turned back along the old pathways then all the kids on Earth might do the same. And they were the future, weren't they? True, they *were* only kids, all of them. But they were capable of seeing things that grown-ups were blind to, just like he'd written in his story. And if they glimpsed the truth and turned their backs on it then what hope was there for their own children and the future of humankind? He glanced behind at the others again. Kit grinned back and put up her thumb reassuringly. He smiled back, feeling taller. But Baz was walking with his head down. Gareth felt sorry for him, trailing in Roddy's footsteps. There was hope for Roddy. He was walking with his chin up now, striding forward with a more determined air. Seeing him raised Gareth's spirits. If only he could share his faith with them, break into the darkness that bound them.

Catching his look and sensing his struggle, Longspear moved forward and gripped his shoulder as they walked. "Fight for them," he said, gruffly. "Lock them tightly in your heart, for once they are driven from your memory the Tuatha are lost for ever. Take courage. You have come this far."

"But now we are four," said Gareth forlornly.

"Then we must double our resolve and strive to convert the useless ones. Maybe it is in you to strengthen your army by multiplying its power. Imagine what five believers might do." He said no more, for suddenly, a raucous cry spilled into the air and thirteen black birds fell from the sky like curses and moved in on the children, swooping and diving at them, driving them into the trees.

Screaming and yelling and waving their arms about to ward off the ugly birds, the five travellers disappeared into the deepening darkness of the forest, and the cries of the creatures became a hideous, mocking laugh.

Chapter 20

Shapeshifters

"Still no birds," said Kit, as they moved deeper into the covering darkness of the trees. "Real birds, I mean, not those horrible black things. Birds are like dogs, did you know?"

"What on earth are you talking about?" asked Roddy.

"Birds," said Kit. "They sense things like thunderstorms .and bad places." She whispered the last, aware that Baz, clinging like a shadow to Roddy, had pricked up his ears to listen.

"Great!" said Roddy. "Have you got any more precious thoughts to cheer us up with?"

"Sorry," said Kit. "But it's no use pretending we're strolling through the park on a Sunday afternoon, is it? We've all got to be on the lookout."

"What for?" wailed Baz.

"I don't know, do I? You've seen what Morgana is capable of. Your guess is as good as mine."

Before them, Gareth had stopped. He held out his arms to halt them. "There's a path," he said, pointing. "Look."

"It's heading in the wrong direction," said Roddy. "I thought we wanted to go north."

"We do," said Gareth, "but-"

"'Tis no but the trail of a bawson," said Longspear, "but 'tis the only trail I can see."

"We have no choice but to follow it," said Gareth. "Can't you see the wood is getting thicker and more tangled by the minute?"

"Could be a trick," said Roddy.

"It's our only hope of getting through this lot," said Gareth," and I think we're going to need torches. How many have we got?"

Baz looked accusingly at Roddy. "We didn't bring any torch, did we? Where's the moon now, Spinksy?"

"Shut it, Baz! How could I know we'd end up in a place like this?"

"Then we've got two between us. I'll go in front with mine. Roddy and Baz can follow me. Kit, you and Mr Longspear can bring up the rear."

Baz stuck his hands in his pockets and stared at the ground. Kit and Roddy nodded. And so, they set off again, walking in single file as one does instinctively, following a narrow track over strange ground. It led them around curiously-shaped boulders, remnants of another time. It circled thorny bushes and saved their feet from dips and holes they might not see. When Kit stepped from the path to offer words of encouragement to Baz, her toe caught in a root-snare and brambles clawed at her legs.

"Just like a girl!" sneered Baz when Kit cried out.

"I was shining the torch for you, limpet!" she said crossly. "And anyway, I wanted to tell you something."

"What?"

"That I'm sure we'll find Carter. I know he'll be OK."

"How? How do you know? Been here before, have you?"

"Of course not. I just know, that's all."

"Yeah, sure." He sniffed. "Well, thanks anyway, Talbot."

Before them, the forest seemed to swell, thicker and darker, bringing its own night as they burrowed into it, leaving daylight far behind. On and on they trekked, eyes on the path and the person in front. But no matter how far they walked there were still some tiny patches of light behind them, scraps of sunlight, caught like pale rags in the mesh of trunks and branches, while ahead loomed a solid wall of darkness. Gareth was puzzled. He stopped and waited until the others caught up. "We don't seem to be getting anywhere," he said.

Baz was about to clap his hands in mock applause when the turn of Roddy's head stopped him.

"I told you it was the wrong way," said Roddy.

"It was the only path," said Kit.

"Have you noticed something?" asked Gareth.

Roddy nodded his head slowly. "The light's been behind us all the time," he said.

"By now," said Gareth, "the forest should be thicker behind us. It doesn't make any sense."

Kit burrowed into her rucksack and pulled out some chocolate bars. "It would," she said, snapping them in two and handing them around, "if the trees were moving with us." She munched on the chocolate and shuddered at the thought.

"Come off it, Talbot!" said Roddy.

"OK," said Kit. "It may sound crazy, but the rules here are different. You've seen that. Anything can happen, and because we are fighting an enemy we don't understand we have to be prepared to think differently, to accept things we thought impossible."

"She's right," said Gareth. "Can you think of a better explanation?"

"But trees can't move, can they?" said Baz, feebly, and earned himself a withering glare from the dwarf.

"Just because they *look* like trees …" said Gareth.

Longspear nodded. "Acknowledge the size of your enemy and courage will strengthen your arm to match his." He tugged impatiently at his beard. "And if, indeed you are right, then the shapeshifters are discovered and will pretend no longer. Soon, their purpose will be known."

"Right!" said Gareth, willing his feet forward, his torch searching for the path.

"Into that lot?" said Baz, unable to control the tremors in his voice. "But if they're not trees?"

"Decisions come easy when there's no but one choice," said the dwarf helpfully, "unless you prefer the company of Scathack and her sniddlebog cronies." Then he turned his back on them and leapt away through the darkness. "Aroint!" he yelled as he went, "'tis weary I am of this tangled forest."

For a moment, Roddy and Baz hesitated.

"Here," said Kit, thrusting her torch at Roddy. "You can stand here dithering if you want to, but I'm off." And she set off after the other two.

Baz gripped Roddy's arm. "I hate the dark, Spinksy. I know I'm a wimp. But it's the truth. This Tara place, it's just a load of rubbish. We're having a nightmare, aren't we, Spinksy? We can go back, just you and me. It's him they want. He's the one who got mixed up in this. It's nothing to do with us. It's none of our business."

"That's what everyone thinks," said Roddy. "But they're wrong. You're wrong. If it is a nightmare then it's one we have all helped to make." He pulled Baz after him, shining the torch for them both. He could see the light from Gareth's torch growing fainter by the second, but beyond it, just for a moment he saw another light glimmer and vanish.

177

"Maybe they're right," he added, "Gareth and Kit. It does make some sort of sense. Remember that talk about the Titanic?"

Baz's face was blank.

"Oh, never mind. Trust me! We can't go back without them. We have a job to do, of some sort, a challenge, and anyway, we have to find Carter. That's our own special challenge. We can't go back without him now, can we? What on earth would we tell his mum? They'd lock us up for loonies. Come on, Baz, we have to move faster. It won't go on for ever. There's a light. I saw it, way ahead of us. I think it's that Tara place." And he began to run, a terrified Baz hard on his heels.

There was something different in the air now, a humming and vibrating that made the children want to hold their heads as they ran. Then the forest broke its unnatural silence and in place of it came a wild cacophony of sound. Trees screamed and cracked, the floor of the forest heaved and groaned as roots tore free and dragged their massive bulks across the ground.

On ran the five, leaping and dodging roots and branches for as long as they were able, trying desperately to stay clear of the shifting trees. Only Baz hesitated and stopped for a moment to look longingly at the patches of daylight, still visible behind them.

Gareth kept his eyes and his torch on the way ahead. Kit gritted her teeth and thought of Tara, wondering how it would feel when they finally stood before its massive gates.

Roddy fought to keep the flickering light alive in his mind.

Baz felt more and more certain that if he turned back he would leave this terrible dream behind. It was nothing to do with him. He never wanted to come in the first place. Why should he risk his life? He couldn't make any difference. It was all a mistake. If he turned now, he would find himself at home and Carter would be there, waiting to play football.

Suddenly, out of nowhere, a twisted trunk lurched towards Gareth; its rough bark scraped his hand. He lifted his torch and shone it in a wide arc. Before them, tree shapes were moving over the forest floor like demonic chessmen, dragging the undergrowth with them. They were taking up positions like an army, closing ranks

Above the children's heads, branches bowed and swept the darkness.

"Down!" yelled Gareth, dropping to his knees. For now, the tree-shapes were leaning low across the path, and the widest way through was close to the ground.

Kit crouched behind him and crawled forwards, then Longspear, struggling to squeeze his wide girth through, lashing at the looming trees whenever he could, uttering curses that only he and the trees could understand.

Roddy pushed through next, dropping on to his stomach and wriggling like a commando, all the time holding the torch so that Baz could see what was happening.

"I can't get through there," wailed Baz, who was almost as wide as the dwarf. "It's getting smaller. I'll be crushed."

"Not if you get a move on," yelled Roddy. "Come on! Breathe in and I'll pull you through."

"No!" said Baz, resolutely, now. "Look, there's another way, an easier way. It's wider there. Give me the torch, Spinksy."

Roddy hesitated, glanced behind him and aimed the torch.

At the same moment, Gareth turned and saw what was happening. He screamed, "No, Baz! No, you idiot!" For Baz had caught the torch and turned and was running back

179

the way they had come. Roddy made to go after him, but the dwarf gripped his arm and shook his head.

All around them the tree-shapes heaved and throbbed, drawing in their branches, absorbing their roots. Out of their darkness, red and amber eyes glowed dully as they took on new forms, more hideous than before — bat-like, bird-like, serpent-like. Some sank to the ground, others lifted into the air, seeming to take the roof of the forest with them as they beat noisily through the real trees away from Gareth and the others, following Baz.

He didn't even see them coming, though the others yelled, so intent was he upon the path that would take him home.

When the creatures reached him, along the ground and through the air, they joined forces like the rivers in a flood, and swept him away.

Chapter 21

Baldor

The others watched helplessly as the winged torrent lifted the night from the forest. Although they couldn't see it, the darkness became a single shadow that glided away across the plain. Without its malevolence the forest became a friendly place. Summer leaves whispered overhead as daylight flooded through them and washed away any remaining patches of shadow. There were birds, too, bright flurries of them, darting and singing in the topmost branches.

At the back of her mind, Kit heard them and was glad. But the others seemed unaware. They could only stand, staring at the place where Baz had been.

Gareth slid his rucksack off and sat down, his head bowed. For once, Kit could think of nothing to say. She opened his rucksack and took out the sketches so that she could look at the boy and his companions on the hill, at the spires and towers of the city carved from rock.

At last, Roddy turned to Gareth and Kit, his fists clenched tightly in his pockets. "All this time we've been mates," he said, "and I never knew he was so scared of the dark." He looked up. "You seen those birds?"

Kit nodded and smiled. She was glad he had seen them, too. She believed they were like the music and the light from the city.

Roddy had a different look about him now. He bent down to look at the pictures. "Looks like quite a place, this Tara," he said.

Kit nodded.

"I think I saw a light," said Roddy, "when we were in the forest." He turned away, looking again at the place where Baz had been.

Gareth lifted his head and looked around him. "We have to keep going," he said. "Where's Longspear?"

They saw him kneeling some way back along the path, bending low and tapping the ground with his stick. He jumped up and ran towards them. At the same moment they felt the floor of the wood tremble, and above them the birds scattered in all directions like the shards of a shattered rainbow.

The sound reached them then. At first it was a low rumbling like a roll of distant thunder, but, as it grew louder, they recognised the thudding of hooves.

"Baldor!" muttered the dwarf, "or my nostrils betray me. But what should bring him here is a mystery to me. He and Morgana have never shared the same mixen heap, for Baldor is of a race older than Time. His nature rises not from the workings on Earth, but from a conflict beyond the stars. The memory and scent of him comes to me from those whose lives are spent, though I cannot see clearly what part he has in all this."

Gareth was breathing deeply, remembering Grandy's birthday present. As they ran he yelled to the dwarf, "The Stone. Baldor's fate lies with the stone. At least that's what he believes."

"Pah!" yelled back the dwarf. "Then he vies with Morgana for possession of the stone. And he follows us. He must have knowledge that the stone is moving. But how can I fight him with only wood in my hand?"

Two minutes of running and they were clear of the trees and climbing a hill. On the crest of it they stopped and sank to their knees, gasping and panting.

"Look! Look!" cried Gareth.

Beneath the northern skyline, against a backdrop of dark mountains, crouched like a waiting panther, shone the pale light of the city. He rubbed his eyes and saw it still, shimmering like a mirage. The vision made him stronger, drove the ache from his tired limbs. When Carter had been taken, and then Baz, his mind had been squeezed dry like a sponge, ready to soak up doubt and despair. He'd wondered if the city were there at all, or if this was some terrible joke, triggered somehow by his meddling, his longing for an adventure. If so, then the dwarf wasn't on their side at all, but was leading them into a trap where they could be picked off one by one, according to their weaknesses. He closed his eyes to banish the thought for good, and when he opened them he saw Longspear's eyes fixed firmly upon him. Blue eyes, sharp as ice. Frank, honest eyes that seemed incapable of deceit. Gareth shook his head, heartily ashamed, and the dwarf nodded and grinned. He knew Morgana's ways, how she filled empty spaces with diseased thought, so the mind turned in on itself and was lost.

The pounding was heavier now, as though the riders were growing in number. The noise was all around them, a clamour that rang through the air and thudded through their heads.

"Come on!" yelled Gareth, grabbing Kit's hand.

The other side of the hill was stony, hard on their feet. Boulders littered the ground like pebbles tossed from a far-off mountain. Among them, gorse bushes sprouted, spiky and bright with yellow flowers.

The pounding was different now, as the riders left the forest and galloped up the hill. Then the beating ceased altogether, and the children, at a cry from Longspear, dived for cover behind the nearest stone or bush.

Behind them, the hill wore a jagged crown of riders, stone-black against the leaden sky. In their midst, one rider towered above the rest. From the wild mane of hair that framed his great head, two branched antlers cut dark grooves into the light.

"What *is* he?" hissed Roddy.

"An ancient warlord," said the dwarf, "who knows no time and is drawn by the stench of war and the rattle of death cries. His army grows with every wandering spirit he finds lost on the battlefield."

"Did Morgana summon him?"

"Perhaps," replied the dwarf. "She has the power. But if he comes to her bidding then you can be sure he has reasons of his own."

"Lia Fail," whispered Gareth, "the Stone of Destiny. It carries the knowledge of what he once was and the knowledge of what is to be. He needs to find it and knows we will lead him to it. He rides with the wind."

On the crest of the hill the beasts were restless, champing and snorting as they reared and pranced and tossed their great heads. Watching them, it was easy for the children to picture their blazing eyes and foam-flecked lips, curled back in a thousand screams.

The dwarf pulled Gareth close to him and pointed. "We stand at the edge of the Field of Moytura, last great plain before the City of Tara. My blood is telling me that only two will leave their footprints in its soil, and I have hopes that Caladbolg and Answeror are free, and that the Dagda will hear your cries and awaken. Go swiftly now. The riders are soon upon us."

Gareth was horrified when he understood what Longspear meant. "We can't go without you and Roddy!"

For answer, the dwarf gave him a hefty shove. "Run!" he yelled. "Or else we lose all."

Now, the riders were spilling over the summit of the hill, as far east and west as the children could see; waves of darkness moving slowly down like an eclipse. Any moment now and they would give the horses their heads. The children could smell them, could hear the rattle of harness, feel a new chill in the air.

Kit and Gareth ran then, torn between the knowledge of what they had to do, and the need to stand together with their friends. They rounded a small hummocky hill and turned briefly, compelled to look back.

They saw Roddy, a tall, straight figure beside the squat form of the dwarf.

"Roddy!" screamed Kit, for the tide of riders was moved swiftly now, bearing down upon them like a tidal wave.

Roddy turned. "Run, Talbot, run!" he yelled as the two figures disappeared around the low hill. And in that moment he saw it again, a pale light touching the distance like the first silver thread of a winter dawn. The vision sent a new determination pulsing through his veins and he planted his feet firmly on the ground.

As they galloped nearer, Roddy saw them clearly. If he had *wanted* to run it would have been impossible, for, as he stood, he felt as though his blood was turning to ice and his feet were frozen to the ground. His head was spinning; he squeezed his eyes shut for a moment – opened them – and stared. Beasts with heads of horses, wild red eyes and streaming manes. Their backs were armoured with scales, their hindquarters tapering to thick, muscular tails. As they came, black hooves struck sparks from the rock and he saw their necks and legs, shiny with sweat and flecked with white foam.

Roddy glanced at Longspear. What was he hoping to do? They must be mad. If they didn't move now they would be crushed like beetles. But the dwarf was rooted to the ground, legs planted well apart, stick held up before him with both hands. The fierce expression on his face said it all. He would halt the enemy – or die in the attempt. He was just like the Yorkshire terrier next door but one. No bigger than a pigeon but thought it was a Rottweiler. Roddy almost smiled. Then he faced the riders as they bore down on them.

In the fragment of a moment he saw an army of the slain; their faces were pale, their bodies dark with wounds. Some wore helmets, plumes, sashes. Some wore only animal skins; others were cloaked. However they were clothed, shreds and tatters were pulled away by the wind and grey hair blew like cobwebs behind them.

Instinctively, Roddy leapt sideways and dropped behind a rock. He wondered if the riders had even seen them.

At the same moment, as the first serpent horses were upon them, Longspear leapt into the air and spun like a top, lashing wildly with his stick and screaming at the top of his considerable voice.

At sight of him, the leader's mount reared and struck the air with his flailing hooves. Baldor held him for a moment, then let him plunge earthwards to circle the dwarf as he threw back his massive head and roared with mirthless laughter.

"Are there still dwarfs?" his voice boomed. "I thought they had been trodden underfoot long ago, food for worms."

Filling his chest and making himself as tall as he could, Longspear continued to lash at the beast that towered above him.

"Meddlesome as always, I see," snarled Baldor. He turned the beast sharply. Its great tail curled around and flicked back, striking the dwarf with a sickening thud, flinging him to the ground.

"Back to your rock-chipping, dwarf! You keep me from my business."

"And what can be your business that you stir from your sluther-swamp and ride to Tara?"

Baldor scowled and lifted his head to search the sky. "'Tis a matter greater than dwarfs can think on, Ugly One. But tell me, does the Stone move, or has she powered the wind also to lie and do her bidding? Answer wisely and I might spare your brains."

Longspear lifted his head painfully. "What can a poor dwarf know? The wind will not trust him with its secrets."

"Then why are you here? And where do you journey from? What message do you take to Tara?"

"I know the Old Ones are stirring. Morgana raises them all. They march to the beating of her drum. And is the mighty Baldor nought but a twitch-clog crawling in the leather of Morgana's shoe?"

Baldor threw back his wild mane and snarled as his mount reared into the air and came down, narrowly missing the dwarf's head.

"You tread in swampy ground," he roared. "And your brains are scarcely worth saving if you believe Morgana's boast. 'Tis the Stone, the Stone that moves them, and I, Baldor, have greater need of it than most."

"Then ye must find it," roared Longspear, in as big a voice as he could muster, "for none has seen or heard of it since it was lost and a torrent washed the land."

"And what of the boy?" roared Baldor.

"Boy? What boy? I know of no boy."

And the dwarf, unable to rise, buried his face in the dust and covered his head with his arms. To die in this way, beneath the feet of his enemy, was more than he could bear.

Baldor, knowing the resolute nature of dwarfs, bellowed at the sky and pulled back his mount. "Out of my way, Barmskin!" he roared. Hooves pounded on stone, shooting fire. Then the animal reared once more above Longspear's battered body.

"Finish it, Geldor!" he commanded. "I'll have no more dealings with cankered runts who smell of humankind."

Without thought, seeing the imminent death of the dwarf, Roddy darted from behind the rock, yelling wildly and wielding the only stick he could find.

Baldor hauled back on the reins and spun in mid-air before hooves crashed down on bare rock. "What have we here?" he roared. "'Tis too puny by far for elf or dwarf, though 'tis no less ugly." He reached down, and with an enormous, clawed hand, hoisted Roddy into the air.

"What boy, indeed?" he yelled, his laughter enclosing Roddy's mind like a tomb. "Don't waste your last thoughts on him, dwarf. Be sure I shall treat him as my own, at least until the Stone is in my hand."

Longspear pressed his hands to the earth and raised his spinning head. Through clouds of dust and flying stones he saw a flurry of burnished hooves as the terrible riders galloped past. He caught a fleeting glimpse of Roddy, sitting astride the biggest, wildest of the beasts, hanging on to Baldor's cloak for his very life.

"Run, Gareth, run!" whispered the dwarf. "Run like the razzored[4] wind."

---

[4] angry

Chapter 22
The Dagda

There was no breath for speaking as Gareth and Kit ran on. Each tried not to think of the two they had left behind as they rounded another rise and went down, dodging thorny bushes and leaping over rocks. They listened for the screaming of horses and the pounding of hooves, ready to dive for cover if the horsemen appeared. Soon, the ground levelled, the rocks and bushes were fewer, and before them, flat as a desert, stretched the Field of Moytura. Beyond it, at the edge of the world they could see, were the black Mountains of Urd and between the two, Gareth and Kit glimpsed the towers and spires of Tara.

Though the rocks were fewer, between the hill and the flat, treeless plain, one boulder remained. It was a curious shape, as though wind and weather had contrived to carve it in the likeness of a man. Soil had gathered in furrows and sculpted crevices and, from the soil, saplings sprouted at crazy angles like spiky hair.

They edged towards it. Still no hoof beats. Relief was mixed with concern. How had Roddy and the dwarf managed to delay them?

Perhaps they're not following us after all," said Kit, hopefully, knowing their thoughts were the same.

"And now there are two," said Gareth.

"And we haven't found any of the treasures. We don't even know where to start looking. How could we? What on earth are we supposed to do when we get to Tara – if we get to Tara. Whatever game she's playing, I think Morgana is winning."

"No!" said Gareth, gripping her arm "You must never think that, let alone say it. Don't you see, that's how she works? She gnaws at your thoughts until there's nothing left, and then she fills your mind with darkness. That's the only way she can win – and you can't let it happen!"

Kit grinned at him then and Gareth sighed with relief. "Anyway," he said, "perhaps, somehow, the treasures will find their way to us. Perhaps, between us, without even knowing it, we already–" But he didn't finish.

All around them, stones were moving, rolling to and fro. And beneath their feet the earth was groaning, shifting. They gripped each other and sank to the ground, looking anxiously back towards the hill. If the riders came now – but, while the rocks trembled and moved, they were safest out in the open. They crouched, afraid to move, afraid to think, until stones crashed against them and they had no choice but to run.

"Over there!" yelled Gareth, pulling Kit to her feet and pointing at the strange mass of rock, standing like a sentry at the edge of the Plain. It was the safest – and most dangerous – place – and Gareth was drawn to it. As they moved, the ground lurched and heaved beneath them and the rocks cried out, filling the air with a deafening roar. Then all was still, and a silence, heavy as night, settled around them.

They drew near to the rock, amazed at its size, its strange, sculpted shape. Now, they could see ridges like steps in the stone, and, above them, a long, low cave.

Gareth put a foot on the first step and recoiled sharply as the step melted and took on a different shape. He fell backwards and knocked Kit to the ground. As they lay in its shadow, the mass of rock began to move, grinding and groaning as it did so. Ripples moved jerkily through its face, contorting the features. Then it heaved and shook and showered the children with crumbs of stone and soil.

Above the huge cave mouth an enormous, ugly nose appeared, and above that two black eye-holes opened beneath a bank of brows.

Gareth and Kit scrambled further away as two massive arms separated from the thick bulk of the body and the body itself lifted from its squatting position.

They huddled together as the giant's head hung over them, its black eyes like holes in space.

"It's the Dagda," whispered Gareth. "I didn't expect he would be so."

Kit gasped. "But he's on our side, right?"

Their voices were silenced.

"Who wakes the Dagda?" The sound was like the boom of waves thundering through a subterranean cavern.

Gareth stood up and with his hand on his chest, said, "Gareth, son of Gwydion, sent to help the Tuatha de Dana in their fight against Morgana and the evil that overflows from our world."

"Hmmm!" growled the Dagda. "And your companion?"

Kit leapt to her feet. "Katherine Iris Talbot. Kit for short. We come to find Mariandor and restore the Light."

"And the fate of the Tuatha rests in *your* hands – when Dagda and prince Lugh were powerless to help them?" He threw back his head and roared like a hurricane. "I have never set eyes on such a pair of wammocky creatures."

"What does he mean?"

"Scrawny, I think."

191

Kit was indignant. "Size didn't help you much, did it?"

"Err, no," grumbled the giant, whose colour was improving by the second. And he showered them with dirt as he chuckled like a mountain stream. "I'm hungry. Where is my cauldron? Have you stolen it?" he managed to get out between roars and noisy, belching sounds.

"Morgana has it," said Gareth.

"Ah, Morgana. The name leaves a vile taste in my mouth. And what of the other three? Does she possess them also?"

"We believe that the Guardians have held them since they were lost at the last great battle. But the Guardians are moving."

The Dagda sighed and the ground beneath him trembled. "It returns to me in pieces," he groaned, "the memory of that terrible day. We knew not how great the Evil had become. It was not within us to imagine such power. And she is risen again? Then the evil must be awesome, even greater than before." He shrugged his massive frame and the children covered their faces against the dust and debris that fell upon them.

"But you are come," he roared, "from a world that is slow to learn the old lessons. And your footsteps, no heavier than a dew-fall, have woken the Dagda. Then all cannot be darkness." His head fell on to his deep barrel chest and he groaned again. "She has the cauldron, you say … and the stone, Lia Fail. Something returns to me about the stone. Ah! Now I have it. The stone was removed, and concealed. No. No!" he roared. "Not concealed but given to one whose size and strength should have protected it. Dagda, the great one! Pah! Dagda the fear crow, left behind to scatter birds."

Gareth and Kit glanced at each other, but the Dagda twisted his gnarled and knotted face and shook his great head.

"My thoughts stayed with me," he said, "hung around me like dreams. But strength I had not. After the battle the rains came and the flood engulfed me. Salt water, tears of the oceans, tears of Nwyvre, that his people should be treated thus. In his anger – or his sorrow, I know not which, he took back the stone, plucked it with his tears and carried it away." He lifted his head, listening. Then he looked at the children. "And you say the Guardians are moving?" His nostrils rattled as he sniffed the air. "Others too, if my senses serve me right." He sniffed loudly again. "Baldor, 'tis Baldor and his whey-faced scum. Is it you they seek? If so, then the Dagda's time has come. Be gone! Have courage and trust all things you hold closest to your hearts. They will serve you in your hour of need."

There was a distant drumming, as of trotting horses. The ground stirred and the air moved about them as if it too were telling them to be gone. They had tarried too long.

The Dagda lifted his right arm and they saw that he wielded a massive club that had lain by his side. "Go," he roared, "while I amuse myself with Baldor and his creatures."

Gareth and Kit began to run. Then Gareth turned and yelled back. "We have a friend. He's with Longspear, the dwarf – and Baldor may have them both. Help them, if you can."

"Longspear? Did you say Longspear? 'Twas a Longspear who plucked the stone from its place and brought it to the Dagda for safekeeping."

"They stayed behind to give us a chance."

Ah!" bellowed the Dagda. "Brave warriors, all. Now, be gone!" And, with that, he lifted his club high into the air and brought it crashing down to make a deep furrow in the ground.

Gareth and Kit held hands and ran as the great club smashed into the ground again and again. Each time, the

Dagda drew it back, making channel after channel, intersecting like a gigantic noughts and crosses board. Zigzagging through the channels, the children ran, hidden from all except the black bird that appeared from nowhere and watched from above.

They could hear the Dagda's roar, but they didn't see Baldor and his grey riders gallop in confusion through the maze.

On and on they ran until they heard the pounding of hooves once more. They stopped, sucking in great lungfuls of air. Behind them, dust clouds were rising from the Plain. There were no more furrows to hide them. Suddenly they were out in the open with nowhere to hide. They looked all around in despair. Then the ground gave way beneath their feet and another furrow appeared, crossing theirs at right-angles. But even the Dagda's long arms could not reach this far. If he was not helping them, then who was? No time to consider. They turned down it, clinging to the cover it gave. Like a valley it grew shallower and when it came to an end they saw trees and flowers and a white, wooden fence. In the fence was a gate that creaked as it swung to and fro. Its very ordinariness invited them to pass through.

Chapter 23

Morgana's Lay

Kit couldn't help shrieking with delight when she saw the garden that awaited them beyond the gate. She didn't stop to consider the unlikelihood of such a garden existing here and now, when they had caught no sight of it from the hill. Longing for something normal, she had wanted it to be there. And her wish had been granted. It was her refuge — and it was perfect.

The garden lay before them like a piece of Paradise, a rumpled patchwork bedspread tossed down from the sky for them to sink into and rest. Colours tumbled over colours, yellows and purples straying across the crazy-paving paths, overflowing on to a perfect pillow of emerald green lawn. All around the garden, leafy trees were frothy with blossom and in one shady corner, sunk between lush banks of moss and fern, a clear pool shone like a mirror, offering an upside-down version of the cherubic boy who stood a on a pedestal at the centre, flute in hand, poised to play.

Kit had had enough of being careful, of constantly being on the lookout and running from danger. Adventures were all very well, but she so just wanted to be carefree Kit again — and this was her kind of place, just like her room — a kind of welcoming muddle, all soft lines and colours. Like Grandma's parlour, too, full of patchwork cushions and crocheted throws and the comforting smell of lavender. It made her long for home.

Her first instinct was to fling open the gate and run along the path, touching and smelling the flowers, dipping her hands in the cool water of the pool. Surely nothing so lovely could be bad. As her hand touched the gate, Gareth grabbed her arm.

"We have to go through it!" she yelled at him. "There's nowhere else to go."

"No we don't. We have to look for a way around."

"But Tara is in front of us. We have no time to go around. And someone is hunting us – or had you forgotten?"

"It's another trick. I know it is. For goodness sake, Kit! We were five, remember! Now we're down to two. And so far we've achieved absolutely nothing."

"That's because we're holding you up, me and the others. You're different, Gareth. You can do this on your own. You don't need us. We shouldn't be here."

"That's absolute rot and you know it." Gareth frowned and pointed. "Look at that!"

In the furthest corner of the garden, almost hidden in a grove of tall trees, was what appeared to be summer-house. A flight of white-painted steps rose towards it.

It was too much for Kit. "Perhaps someone lives there," she said hopefully. "Perhaps this is where we'll find the stone. It has to be, don't you see? There's nothing left between here and Tara."

"But we saw no sign of it from the hill," said Gareth. "Wait a minute and I'll soon tell you whether it's real or not." He made a move to take the rowan wood from his pocket, but Kit couldn't wait. The call of the garden was too strong.

She could think of nothing now but losing herself in the smell of the grass and the leafy shade. She wanted to leave the ugliness and evil behind and melt into the cool, moist earth, to fall asleep breathing the scent of roses. She tugged her arm free and flung open the gate.

"Come on, Grumbleweed!" she called, playing dodge the cracks as she ran down the crazy paving path towards the pool, stopping once to smell the lavender and once to pinch the head of a snapdragon.

Gareth rested his hand on the gate. He looked at the sky and all around him. Perhaps Kit was right and there was no danger after all. The peace and normality of the scene was like a drug, swamping their senses, making them want more. He suddenly felt tired, drained. What time was it? His watch had stopped at nine-thirty-five. Perhaps time itself had stopped while they were in Tir na nog. He looked back at the garden. Nothing stirred. Not a leaf so much as trembled. There were no butterflies, no birds, no hum and buzz of insects. The garden was empty of life, just as the forest had been when invaded by Evil. Kit, of all people, should have noticed that.

There were flutterings in Gareth's stomach, alarm bells jangling in his head. His hand still held the rowan wood. The stone it held – he had given it no name, told no one of its existence. Ergyriad had said it would protect him, warn him of Evil. If he used it now, would Morgana be aware that he had something of power in his possession? He would have to take that chance if he was to see the true nature of the garden and save Kit.

He held the rowan wood in both hands and stared at it. It was as if he were seeing it for the first time. The pattern scored in the yellow rim was no longer just a series of lines and swirls but words written in the Old Language.

"When five win through

And five stand true
Beneath the silver tree
The stone will sing
To choose our King
And Tara will be free."

"But we're only two now," whispered Gareth, and the thought weighed heavily. He looked at the garden again and saw it with different eyes. Trees bulged outwards and flowers around the edges blurred and slipped out of focus. It was like looking through a goldfish bowl. If he looked through the stone now, what would he see? Was he strong enough to face whatever lay before him? Was it ever a good thing to know what lay just around the corner?

"Acknowledge the size of your enemy," Longspear had said.

Slowly, Gareth lifted the rowan wood to his eye and looked through the golden stone at the 'wonders' of the garden. What he saw gave him such a shock, such a sickening jolt, that he stumbled backwards. As he flung out his arms in an attempt to save himself, the rowan wood flew from his hand.

There was no garden. It was an illusion feeding on their weakness, their need. If once there had been, then, like Eden, it had been destroyed by Evil. Now, black, skeleton trees circled a wasteland of ugly black rock and barren soil. And there was Kit, fooled by it all, lost in the perfection of what she wanted to see. She moved jerkily, like a puppet, walking away from a pool of bubbling mud, smiling like a doll and wiping her mouth with the back of her hand. She looked towards him, then back at the decayed shell of the house, pointing and beckoning him to join her.

Away from her, another movement caught Gareth's eye. At the centre of the pool, where the cherub had been, was a black, shapeless mass that seemed to be melting like wax, flowing downwards and outwards. At its centre were two pools of sickening red light, and they were following Kit.

The moment he hit the ground, Gareth was leaping to his feet again, searching frantically for the rowan wood. He groaned with relief when he spotted it, grabbing it and stuffing it hurriedly into his pocket. Then he flung open the gate. Something happened then, in that moment of crisis when the rowan wood left his hand. He felt weak when the realisation hit him and his heart pounded like a drum, beating painfully against his ribs. "Idiot!" he hissed. "Dumb, stupid idiot!" Then he raced after Kit.

She was already climbing the steps to the summer-house, completely unaware of the darkness that hunted her and the wasteland that lay all around. Now, with the help of the stone, Gareth could see it all and his nostrils filled with a sulphurous smell that could choke him.

"Kit!" he screamed.

But Kit just turned and smiled.

He was losing her.

"Kit, wait!"

Now, she was lifting her hand to the carved wooden knocker. It was a beautiful thing, a dove in flight, Peace knocking at the door, asking to be let in. She turned and smiled back. Who was this boy? And why was he always so serious, so hard to please? She was tired of him, tired of this silly adventure. She wanted to go home. Somewhere, there were hens to be fed, a pony to groom.

"Kit!"

Gareth leapt up the steps in one bound, aware of the jagged splinters of wood where the rails had been. Kit was leaning on the charred and blistered door, watching him with something like a sneer on her face. He grabbed her arm and yanked her back down. Behind them, the rotten wood gave way and a green fungus burst upwards.

"What are you doing? Let go of me! Let go of me! You're nuts, do you know that? Completely bananas! Let go of me or I'll kick you so hard."

She stumbled then and lashed out angrily at Gareth. He pulled her to her feet and dragged her further from the house.

"Run! Run, you idiot!" he yelled at her, aware that the garden was closing in on itself and on them – and at its centre were the two fluid red eyes, swimming in the blackness, circling them.

"Run!" he cried again, desperately, this time. "Run!"

It was all he could manage, for his mind was leaping between the darkness that surrounded them and the knowledge that was new to him.

He hauled Kit away from the patchwork garden and the scent of roses. Together, they turned their backs on the serpent that poisoned the Tree of Light. There was no time to stop or look back until Gareth was sure that they had cleared the heap of rubble that marked the boundary of the garden. Once over it he relaxed and Kit shook off his hand violently, gasping and furious, angry tears mixed with dirt on her face.

"What did you do that for, Gareth Jones? Who do you think you are, anyway, always telling people what to do, always thinking you're so clever? For your information, there was a woman in the house, a lady. She looked really nice, like someone I know. She might have been able to help us."

Gareth didn't answer, didn't even look at her. His hand was held tightly against his chest and he was staring back to where the garden had been.

"I'm talking to you!" screamed Kit, thumping his arm. Still, he didn't answer, only stared.

Clenching her fists, Kit at last turned and followed the direction of his stare. Now, finally, she saw what he saw. Morgana was discovered. There was no need to continue the illusion. Through blackened trees, Kit saw the jagged outline of a ruin that crumbled further even as they watched. The garden was a battlefield, blackened and bare. Fires smouldered where roses had been, and a blanket of sulphurous smoke hung over it all like a shroud.

Kit sagged like an old rag doll. She looked down at her fist, still tightly closed around the snapdragon. When she opened it a puff of grey ash blew away.

"It was her, wasn't it?" she said, in her smallest voice.

Gareth nodded and pulled her to her feet.

"You should have stopped me," she said weakly.

"Fat chance," said Gareth. "I tried, remember?"

"You should have tried harder if you were sure. You know how bossy I can be. I'm useless now, aren't I – just like Baz and Carter?"

"You're still here."

"Only just," said Kit. "Only because you saved me. And only for the moment. We're not strong enough, are we? That's what this is all about. Not strong enough to make a difference. How could we ever think we were?"

The flatness in her voice and the dull, beaten look in her eyes set alarm bells ringing in Gareth's head. This wasn't the Kit he was getting to know. He shielded his eyes and stared into the distance, across the wide Plain of Moytura to the dark ridge of the mountains.

"'Bring the Keeper home.' That's what the riddle said, wasn't it?"

"Huh?" Kit was following his look, straining to see something, struggling to remember what it was she was searching for.

"At first," said Gareth, "I thought I was the keeper, but I was wrong. Tara isn't my home."

"Tara?" said Kit, weakly, shaking her head.

"Yes! Tara! Tara! Remember? It's not far now! Look! If you shield your eyes you can just make out a faint haze in the distance. Imagine how amazing the city must be, its walls threaded with veins of pure white quartz, shining like silver."

Kit shook her head. "It's as far away as ever," she sighed, "if it's there at all. Probably a mirage, an illusion, just like the garden."

"No, "said Gareth. "It's there all right. I have never been more certain of anything."

Kit's face was blank, empty. "I'm tired of all this," she said. "Tired of running and getting nowhere. It's like playing a game when the other side is making up all the rules. I don't believe we can ever win. Look at us! We're a mess! The whole world is a mess! It's too late! We haven't found the stone. We don't know where Mariandor is, and all the time Morgana is watching us, prodding us about like some mouldy old professor poking a bug under a microscope. When she's finished playing she'll pour us down the drain and we'll be swimming there for ever with Baz and Carter and Roddy and the dwarf. Can't you see we haven't got a chance?"

Gareth couldn't believe his ears. "That's not true, and you know it! We can win! We have to win! We have to try, anyway, not just sit down and give up. If we fail, then everyone fails, and we can't allow that to happen. We have to go on."

But Kit just shook her head again. "We've failed," she said. "Why are you too stubborn to admit it? We didn't believe enough – and now it's time to go home."

"It's not that easy," said Gareth, "because it's not what *she* wants. You'll never go home until this thing is finished, one way or another." He stood, resolute, his eyes towards Tara.

"You're seeing things," said Kit scornfully. "You and your crazy dreams, dragging us all into this nightmare. It's all a trick! There's nothing there but a ridge of black, ugly mountains – and this whole thing is a horrible, cruel joke."

"You know it's there as well as I do," said Gareth quietly. "You've seen it as well as I have. You know in your blood and your bones that it's real. You heard the music from the sea. You saw the birds before anyone. How can you say now that you no longer believe when you know in your heart that you do?"

Kit hung her head and sighed.

"Come on," said Gareth, offering a hand. "Best foot forward, huh? We can make it, just the two of us. We can reach the city and save the Tuatha. I know we can. But we must go now."

"I can't," said Kit, "and that's all there is to it. You'll have to go without me, Gareth."

"I don't understand. You were always better than the others. You wanted to come as much as I did. You can't stay here."

"Why not? I'm tired. I want to lie down."

Gareth stared at her, realisation finally dawning. "I saw you wiping your mouth. Why were you doing that? Kit, did you drink the water? You did, didn't you? You drank that filthy water in the garden."

She scowled at him. "So what? I was thirsty."

"Oh, Kit! You idiot!"

203

She shrugged and yawned. Gareth shook her and pulled her forward. As he did so, he saw, behind them, columns of darkness rising from the wasteland, spiralling upwards, twisting together in the sky, blotting out the light.

"Come on!" yelled Gareth, dragging her until she almost fell over. "Now, we've really got to run for it – for our own sake – for everyone's sake – and for Mariandor. Think of Mariandor, Kit. If you can still see her then you'll make it, I know you will."

"She's gone for ever," said Kit flatly. "Mariandor is dead. That is why Morgana rules and the Light is fading. It's the same everywhere. There is just too much darkness."

Her words shook Gareth, cast shadows in his mind, but he cried out against them. "No! Mariandor lives – though she is trapped like a fly in amber!"

As he spoke the words a low ripple of laughter echoed about them. Other voices joined it, weaving the air, sniggering, whispering, chanting. Words they couldn't understand, strung together in chains, rising and falling and winding about them, weighing them down like a terrible curse.

Suddenly, Kit jerked into action, looking about her like a startled rabbit. Together, hand in hand, they ran. As they moved, the darkness in the sky grew wings and monstrous head and serpent tail. They fled beneath its shadow, knowing they could never outrun it, dreading the moment when it tired of the game and fell from the sky.

And fall it did. When their legs were weak and their breath came in painful gasps it plummeted like a stone. They crashed to the ground, arms over their heads, waiting for claws to strike and tear. They felt only the powerful beating of scaly wings and the wind that came with it, sucking them backwards. They scrambled to their feet. "She can't hurt us!" yelled Gareth. "We must remember that. She can only weaken us from the inside, like she did with Baz and Carter. We can beat her, I know we can."

They scrambled to their feet and ran again while the creature flew in circles above them, hammering the air, lifting the dust in choking clouds from the Plain. And now, the wind grew stronger, holding them back like an invisible wall. They gripped hands again, Gareth moving in front, taking the brunt, praying he could pass his faith to Kit, that together they would be strong enough. We're like salmon, he thought, battling against the current. Determination and belief, that's all it took.

He heaved himself against the wind with every ounce of his physical and mental will, secure in the knowledge that he could beat it, and suddenly he was through. But the wall of wind was between them now, pulling Kit away.

He tried to tighten his grip on her hand and on her mind. He must pull her through. It was his fault she was here at all. She wasn't weak. She wasn't a coward. She deserved to win. Kit! Kit! But their hands were numb with cold and gripping – and Kit's resolve had been poisoned by the water in Morgana's Lay. Gareth knew he must be strong enough for both of them. He focused his thoughts, concentrating on the stone that had been entrusted to him by Ergyriad. The peregrine said the stone would protect him. He turned his back into the wind, thrust his hand in his pocket, took out the rowan wood and pushed it towards Kit.

As her right hand reached out to grasp it, her left slipped from Gareth's grasp.

Chapter 24

Morgana

"Kit." He heard the scream but didn't recognise the voice as his own. He saw a look of terror on Kit's face. Then she and the wind were gone, and the dark shape in the sky was just a rain cloud blowing away towards the horizon.

Gareth sank to the ground, staring at the cloud until it was a faint smudge in the distance. She had taken them all. She had played on their weaknesses and snatched them away from him one by one. Now, his task would be impossible. Kit was right after all. He closed his eyes and leaned back, believing that, if he fell asleep now, his head pillowed on a tussock of spiky grass, he would wake up on Rundle Hill with the moon still high in the sky and the wind on his face. The stones would be gone, the dwarf too, but Kit would be there, and the other three. It was so easy. This was just another dream or one of those computer games he'd heard about, the ones that get inside your head so you think you're really there. He felt himself drifting, falling deeper and deeper, when suddenly his eyes flew open and he blinked at the unaccustomed brightness of the sky. High above him a tiny speck was circling.

"You are not alone!" said a voice in his head. "You will never be alone!"

"Ergyriad!" Gareth felt like crying. "Ergyriad!"

"I am here, Son of Gwydion. And the thoughts of your companions flow together in the river of light and understanding. In their dreams they can see Tara and the Children of the Dawn. They know now why they were chosen. For, if such unbelievers can step along the path then the way lies open to all the Children of Men.

"But they lost their way, Ergyriad, and now she has them."

"She has their bodies," spoke the falcon, "but the Light can penetrate through the tiniest crack, and thanks to you, the seeds of truth have already taken hold even though you despaired of them. All is not yet lost. Have courage. That which you believe is gone will be restored to you."

"But where are they, Ergyriad? I have to find them before I go on to Tara. We must be five."

"Sleeping," said the voice in his head. "Locked in stone."

"Where? Ergyriad, please tell me where I will find them."

"Beside the straight path." But the voice was fading now. "Nothing … can … be … lost … when … there … is … a … rock … to … hold … it … fast."

"Ergyriad, wait!" But he knew the peregrine had gone.

Gareth stood up. His legs were aching and heavy, but somehow, of their own accord, it seemed, they took him towards Tara.

As he walked he thought about the golden stone. He'd mentioned it to no one and felt guilty about not sharing it with Kit, but the risk had been too great. Did Morgana know what it was he carried? Was the Scald-Crow cleverer than Grandy believed? And was Morgana now trying to trick him into giving it up? If Kit had grasped the rowan wood she might have been saved – or the rowan wood might have been taken with her. What would Morgana do

207

next? If she was looking for a chink in his armour it wouldn't be difficult. He felt as full of holes as a colander – and now he was journeying to Tara alone.

Lost in thought, he was unaware of the change in the landscape. Suddenly, the ground slipped away before him into a shallow, dish-like hollow, undetectable from a distance. On the opposite slope was a group of three standing stones, huddled, like old men complaining about the weather. At the bottom of the dip a sickle-shaped pool, uninfringed by reed or tree, threw back a piece of grey sky.

Gareth stopped to take in the scene and to weigh its meaning. His attention was taken by a fourth stone. It had stood apart, but now moved towards the pool. Not a stone after all but a figure – and one he knew well.

"Kit! Kit!" Relief overrode every other emotion or thought. Gareth was running towards her when he remembered Morgana's tricks and slowed to a walk, watching Kit carefully as he drew nearer.

Her face was expressionless, unmoving. She didn't lift her head to look at him, only gazed, motionless, into the black mirror of the pool.

"Kit?" Gareth said in the kind of soothing tones he would use with a strange dog.

There was no response.

"Kit, are you OK?" he asked, unable to control the trembling in his throat.

She shook her head in slow motion and pointed at the water.

Gareth took a step nearer and leaned forward to look into the pool. From the smooth, dark mirror only one clear reflection stared back at him. Beside it, deeper in the water a grey shadow moved in circles.

"Bring me back," pleaded Kit, in a voice that belonged to windswept moors and lost, lonely place. "What you see before you is nothing but a shell. The Kit you know is locked beneath the water."

"Then tell me what I must do," said Gareth, "but first, look at me so that I know it is really you." Still, she did not lift her head. "If I take my eyes away from the water the thread that joins body and soul will be snapped, and I can never return. Only you can save me."

"Tell me what I have to do."

"Break the skin upon the water."

Gareth's thoughts raced. "How?" he asked. "With a stick or a stone?"

"Only wood of the rowan tree has power enough to break the spell."

"But there aren't any rowan trees here."

"Then you must think of something else. You're a smart boy. Surely, you carry *something* with you, a charm of some kind. Hasn't your grandfather, Merlin, given you anything - anything at all?"

Gareth started at the sound of Grandy's old name. He glanced around at the three huddled stones. "If I have anything," he said, "it belongs to Tara and is not mine to give away."

"I knew it."

Gareth was shocked at the undisguised sneer in her voice.

"You carried it with you from the hill and told no one. It is not one of the Four Treasures – and yet it is a source of power, the only reason your mind is still your own." Then the sharpness in her voice was replaced by a pathetic whining tone as she pleaded with him. "Save me! Name the source of the power you carry and cast your charm upon the water. If you do not, my face will haunt your dreams."

Gareth was silent. If only she would look him in the eye.

"Name it! Name it!"

Gareth was cold. His hands shook; his feet felt numb. He was picturing Kit in the barn, whooping with delight as she dropped on to the bales. Wherever she was, he had to save her. He would rather die than go back without her. She was special. She had guts, as good as any boy. But if this wasn't really her, what then?

Slowly, he slipped his hand into his pocket and drew out the rowan wood, his fingers sensitive to the words carved by Lugh Lamphada all those years ago. "Here," he said, his voice cracking with the effort as he thrust the tube towards her.

Kit stood her ground, but Gareth saw the sinews tighten in her neck – and he knew for sure.

"You must do it," she purred. "You must name it and cast it into the pool, or else, whatever you believe, Morgana will never let us return."

Gareth lifted his hand, but he had no intention of releasing the tube. "And send it to the centre of the Earth?" he said. "Never! If you want it, you must take it. But you can't, can you? For in the moment of touching it, even touching the rowan wood, before you cast it into that pool that isn't really a pool, it would drain your power."

His hand shot out towards Kit and she flinched.

"No, on second thoughts, I shall keep it for the time being and I shall name it only when I stand before the gates of Tara."

Kit turned to look at him then. The nose was the same, chunky and freckled; the mouth and ears were hers. Only the eyes were different. For eyes can never lie. They mirror the true nature of what lies beneath the skin. They cannot hold the deception. The friendly sparkle that was all Kit's was absent. In its place lurked a gleam of reptilian coldness.

In that moment of absolute certainty Gareth tried to return the rowan wood to his pocket, but his arm would not respond. He had neither the strength nor the will to lift it. He felt as though he was slowly freezing and he could sense something moving around his feet. Out of Kit's face the inhuman eyes considered him and the mouth, no longer Kit's, was frozen in a sneer. He tried to look down, to see what was crawling, but could not, and now it was moving upwards, coiling about his legs.

Gareth fought to control his fear. But there was something behind him now, touching his head, his neck. He shuddered violently and kicked out as hard as he was able, in a desperate attempt to shake the thing off. The effort, against the weight that held his legs, threw him off balance and he fell backwards. For the second time that day, the rowan wood flew from his hand. But, this time, there was no safe landing. Gasping with horror, Gareth saw the tube turning over and over in space, as if in slow motion. But there was something wrong. The tube was incomplete. The horny rim that held the golden stone fast was missing. Then down it came, much faster now, into the waiting pool. He felt a splash of water on his face and saw the mirror break.

Gareth laughed, nervously, stupidly, his thoughts racing. The tube would float. The weight of the rim was not there to drag it down. Neither was the stone! He jumped to his feet, unhampered now, aware that around his legs there was nothing but a tangle of grass and bindweed. He stepped forward, dropped to his knees and thrust out his arm. The moment he did so, the rowan wood tilted like a stricken vessel and slipped into the black water.

The thing behind him laughed hideously, mockingly.

"Such a good friend," she hissed. "I knew you wouldn't let me down. Such loyalty should be rewarded. What can I give you, I wonder."

Gareth said nothing, only stared at the rings, spreading outwards on the pool.

"Precious, was it? Must have been, for that tiresome bird to guard it so well." Her words were fired at Gareth's back like an arrow. "Name!" she screamed at him. "I need to know its name and from what source it came."

She didn't know! Ha! And he certainly wasn't going to tell her. "It came from the air and the rock, from the sea and the stars. It came from the four corners of the earth. And it came from me."

"From you?" Laughter then, discordant, grating, nerve-shattering, like nails on slate. "You are nothing but a runt, a pot-boy, a thief. When the moment is right I shall give you your reward."

Gareth rose then and turned to look. The figure behind him no longer looked like Kit. The face was a grey mask, melting and flowing like candle grease. The body, a shapeless dummy the colour of mud, had slumped to the ground and was reforming as he watched.

At the same time, the group of stones began to move and change. Chiselled edges softened, harsh lines became rounded and colour flowed through them as though life was being poured into them from above. In moments they were recognisable forms.

"Kit! Baz! Carter!"

Morgana and the lost stone were forgotten as Gareth ran towards them. "I've never been so glad to see anyone – even you two."

Kit tried to smile as she rubbed her arms and legs. "I've been asleep," she said. "It feels like years since I saw you." And she gave him an awkward hug.

"Me, too," said Baz, shaking his feet and hands.

"Where's Spinksy?" said Carter.

"Long story," said Gareth. "You've missed half the fun. But I think we'd better move." He pointed to where Morgana was twisting and stretching like a metamorphosing insect.

"Yeuk!" squealed Kit. "I'm out of here."

They didn't wait to see Morgana in all her hideous glory, but, as they ran, they felt her shadow fall upon them and waited for her anger to overtake them. Instead, Morgana's laughter burst around them like exploding glass.

"Fools!" she screamed. "Do you really believe you have got this far because you are noble and brave and clever? Hah!"

The children stopped in their tracks and watched her. Morgana lifted a long, thin arm and pointed beyond them. When they turned, they saw, where the city should have been, a lifeless grey ruin against the black mass of the ridge.

Kit swallowed a lump in her throat. "We're too late!" she whispered.

Morgana shrieked with laughter. "A sense of humour," she purred. "I like that, considering how ridiculous you all look. Too late? Too late by a thousand years, by ten thousand years! What your feeble eyes have seen was the glow of a dying star, a star whose light was extinguished long before you miserable scurricks were wriggling on the planet. For centuries now, the sun has risen on a ruin. The people you think you are going to save were too weak to survive and their lives have been snuffed out, blown away with the dust of their worthless past."

She swept her arm towards the Black Mountains of Urd. "Behold, the last stronghold of the spawn of Nwyvre." She spat out the words.

"You're lying!" said Gareth. "We've seen Tara, really seen it, not just in our dreams. Our quest has brought us this far. We know it's there, waiting for us."

"We know in our hearts that it's real," said Kit.

"Hearts! Hearts! What use are hearts. I have no need of one. Instruments of the spineless. And can you trust them — any more than you can trust your halfwit eyes that see only what it suits them to see? Believe me, my dears, playtime is over. It's time to switch off the game and go home. This is no place for children. You belong at your mothers' knees listening to fanciful stories about nookshotten wizards and meddling dwarfs who send gullible children on journeys that a wild goose would scorn."

Kit was breathing heavily. Her legs felt as though they belonged to someone else. Nevertheless, she looked Morgana in the eye and said boldly, "I don't believe a word you say."

Then, Baz and Carter stepped forward together. "Neither do we," they said, lifting their heads and chests in defiance.

Morgana spread her long, thin fingers on her bony hips. They saw the gleam of red stones, like drops of blood against the white of her scrawny neck as she threw back her head and screeched with laughter.

"What about the Treasures?" demanded Gareth. "Even if you are right and the Tuatha have gone, we might yet restore the Treasures to Tara. And then who knows what might happen?"

Morgana lifted her hand and studied her crimson fingernails. "Impossible," she hissed. "Ask your friend, the dwarf, when you see him, if you ever do see him again. He will tell you how a Longspear snatched that nasty green bauble from under Baldor's nose at *my* bidding — and how he lost it in the endless caverns beneath Urd. By now, it will be on a thousand shores, ground into sand by the oceans. Its fate foretold the fate of those who would believe in it. 'Twas nought but a worthless lump of rock woven about by tales. As for the cauldron of that great maggot-

214

heap − it rose to my bidding, wiser than its master. And even as we speak, the lance and the sword are flying to my hand. When I am finished with them they will never again see the dawn or sunset of another day, and the elements themselves will bow to my whim − while the Sleepers − Ah! My good dear children! The Sleepers will sleep on undisturbed. Who would have the heart to waken them?"

Inside each child a battle was raging. In spite of their bravado they felt tiny, insignificant. The odds were stacked against them. How could they change anything, make any difference? Against so much Evil, so much Darkness, they were like ants in a flood. They looked at each other, their minds sharing the same image. It gave them strength.

"Have you ever watched ants?" Gareth asked the others. "They simply never give in, no matter what. Whatever the odds, they work and fight to the end, and every single one has its own special part to play if the colony is to survive."

Kit turned suddenly to Morgana. "What about Mariandor?" she said. "What have you done with her?"

The name alone was poison to Morgana. She snorted, her eyes darting to and fro like those of a lizard, wary of its enemy. "Lost!" she croaked. "Gone! The Darkness holds her fast in a place where none, none can venture."

Gareth watched her closely. He felt something inside him growing. He sensed her uncertainty, spotted the chink in her scaly armour. "Not even you," he said, "because the Darkness did not take her. You ordered the Scald-Crow to take her to Sinadon, but even you cannot command mountains. You over-reached yourself, Morgana. You are too proud. The Guardians saw her danger and led her away from our world until the time was right for her to return. You lost her and the world did not deserve her. You have grown in power because she has gone, but the children of the world are tired of the dark. They want to touch the

Earth again and feel its blood flow through their veins. In spite of you, the song of Mariandor has managed to stay alive, and the dream of the Tuatha lives in us all. Mariandor will return. Nothing is more certain. We will build a bridge to Tara and nothing, nothing you can do or say will stop us."

The others cheered and Morgana began to shake. Her shoulders twitched convulsively, her nostrils dilated and they could smell the hatred oozing from her skin.

"You bore me!" she said at last, through clenched teeth. "You are worms sucking the last blood from a long-dead carcase, hoping it will give you life. Your chance has gone. Your people have no champions. They no longer dream of elvish folk, nor search for the gateways to their realm. The old pathways are choked with burdock and briar and the roads they build lead them to destruction. They trip along them like children going to the fair. The game is all but won. Perhaps, when they have drowned in their own despair, a new race will grow, a more fitting opponent for Morgana. For now, there are none. Even Baldor has left the battlefields to me for he has been chasing fools, hoping they will lead him to the stone they call Lia Fail. Through time he has followed the scent of death like a witless hound. Now, he fears the blood in his nostrils might be his own. And all roads lead to Tara. Feast your imaginations if you can – and picture the earth and all its shadow lands, the stars and the universe, all under my control."

"Never!" yelled Gareth. "Never! Never! Never!" Then, quietly, "You can never extinguish the light – because if you did then you would die too. But you are too stupid and vain to understand. Light and dark are in all things. They come from the same source. One cannot exist without the other, for all things are weighed on cosmic scales which balance opposites. Without the light, the power of the dark has no substance and would cease to be. Right now, the balance is all wrong and it's up to us to put it right."

He spoke with such authority that the others echoed his words.

"You can never win!"

"Never! Never!"

Waves of loathing spilled over Morgana's face, distorting her bloodless features. Her bony chest heaved, and for one terrible moment the children saw her body arch and take on a different, unspeakable shape – monstrous, non-human. They could hear her breath rattling as she fought to control her anger. All in a second she was Morgana again, her mouth moulded into a smile, her eyes colder and darker than a subterranean pool.

"Go!" she muttered, her voice thick with menace. "Visit your monument. Drag this fiasco out – and I will have you all, caught like moths in a candle-flame – or maggots in a corpse." She grimaced and waved her arms at them. "Go! Go! It sickens me to look at you. Finish your ridiculous game and see for yourself where the real power lies. If you are lucky, and I spare your wits long enough, you may glimpse the chaos that is the future of the world."

She slashed a smile at them, her red lips curling back into a lupine grin. Then she snapped her fingers and shrieked with laughter as she turned her back on them and strode away.

Chapter 25

Tara

"Do you believe her?" asked Baz as they walked. "Are we really too late? I've tried but I can't see anything now, not even a ruin. All I can see is the mountain."

Gareth shrugged. He felt like a burst balloon, flat and useless. "No," he said quietly, but with none of his previous conviction. "We're not too late. We can't be."

He put his hand inside his anorak. Perhaps the stone had fallen out in his pocket and wasn't lost after all. His hand felt only flat emptiness and the enormity of what had happened hit him like a fist in the stomach, sending waves of panic to his throat and head. "Grandy knew," he said weakly, "and Longspear knew. We must believe in them, even if we doubt our own judgement."

Baz stared at him. "What's up? You OK? You were great back there."

Gareth shook his head.

"You look like you've seen a ghost," said Kit, and she almost made Gareth smile. They'd all seen much worse.

"I wish the dwarf was here. I miss him. He was kind of cheerful, even if he did have a sharp tongue."

Gareth stared at the ground intently. "I've lost something," he said. "Something entrusted to me, something I had to take to Tara."

"What kind of something?" Kit sounded upset. "Not one of the Four? You said."

"No, not one of the Four. But something equally important. A stone. Don't look so put out, Kit."

"What kind of stone? And why didn't you tell me? I thought we were in this together. Didn't you trust me enough?"

"No. I mean no, that's not the reason. I was supposed to keep it hidden and breathe no word of it to anyone. If Morgana knew what it was I took to Tara, she wouldn't have stopped at playing games. Grandy gave me the rowan wood to protect it. Then I took it out of my pocket to prove to you that I was right about the garden. Ergyriad said I was worthy of the task, but he was wrong. I fell and dropped the rowan wood. The stone must have fallen out but I was in such a hurry I didn't notice. I have lost it and we have nothing to take to Tara but ourselves."

"But if it's not one of the Four?" Kit stared at Gareth open-mouthed.

He read her thoughts and nodded.

"What about Lia Fail?" asked Kit. "Was she lying about that? Surely it's not in pieces at the bottom of the sea."

"No, but if I'm right, Lia Fail could already be in Baldor's hands."

"Who's Baldor?" asked Carter. "And you still haven't told us about Spinksy and the dwarf."

"Baldor is a warrior, sort of," said Gareth. "He and his zombies were following us. He thinks his fate is somehow linked to the stone so he's after it, too. When they were chasing us, Roddy and the dwarf stayed behind to delay them. I don't know where they are now."

"Wicked!"

"You mean Spinksy's a hero?"

"Did you scrump some of Kit's apples, you and Roddy?"

Baz glanced at Carter and shrugged. "It was just for a dare," he said, "a bit of fun. We only took a couple, Carter and me. But there was a big one right at the top. You know Spinksy. Well, Talbot does. He doesn't like anything to beat him. Likes to show off a bit sometimes. He climbed up and got it. Then we heard someone coming so we legged it quick."

"Was it my mum?"

"Didn't wait to find out. Funny if it was, though, 'cos your Jasper legged it faster than we did. Anyone'd think he'd been pinching the apples."

Gareth nodded at Kit. Their eyes spoke the same thought. Morgana.

"What's with the apples?" asked Carter. "I wish you'd tell us what's going on. Baz and me, we really haven't a clue."

So Gareth told them something of the history of Tara, of the battle between Good and Evil, Grandy and Ergyriad, the dreams and the golden stone. But the secret of the stone he kept to himself.

"But the other stone, the one you called Lia Fail – you think Spinksy's got it."

Gareth nodded. "It makes sense. The best apple at the top of the tree. The green light I saw in my dream. But what made Morgana look there? We didn't know, not then. No one spoke of it."

Kit gasped. "The diary. Grandpa Joseph's diary – and the name, Gwydion. That's where I'd heard it before. How could I have forgotten that? I told you the rest of it was about the war, but he wrote about something strange that happened when he was in the trenches. A soldier had suddenly arrived from another trench. Grandpa'd never seen him before – but when they were running and Grandpa was shot, the stranger dragged him back to the trench. He saved his life – and then he gave him something. A piece of good luck, he said. Then he told Grandpa to make sure the gift never fell into the wrong hands."

"What was it?

"He never said, but he did say he had hidden it in the orchard."

"Lia Fail," said Gareth, "buried among the roots of an old apple tree and fed by the spring that bubbles up from who knows where. Protected by the Guardians until the time was right."

"And that's how Morgana knew. That's what she was looking for. Those shadowy things – the ones in your garden and the one in our drive – they've been watching us, trying to figure out how we all fit into this and what power we have." She shuddered. "While I was out in the storm he must have sniffed out the diary. I told you it was on the floor."

"But why your Grandpa? It doesn't make sense.

"In our old lives this would sound crazy – but here it doesn't any more. Grandpa Joseph was a believer. He'd seen the dwarf more than once and walked with elves on the hill – or with the memory of them. Grandma told me that."

"Weird!"

"I always thought it was a lot of old nonsense."

"We have to find him," said Gareth. "We have to find Roddy and Lia Fail. There must be five of us standing before the gates of Tara."

"Right," said Carter. "Let's go find Spinksy. I'm not afraid of that old bag of wind."

221

"Me neither," joined in Baz. She's just like Mrs Crabbe at the chip-shop, full of boasts and hot air. Pinch her and she'll go pop."

"Yeah," agreed Carter, "I know what you mean."

"So we're all in this now," said Kit. "I mean really in it, body and soul."

The others nodded solemnly.

"OK." said Kit. "Let's join hands and put our heads together. We are stronger now than we have ever been, even without Roddy and the dwarf. Morgana's tricks and games have proved to us that Tara and the Children of the Dawn are there, waiting for us. She wouldn't have gone to so much trouble if there had been nothing to fight for."

The three boys looked at her and Kit smiled at Baz and Carter for the first time out of true friendship. "You're wrong, you know, Gareth. We have plenty to take to Tara."

They stopped and stood like the four points of a star. North, South, East and West, arms out in front, hands clasped. In his mind, Gareth could see Ergyriad. He could feel the glare from his eye, the power of his purpose. Although he no longer had the golden stone he felt its fire flowing through him. Memory of it gave him strength.

Communicating silently, the four closed their eyes and let their hands fall until their fingers pointed at the ground. When they lifted them again to the centre of the star it was as if they drew from beneath their feet invisible threads of light and energy. When they raised their hands above their heads, slowly, the light washed through them, lifting the last remnant of shadow from their thoughts, opening their hearts to the truth that lies at the heart of all things.

"We must take no Darkness with us," said Gareth, "for if we do we will find its reflection there. Men on earth are trapped in a Darkness of their own creation and draw the shape of the Light in their own shadows. If we cannot see Tara now it is because our minds will not allow it. Morgana

222

would have it so, that we might abandon all hope and turn our backs on the Light for ever."

"I can see it," whispered Kit. "I can see the Silver City. Its walls are shrouded in mist, but I can see through the mist. I can bore through it with my eyes, push it away. And I can see a gate, an enormous gate carved with animals and birds. One of the birds holds an amulet in its beak and there's a lady. She's very tall and beautiful."

"Mariandor," said Gareth. "Are you sure? I can see the walls of the city and towers climbing through the mist, but ..."

"She's there all right," said Baz quietly. "And I've seen her before, in a painting or a dream. I don't know. She's got red hair like me and something shiny around her neck."

"And pearls," added Carter. "Lots of little pearls in her hair."

"She's so beautiful," said Kit.

"But how can you see her?" said Gareth. "I don't understand."

"It's quite simple," said Kit. "We are glimpsing the future – and Mariandor is there."

"Then why can't I see her?"

Kit shrugged. "Only you know the answer to that. Perhaps, now it is our turn to be strong. Perhaps the thing you have failed in weighs too heavily on you. Believe me, Mariandor is not far away and I know we are not too late."

"We can do it," said Baz. "I have never felt more certain about anything."

"Weird, isn't it?" said Carter. "I feel strange, different, somehow not like me at all."

Kit smiled. "It shows," she said. "You were always such a prat!"

"Thanks, Talbot."

"Are we ready, then?" said Baz.

They turned their faces towards the black mountains, whose peaks rose through ribbons of mist. Gareth clenched and unclenched his fists. Something was making his fingers tingle as if he had pins and needles. Arrows of ice and fire shot through his veins and every part of him suddenly felt strong again. It was just like – he hardly dared to think of it – like the glow he had felt at Caer Cadarn.

Kit was watching him, puzzled, but the other two were stamping their feet, anxious to be off.

"What are we waiting for?" said Carter.

"Beats me," called a familiar voice. "Skitterwits, the lot of ye, daddling about as if ye'd only socks to mend."

There were gasps from everyone and shrieks of pleasure.

"Urion Longspear!"

"It's the dwarf!"

"Where did you come from?"

"Out of a tooty-pot, where d'ye think?"

"Are you all right?"

"No. Me head's cracked and I've a fine pain in me thumb, but I'll live to wear out another pair o' boots."

"Where's Spinksy?"

"Ah, now, he's riding away somewhere on a fine black beast of a thing. Could be he's helping Baldor seek out the sword and the lance before they turn to Tara."

"Whose side is Baldor on?"

"None but his own," replied the dwarf. "Light and dark are fused in him and Baldor moves between the two. He rides. He is. It is enough."

"And what about Spinksy?" asked Baz.

"I'm thinking he has something of Ymyr in his blood," said the dwarf.

"What do you mean?"

Longspear rubbed his head. "Bezountee! 'Twas the fault of a dwarf again, letting pride and anger lead his brain astray. If it wasn't for your friend, Longspear would be mashed like a turnip, food for maggots."

"Roddy saved your life?"

"Aye, that he did, and at risk of his own. I'm thinking he has his uses after all if 'tis only the saving of worthless dwarfs. Now my beard is knotted with more than one score to settle."

"Then what are we waiting for?" asked Carter again.

"Let's go find Spinksy."

"Wait!" Kit was looking at Gareth again, at the strange, bewildered expression in his eyes. "Are you OK?"

Gareth was looking at the dwarf, the pain of his failure written in every feature. How could he tell Longspear what he had done? Did the dwarf even know what it was he had carried?

Longspear raised his eyebrows at Gareth's desperate look. The blue eyes beneath them couldn't disguise a twinkle. "Ah!" he exclaimed suddenly, as if he had just remembered something. He thrust a gnarled hand into his tunic pocket, drew it out again and passed its contents to Gareth. "Would ye roll yer eyes over that now," he said, "'twas caught in the stump of a wickey tree and fair dazzled me as I leapt over tussock and tump in pursuit of ye. It was in me to ignore it, being in such a hurry and panicked by the mixen heap stench that came from nowhere and anywhere and nearly finished me. But stop I did, and by your face, 'tis a happy choice I made." He pushed his hand into his pocket again. "I found this too and thought it a pretty piece, though it was covered in mud." It was the rowan wood.

Round as the moon and pale as the morning sun. Gareth stared at the golden stone, unable to believe his eyes. He had felt its power before Longspear had appeared. He closed his fingers around it, whispered thanks and knew, beyond doubt, that his carelessness was forgiven. "I thought it had gone for ever," he said quietly. "I didn't know I'd lost it at the gate. Morgana didn't know either. She thinks the only power we have is our own and she doesn't rate that very highly. She thinks she is safe." He looked hard at the dwarf. "Do you know the secret of the stone?"

The dwarf grinned. "'Tis not fitting for dwarfs to think too hard. 'Twas a Longspear who contrived a plan to save Lia Fail and see how that turned out. Howbeit, if I did have an inkling, 'tis tight in my noddle I should keep it, for the only thing more tiresome than a thinking dwarf is a dwarf who blows too many words through his beard." He shook his staff in the air. "Sucks and sogwashes to Morgana. She hasn't the measure of ye yet." And he leapt away, his injuries forgotten.

Gareth ran his fingers over the golden stone and felt a movement in it, like the rhythmic beating of a heart. He tucked it safely away before beckoning to the other three, who watched but did not interfere or question.

"We go to Tara," said Gareth. "We take the Light back to the Silver City.

"To Tara," said the old Kit, smiling.

"To Tara," said Baz and Carter together.

As they set off after the dwarf, Gareth felt happier than he had felt since this whole thing started. He glanced at the other two boys. They were comrades now, friends, equals – warriors, too, fighting side by side, driven by the same cause, fighting against Evil. Kit guessed what he was thinking and grinned at him. It felt good, this companionship.

They soon caught up with Longspear and together the five tramped across the Field of Moytura, five specks, like grains of sand moving in a wind across the great plain. Around them there was nothing save the empty air, no sound of pursuit, no sense of being followed. The vacant space weighed upon them, filling them with suspicion and dread of the unseen. It was too quiet, but they were forced to listen to the silence, raking it for any change, any hint or whisper that they were not alone. And so, no one spoke, no one dented the silence as they shortened the distance between them and Tara.

Not one of them had any notion of time. Hours, days, could have passed before they came to a river running from east to west.

"Now what?" asked Kit, surprised by the sound of her own voice.

"Upstream," said Gareth, shading his eyes from the mercury brightness of the sky. "That looks like a bridge."

They ran now, until they reached the bridge. It was an ancient construction of massive pillars and slabs of rock. They climbed its wide, shallow steps and stood for a moment at the highest point, pausing to catch their breath. Peering into the bright, clear water, they were struck by its perfection, its clarity – as if they were seeing it for the first time. They marvelled at the way it rushed and gurgled over its stony bed, tugging at fronds of bright weed, eddying and whirling as it moved along. As they watched, tiny fish darted like shadows and lost themselves beneath stones and overhanging banks. Where the river ran smooth, a patch of blue sky had been caught and held like a memory of something lost. Strange, when above it the sky was as grey as November.

Kit looked up, then back at the water. There was no need to say anything. The others had seen it too.

"Weird!" said Carter.

Above them, the sky was becoming even darker now, but beneath them the water had turned to silver – as if it had swallowed the moon.

"The light," said Kit, "it's coming from under the water."

"From the rock," said Gareth. "The rock that holds it fast. One of Nature's memories. We must keep it forever."

As he spoke, a tiny fish, mirror-bright, rose to the surface and sent out a circle that grew and grew. Within the circle, radiating light, was a trembling image of the spires and towers of the Silver City. In a moment, the picture faded, the light died. They looked up and all around them. To the north, a bank of mist was rising. Above it, if they concentrated, they could just make out the charcoal silhouette of a single tower and a crenulated wall. In that moment, everything changed. The plain was charged with echoing sounds that vibrated and crashed into one another as though mountain walls enclosed them. Sounds were tossed through the air, screaming, roaring, tearing the silence apart.

Behind them, as far south as they could see, the horizon was blurred. Darkness rose from it like a poisoned dawn, filling space as it came, closing on them, driving them like the shadowy creatures on Rundle Hill.

From the west another dark curtain was being pulled across the sky. Before it moved a tight coil of black smoke and the ragged, familiar shape of the Scald-Crow.

The children stared at the changing scene. The Mountains of Urd towered through the thickening mist and Tara was lost to them. Beneath their feet the massive stones seemed to tremble as hoof beats thundered from the east and dust clouds rose to meet the darkening sky.

Beneath the darkness, threads of yellow mist had appeared and were writhing and twisting along the ground like streamers caught before a wind. When they reached the river they drew together, coiling about each other, and slid down the bank into the water.

At the first sound of hoof beats the five had left the bridge and headed north for whatever lay beyond the swirling bank of fog. They looked neither east nor west, saw nothing, stopped for nothing – and nothing touched them until at last they came to some steps, bedded in the ground and rising to a great wooden gate. From the gate, the walls of the city stretched east and west but all was silent and as black as the mountain from which it was hewn.

Baz and Carter raced up the steps to the gate. Hanging on massive, wooden hinges, it was taller than three men. Above their heads, a carved eagle hovered in perpetual flight, in its beak an amulet, empty of its jewel.

They banged on the gate with their fists. "Open up, somebody, please!" But the city was deaf to them and no one came.

"It's no use," said Gareth. "They are trapped between Darkness and Light. They cannot answer. It was never going to be that easy, like dropping in for a cup of tea and a chat."

"Then what do we do now?" said Baz. "We are caught like flies in a jam pot."

They turned around. Four children and a dwarf against the shadow of Evil cast by their own world upon the land of Tir na nog and the people who sought refuge there.

The fog was thinning. Baldor and his grey followers were standing silently on the river bank. The children could hear the champing of bits and muffled clomping of restless hooves. They saw vague movements in the mist, and Baldor's antlered head appeared, towering above the rest.

In the sky, the darkness was shifting, thickening into shapes that flew and crawled and fell from the air like the fragments of a nightmare. And the only answer that came to Carter's cry was the hollow, echoing sound of Morgana's laugh. It was worse now, if that were possible, a distillation of all hatred and evil. It couldn't possibly come from the lungs of single being – but Morgana was not a single being; she was the embodiment of all things evil – bitterness, cruelty, ignorance, and hatred. Her voice was the voice of them all, and the shock of it brought a shower of stones raining down from the city walls.

The children stepped forward and watched the coil of black smoke wind downwards like the tail of a kite. As soon as it touched the ground, Morgana rose, tall and skinny, clothed in purple and black, her long, thin neck dripping with red stones, sleeves draping her arms like wings.

"She looks just like a vulture," whispered Kit.

"Only not as handsome!" said Carter, and they all giggled nervously, amazed at their ability to laugh at all.

Morgana turned on them and paralysed them with her stare. Then she threw back her head and laughed again so that the city walls trembled and even the roots of the mountain stirred.

She flung out her sinewy arm and screamed, "Behold, the hopes of the Tuatha! How kind of them to have journeyed all this way for my pleasure. Their reward will come. There are few who will witness the final appearance of the mighty Caladbolg and the toy that is called Answeror. They shall swallow their treat with a sip from the great cauldron of Dagda the Dreary. And when they have done I shall take what they have and leave their bones to rot with the skins of dwarf and elf. Fitting company, don't you think, for the worms that have long inhabited the city."

As she spoke, Baldor and his riders had been approaching from the river bank. Now he stood before her and Morgana grew like a shadow until her eyes were on a level with his. Above her dark, distorted shape her white face hung in the air like a mask.

Geldor threw his head about and pawed the ground while Baldor held him firm and returned Morgana's look with a defiant glare.

"In all your cackling and rambling, you speak no word of the stone Lia Fail. Since we last met I have sought it in all four reaches of the Earth and beneath the long-rooted hills of Sinadon and Bannawg. But there are powers beyond yours that have kept it close and silent. The wind that blows between our worlds carries whispers of the stone. If it moves," he roared, "then it moves to the hand of Baldor. To own it will give me power over Destiny."

Morgana lifted her hand slowly, uncurling her clawed fingers as she did so. Geldor reared and pitched, turning and tossing his head as if he would be away if Baldor loosed the rein. That's when the children saw that he carried more than one rider.

"Spinksy!" yelled Carter excitedly. "He's got Spinksy."

"Ssh!" hissed Gareth. "Listen!"

Morgana's voice then was the only sound, amplified by the towering city walls to fall on the ears of the listeners like the scratching of a rat in an empty castle.

"Is that Baldor the Baleful?" she screamed. "He who has the strength of an ox and the brains of a fish. You have a long memory if you think Lia Fail can save your miserable skin. The stone is nothing to you. It is a worthless bauble, dull as lead and made only for tricking fools. It was a means of ensuring your help, nothing more, and you failed in that as in all things because you hold the Light in your right hand and the Dark in your left and have neither the wit nor the courage to choose which path to take. You

231

are like the wind blowing hither and thither – but you are less than the wind for the wind knows its place and keeps out of Morgana's way."

Baldor made little of her words. He threw back his leonine head and roared. "Baldor's fate lies with the stone! Say what you will. It cannot be unwritten. Who carries the stone?"

Morgana flung her hand towards the children. "Between them, they have it, plucked from a tree whose roots were tangled in the roots of Yggdrasil. Alone, it will do them no good. Take it, if you will. And lose it in the skies of another time. I fear it not. Its power is nothing to me; the knowledge it holds is of another time, chaff on the wind, with none left who can make use of it. The real world has moved on and real power owes nothing to such childish trinkets. Real power is here!" She tapped her head with a bony finger. "And here!" She held out her hands. "The fate of Morgana lies with Morgana. Never has the Dark been so strong. So it should be with Baldor."

"The scent of blood is with me!" roared Baldor.

"Your own," mocked Morgana, "or another's?" She turned to look towards Tara and the children who stood before the gate.

Baldor turned his mount and took several paces north. He looked at Gareth and saw something in his face that brought to mind another time and place. The likeness was unmistakable to one who had looked upon Gwydion, the warrior magician, and seen the light in his eyes. He thrust his great arm behind him and dragged Roddy from his seat. He dangled him at arm's length as he moved forward again. Roddy squirmed and kicked but Baldor's grip was like a steel clamp. And all the time Morgana watched, her face contorted by a malicious smile.

"Is this yours?" roared Baldor. "I found it in the company of a dwarf. It was in me to drop it in the river, knowing it was not the chosen one. But now it seems it would have a purpose. Take him, Dwarf, and persuade your helpmeets to give up the stone."

Longspear darted a look at Gareth. What he held close to him was not Lia Fail. Who then held the Stone of Destiny?

Gareth stepped forward, slipped off his rucksack and began to loosen the drawstring when suddenly, a wind arose, storm-wild and howling as it came. Before it, out of the belly of the sky, billowing shapes emerged, rolling, stretching evolving. A flock of birds, white-winged and silent, sifting the air as they flew out of the cloud and disappeared like mist. A school of whales, wet-backed and glistening, catching the rays from a distant sun as they leapt and sang in the ocean of the sky. A herd of elephants, ambling massively, quietly, grey trunks swinging like pendulums as they grew out of the cloud and lost themselves in the leaden sky. And above them all an eagle flew, carrying something in her taloned feet.

"Aquila!" whispered Gareth. "She comes from the Guardians, from Bannawg and she brings the lance of Prince Lugh."

"Look! Look!" said Kit, pointing in the opposite direction.

From the horizon, a single cloud, like a drift of snow, lifted and was borne towards them. As it neared, the cloud became a white horse, riding another wind, and on its back a soldier king in silver mail.

"Arthur!" said Gareth breathlessly. "He has risen from Llydaw and brings Caladbolg to Tara. What will Morgana do now?"

As the eagle descended and the white horse galloped nearer, Morgana hunched her shoulders and raised her hands before her like a waking bat. When she spoke, her voice was poison in the air. "Lia Fail!" she screamed. "Take it now or death is your destiny."

What happened next and the order of events, remained in Gareth's mind like a confusion of colours in a wild and surreal painting. Who – or what – moved first he never knew.

Baldor galloped towards him and Roddy was dropped like a stone. A clawed hand reached down to grab the apple that Gareth had just removed from his rucksack, the beautiful, big green apple that Mrs Talbot had given him a lifetime ago. Long afterwards, he could feel the raking talons on his wrist and smell the sour, peat bog smell of the lizard-horse. Then Geldor and his rider went wild, rearing, tossing and stamping the ground.

Gareth was aware of Kit's voice. He turned for a moment, saw Carter leaning against the massive gate, Kit's hand on his shoulder. He heard Baz yelling "Spinksy! Spinksy!" But Roddy couldn't get to them. For at the same time the sword, Caladbolg and the lance, Answeror, were falling from the sky, spinning slowly down. They landed halfway between Morgana and the gates of Tara. And the moment they landed, Gareth felt the Dark closing in. He saw Morgana, rigid as a lifeless tree. Only her mouth jerked, pouring words into the air like a snake pumping venom until Gareth felt he couldn't breathe and the air closed about him like the walls of a cave.

In a moment he understood what was happening. Morgana's power was such that she had spun a web of Darkness about the city, enclosing them all, even Baldor. But where was Roddy? Gareth shook himself and tried to penetrate the wall of shadows. He saw the darkness moving, creatures rising from it and Roddy, yelling and struggling, being borne away on a tide of writhing, waving arms. Roddy – and Lia Fail! Morgana must have guessed who carried the green stone, for Yggdrasil had protected it with the apple, just as Nwyvre had bestowed powers of secrecy upon the rowan wood. Her creatures had found the diary, and she had seen Roddy climbing the tree for the biggest apple. She had the cauldron, Lia Fail was within her grasp and all she had to do was snatch the sword and the lance that quivered in the earth before her.

She would have all four of the Treasures and all they had was the golden stone – and the power of their combined wills.

Gareth felt for the stone, dragged himself out of the torpid state that was sucking him down. But the stone was dead, lifeless. There was no beating heart, no warm glow or stirring of life within. He turned. The other three and the dwarf were standing beneath the withered tree beside the gate. Baldor was pacing back and forth, sending up dust clouds, crazy with anger, thrusting his antlered head time and again at the smoky web.

Gareth closed his eyes tightly, his thoughts racing. "When five win through and five stand true." Well, they had won through in one way or another. The five children were here. So were the Four Treasures and the golden stone. Did it matter if they were not together in one hand? They had proved themselves, though only Roddy had been a real hero – and if he was borne across the river with Lia Fail what then?

All of this happened in a fragment of time. Gareth thought of the apple and knew what he had to do. In that same moment, he saw Morgana's face, illuminated by leaping tongues of flame. She had summoned the cauldron and it stood before her now, overflowing with liquid fire. In the light of the cold flames she began to dance hideously, surrounded by tall emaciated shapes that arched and twisted and wound themselves about each other and the fire. In her hands were the sword and the lance. She was mocking them, spitting on them, attacking them with the language of the dark as she leapt, cavorting like a scorpion warding off death.

As Gareth opened his mouth, Morgana was lifting Answeror and Caladbolg. She called on the shades of Darkness, wherever they be, clinging to the corners of our worlds and our minds like cobwebs, finding and filling every empty space. Harnessing that power, she issued into the air such a curse that the flames themselves withdrew and the fabric of time was frozen.

Gareth summoned every shred and tatter of his will and strength. He shut out Morgana from his mind and heard only his own voice lifting above the choking Darkness. His words moved like silver arrows through the chaos of a dream – and reached their target.

"Roddy! Your apple! Throw it to Tara!"

As ice-blue flames licked the air again, claiming the sword and the lance, Roddy fought against the shadows of sinew and steel that held him. In his darkest moment, a seed of light burst and grew in his mind. From somewhere came the strength to seek out the apple, to tear his arm free from tentacles and claws and toss the iron-hard fruit as high as he could into the sky.

To Gareth, it felt as though the universe held its breath. And then he saw it, like in his dream, a soft, green light rising from the river bank like the last flash of a dying firework. It drew an arc in the air, passed through the wall of darkness and fell into Gareth's waiting hands.

He flew up the steps, yelling to the others, rousing them from their trance. They saw what was needed and made a human ladder that Gareth might reach the amulet held in the eagle's hooked beak. No sooner had Lia Fail found its place in the grip of the silver hand, wrought by Lugh Lamphada, than Baldor was behind them, urging his mount to climb the steps to the city gate, and the children were leaping and scrambling for their lives, falling down the steps, tumbling over the walls at the side to the ground below.

Above them now, Baldor was reaching for the stone, the eye of all knowledge that would give him power over his destiny. But the eye of his horse met the light from the emerald-green stone and, as Baldor leaned from his seat, Geldor was blinded and reared into the air, screaming and beating his hooves against an enemy he could not see.

As Baldor's claws reached for the amulet he jerked backwards, lost his grip and was catapulted through the air. His mount, bewildered by the steps and the dazzling light, stumbled sideways, lost his footing and toppled over, crashing down the stone slabs to land, with flailing hooves, on the body of his master.

The children pulled themselves away from the scene. They had scarcely heard Morgana, so intent were they upon restoring the stone. But, when she had seen the green light rising from the darkness that would swallow it, she had killed the dance with one word and screamed at the churning sky. "No, no! He has not the power! There is no power left between our worlds that is strong enough to hold back the Dark."

Rage overtook her. Her body pulsed and heaved as though it would burst, and she assumed another form. She was taller now, darker. Shreds of night hung about her gaunt frame, catching the air like the tattered remains of a cloak on a scarecrow, and the only colour came from the jewels at her throat and the blood-red eyes that swam in the grey globe of her head.

As the children and the dwarf stood now, hands held, beneath the withered tree, Morgana's mind drew in on itself. It was a black hole, refining the Evil on which it fed. Now, it was spinning and tightening until its centre became as dense as the oldest moon. Only then did she raise her skeletal, black-skinned arms and turn to Tara. Only then did she point her finger at the city, at the sky and at the black Mountains of Urd.

But the children were not looking. They were standing in a circle, hands held, eyes closed, linking thoughts. Four children and a dwarf – that made five – plus the Four Treasures and the golden stone. They were all there, standing before the gates of Tara. And they were thinking of the sun, and the light that had shone on Nwyvre's children when they had first come to Earth. They filled their minds with it, drawing it from the earth beneath their feet and from the sky above, and from the north, south, east and west. They became lost in a dream of sunlight – and they *were* the sun at the centre of all things, and the Light was flowing out from them, breaking through the Darkness, reaching out to those who wanted to believe, showing them the path.

But though they believed with every ounce of their being, it was not enough, and the Dark thickened about them like a living, contagious fog, tangible and suffocating. Somewhere, at the edge of awareness, they heard trees screaming, mountains moving, rocks raining down. They sensed they were no longer alone, heard running feet, animal feet, claws, scraping and scratching around the walls. Above their heads, they felt the air stirred by the beating of wings as all the ugliness, greed and insanity of the world descended upon them, hitting the city walls, landing on the battlements with harsh screams and raucous cries.

Without their leader, the grey followers of Baldor lacked substance. They paced outside the Darkness, seeking their warlord, wandering aimlessly, howling at the sky like dying wolves.

Gareth's mind was on fire. Lia Fail was restored and the five were here but it was not enough. And her creatures were swarming up the walls of the city. He could feel Carter's hand slackening its grip. "Fight, Carter! Fight!" he willed, but Kit had felt it too.

"It's no use," she whispered. "She has grown too strong – and we are too late. The Earth is lost in shadow and is losing its fight against Evil. There's no bringing it back. So much Darkness! So much despair!"

"No! No!" cried Gareth. He broke the circle then and felt again for the golden stone. Where had its spirit gone? Why had it deserted him? Was it his fault? Had he failed them all? In his hand the stone felt no more than a pebble from the beach. Suddenly, he wondered if it had ever been anything else. Mum always said he had too much imagination. Why had he thought the stone so special? Why was he here at all? Who were these strangers? He touched the wall behind him. It felt rough, uneven, cold, like the face of a cliff – or a mountain. No city after all. He looked blankly at the faces of the others and they stared back, empty, defeated. Even the dwarf's blue eyes had dimmed.

Names came to him then. Gwion, Taliesin, Gwydion and memories of them rekindled a spark of faith. He struggled, fought to drive out the hopelessness that was smothering his reason. He searched for a foothold, clawed his way back, groping in the darkness for more names to hold on to. Grandy, where are you? Myrddin, Son of Gwydion, help me now. Mariandor! Mariandor! Her name hung about him like a wreath of sorrow. Ergyriad! Ergyriad!

Around them, all was chaos, a heaving, pulsating agonising darkness, bubbling, twisting, reforming – as though the world itself were disgorging its turbulent past, turning itself inside out in disgust.

Within the turmoil the children were contained, apart. Though their minds were slipping, the darkness had not yet devoured them. As Gareth crawled back from the brink he felt a hand on his arm.

"Roddy?" But it couldn't be. "Roddy?"

Gareth grasped Roddy's hand and placed it in Kit's. He put up his own hand, afraid to speak of the hope that now filled his thoughts. He pointed at Baz, Carter, Roddy, and Kit, then at himself, and drew a circle in the air. He shook his head at the dwarf. Longspear nodded his understanding and sat down against the wall, knees to chin, his face set like granite. He was not one of them. Only the Children of Men could build the bridge and bring the light back to Tara, and then, only if the belief they carried with them was strong enough to waken the spirit of goodness and Light, the embodiment of which is Mariandor.

This was Gareth's thought as he stood within the circle made by his four friends and slowly lifted the golden stone above his head.

They closed their eyes, focused, intent as arrows, drawing strength from each other and from the earth below. They were aware of every crumb of soil and blade of grass beneath their feet, as energy lifted into them and through them, and their minds were as one, a bird with silver wings flying beyond the dark.

"WE HAVE MORE POWER THAN WE KNOW," said Gareth breathlessly. "It's now or never! We are the bridge-makers, enemies of the dark, restorers of the Light. We have completed the task and have brought the Keeper home."

Kit, Roddy, Baz and Carter lifted their hands to the centre of the circle, touching Gareth. As they did so, shards of silver light flew from them, piercing the blackness, as fine and strong as cobweb spun through the time and space that separated our worlds.

For a millisecond the darkness lurched and shuddered, cowering from the Light. But still Morgana's creatures hid the city walls, crawling and scrambling, clawing and plucking at stones as if they would reduce Tara to rubble. And still, Morgana grew while the children became aware

240

of the river, churning and rushing, seeping over the banks and lapping at their feet. They dared not look, dared not break their concentration. Like gnats in a hurricane, they hung on for their lives, gripping hearts and hands, spinning their thoughts into a lifeline, casting it towards the stars.

Now, the water washed about their knees, swelling in sinister waves. If they had looked, they would have seen the river turn to blood, its dark waters reflecting the light from Morgana's eyes as she towered above them, bloated with pride, certain of victory.

Within the black cowl of the sky, a crimson moon hung like a battle shield, its eerie light seeping through the darkness, smearing the clouds with blood.

Morgana embraced the Dark. She jabbed her fingers at the sky and lightning burst, crackling from every side. She laughed and the Mountains of Urd trembled to their roots. She breathed in the Darkness, the essence and sap of the Tree of Evil, until she was blacker than the frozen heart of winter. Then a wind rose, lifting her wild, billowing shape above the city of Tara, and the blood-red moon grew brighter, casting her scarecrow shadow upon the city like a long, clawed hand.

Caught in its grasp was the pale sphere of light that held the children. Then the water rose to meet the Dark and they were engulfed.

Chapter 26

Mariandor

In that moment, when the Dark drew on every morsel and grain of its power to snuff out the last hope of the Tuatha, five children, locked together in resolution and belief, enclosed in a sphere of frozen light, hovered in the twilight zone between day and night.

In that fragment of time, the cosmic scales, already dipping dangerously on the side of evil, tilted heavily. Stars, in the great constellations that hung about the Earth, flickered and dimmed and the moon hid its face in a shroud of purple mist.

Morgana lifted a cry out of the darkness, from all the places on Earth where Evil holds sway. It was the desolate cry of empty oceans and poisoned streams, the despairing cry of a people who have lost their way. It was the sound of a world in agony, thrashing and screaming in the throes of death. And, while the Light was suspended there was nothing else – until Morgana's victory rattle rose above the sound to batter the wounded air. All this in a needle-sharp sliver of time. For, no sooner had her cries echoed from the mountain walls than they faded and died. In their place a torrent of anger gushed like a rainstorm and was borne away on a wind that blew from our world.

Only then, when Morgana's monstrous, overblown shape diminished and became earthbound did she awaken to the truth of Gareth's words, that Light and Dark exist side by side and can only be measured one against the other.

Only then, from his shrinking globe of light, did Gareth open his hands and name the power trapped in the golden stone.

"Mariandor, she is defeated – for now. She cannot stand where there is no Light. She is beaten by her own pride. See, how the Dark winds itself about her, like a snake intent upon eating its own tail."

"Mariandor! Mariandor!"

As they whispered her name, the black waters retreated, the stone shattered in Gareth's hand and from it a golden light rose and grew above the city, banishing the Dark, shrivelling its creatures, bringing back the day.

The children unlocked their hands. Roddy reached out to help the dwarf to his feet and they all turned to gaze at Tara, at her dark walls, threaded with veins of shimmering quartz.

They saw Lia Fail, its brightness held fast in the silver hand and beneath it, before the gate, a lady dressed in a robe of emerald green. Her skin was pale, her copper hair dressed with rows of tiny pearls and at her throat a necklace of emerald and gold.

"Mariandor."

Her name was like music, and as they spoke it, half afraid that she would disappear, the sound was echoed by a voice that came from the silver tree, where now, buds were unfurling and a tiny bird stretched its frozen wings.

"Mariandor."

Gareth spoke her name out loud, not quite able to believe that he and his unlikely companions had succeeded, that for the moment at least, they had restored the balance and built a bridge to Tara. This time, as he spoke, the notes were echoed by another sound, a sweet-tolling bell, magical, unearthly, sprinkling the new air like summer rain, cleansing, purifying, Lia Fail.

As they listened, spellbound, they were aware of a shaft of sunlight escaping through a gap in the thinning clouds, and out of the beam, warmed by its glow, an army moved to Tara.

Gareth and his friends could not speak. They were spectators now, watching the threads of a story unravel. They saw the massive gates swing open as the army approached. They saw a king – old, grey and smiling. He was offering his hand – and his silver crown – to the young soldier who climbed the steps. The bell-song was louder now, jubilant. From inside the city voices called out, "Lugh Lamphada, Samildanach[5]. Hail, King of Tara."

As the stone sang, the lance, Answeror, and the sword, Caladbolg, rose from the cauldron and flew to the new king's hands. As he held them aloft and pointed them at the sky a great cheer rose and suddenly the children were aware of hundreds of faces peering over the walls.

They uprooted themselves and began to climb the stone steps for a second time. Surely, they too could enter the city. After all they had been through surely someone would speak with them.

Half way up they stopped, feeling the gaze of the lady's dark, almond eyes upon them. She held up her hand and shook her head.

"You have achieved more than you know and a new light grows and flickers in every corner of your world. But the time for you to meet is not yet. Though the bridge is built, it must yet withstand the attack of waters that would wash it away, dark waters that rise and fall like the tides of the oceans and the waxing and waning of the moon. There

---

[5] Strong-armed and many skilled

is much work to be done before the body and spirit and imagination of the people of your world are one. Only then will they be ready to listen with open hearts to the wisdom of Nwyvre's children, a wisdom born with the first light. Preparing them, waking them to the truth that will free them for ever, is my life's work. Let it be yours too. Tell your children and your children's children what has happened here today. Feed their dreams with stories of the stars. Show them the magic of the world in which they live and teach them to love its creatures. Help them to follow the path to the Light."

She smiled then, a smile they knew they would never forget. Mariandor, Keeper of the Light. It was all the thanks they needed; though, if they were honest, succeeding was enough. They heard another voice then, the gruff, unmistakable voice of a dwarf.

"Longspear? Is that my old friend? Longspear. By my britches, the wanderer has returned."

Longspear leapt up the steps, fifty years younger, as the children turned to go down. One by one, he gripped their hands, shook them vigorously, nodded his head rapidly, unable to speak, and slipped through the gates.

The children looked at each other and turned to take a long, last look at Tara, its spires and turrets reaching up now into a cloudless sky. They heard voices, reed-thin, lifting on the breeze, and the joyful song of the bird in the silver tree. Then the wind that blows between our worlds took them and they felt themselves melting into the air like flakes of snow.

***

They woke on Rundle Hill, autumn's chill striking through their clothes, and rose slowly to their feet. The air was still, keeping its secrets, and a pale wisp of silver cloud was drifting across the face of the moon. Strange, but no one could think of anything to say.

They moved into the trees, isolated, like figures kept apart in a dream, unwilling to leave it, uncertain about which was the reality.

"What time is it?" said Carter at last as they reached the bridge.

Gareth turned his wrist towards the moon. "Nine-forty-five," he said.

"Better be getting home then," said Roddy.

The others nodded.

On the bridge they stopped to look back at Rundle Hill.

"It's not over, is it?" said Kit.

"No," said Gareth, "it'll never be over, but it will get better, you'll see. It has to."

Kit nodded. "I hope I'm still here," she said quietly, "when they return."

They saw the moon's unbroken face in the dark water of the stream and lifted their heads to look at the sky.

"Wow!" exclaimed Baz. "Have you ever seen so many stars?"

***

On the other side of the hill, Will Gresty was checking his sheep. He could see them clearly in the moonlight, pale patches against the nameless colour of the field. He allowed his eyes to wander along the hedge line, down to the river, across Rundle Hill. Satisfied that all was as it should be, he turned homeward.

"Ah well, 'tis ours again – for the present," he murmured to the dog at his heels.

246

Above his head, a black bird with yellow eye settled to roost in the forked trunk of a naked poplar tree.

Ends